BHRIGU MAHESH, PHD

BHRIGU MAHESH, PhD

THE WITCH
OF SENDUWAR

NISHA SINGH

PARTRIDGE

To order additional copies of this book, contact
Partridge India
000 800 10062 62
orders.india@partridgepublishing.com

www.partridgepublishing.com/india

Contents

1. Prologue...xvii

2. Bhrigu Mahesh 1

3. The Mystery 21

4. The Investigation 39

5. The Suspects...61

6. The Trap...141

7. Men Behind Their Masks 255

8. Epilogue.. 307

ACKNOWLEDGEMENTS

Now that this book has been published, I recall the one year that I have spent writing it. It has been the most memorable year of my life as I was finally telling a story that the world would love to stop and listen to. But with every dream comes many challenges, many obstacles that need to be conquered daily. I, too, experienced my fair share of them, and had it not been for the support of my family, I would be a dead duck in water. I sincerely feel that my family has worked alongside me to make my dream project come true and if it were not for their love, care, devotion, and unshakeable faith in me and my talents, I would never have been able to evolve as a writer.

I want to give my first thanks to my mother, Mrs Vinni Singh, who is the one lady who doubles up as an army for me. I feel very proud to say that I had the privilege of having her as my English teacher at school where she taught me great works from great writers including Shakespeare. She was the person who started my love affair with words. I remember as a kid I always used to come running to her with a difficult word whose meaning was a total mystery to me. I was always awestruck at how she used to know the meaning of each and every word. It was like decoding a particularly difficult cipher. She has been my guide, my guardian, the love of my life, and my one-woman army. Whatever I am today, I owe it all to her. She is not just my mother, a most amazing and wonderful teacher who can inspire a generation, but a joy to live every day with. In short, she is my greatest gift from God.

My father, Dr Arvind Kumar Singh, is a surgeon and he has the hands of an artist—long, slender, and delicate—and that's why he performs surgery like an artist. He was the reason I loved the field of medicine, which resulted in me graduating as a pharmacist. He has taught me values like discipline, punctuality, honesty, and a never-say-die attitude. Some people might wrongly class him as a workaholic seeing his patients dance around him like bees around a honeycomb, but I call him a person who is very passionate about his job and dedicated to serving humanity with his gift. I have also inherited the same burning passion and dedication towards my work from him. He always wanted me to follow my heart and work hard. That's exactly what I did and here I am today, with my dream shining as a beautiful reality before me. You are great, Dad!

Next in the line is my sister Neha Singh, who is serving as an officer in the elite Indian Air Force. Although she is my little sister, I have learned many lessons from her, too. She has taught me the true meaning of the adage 'When the going gets tough, the tough gets going'. She has such a resilient spirit that nothing can ever break. Her humour, her wonderful wit has always left me in splits and every day with her is such fun that I almost lament when she stops talking. My sister and I are as thick and thieves and almost all the time end up completing each other's sentences! Had it not been for her support and the sheer happiness she brings into my life with her love and adoration, I would not have any reserve of energy left to write.

Last but not the least comes my grandfather, late Dr Vijay Kumar Singh, a cardiac surgeon and F.R.C.S. from Edinburgh, U.K. Although he is no longer with us, he will continue to live in our memories. My granddad was an iconic man. I remember his dazzling smile, bright countenance, and a spirit of strength and character that shone brightly through his eyes. His wonderful career as a cardiologist ended when he was diagnosed with Parkinson's disease. He never for once let any worry sully his handsome features. He took the crippling disease in his stride and fought valiantly against it like a true soldier. Even in his last days when his senses and muscles failed him, he would never fail to register a joke and tried to laugh as hard as his failing muscles could allow. He was a true hero, a philanthropist, and a man with a heart of gold. My mother is in every way his spitting image.

I also thank the Almighty for his blessings. He has indeed been very kind and watched over me so that I never lost hope in the path of pursuing my dreams.

Nisha Singh
19-02-2016

DEDICATION

I dedicate this book to the memory of a great man whom I call my grandfather and whom the world called Dr Vijay Kumar Singh. I know he must be smiling among the shining stars, watching over me and guiding me through every obstacle.

FOREWORD

I now want to write a thing or two about mystery and why this genre inspires me more than anything else in the world. I am a firm believer of the fact that mystery is an essential ingredient of a rich, healthy and colourful life. Imagine a world where there was no mystery, no suspense, and no intrigue. Wouldn't it be rather dull and not worth living? That's the only reason why, in everyday life too, we try our best to search for mystery in the lives of people around us. 'Oh my god!' we say 'Mr.so-and-so's son is going to marry? Well, who's the lucky girl?' We become restless until and unless we find out who that "lucky girl" is, but, mind you, as soon as we come to know of her identity, we lose interest. Why? Because the mystery is solved and there's no thrill anymore. Well, I might sound like a sensationalist, but the truth is, however we might resent this, it is true. Human beings are wired to gossip because it is a precursor to mystery; as we try to unravel the motivations behind what people do and why they do it. And there's nothing wrong with it. Studies have proved that a good gossip is actually good for our heart! A good puzzle not just makes slaves of our brains but also provides the fuel, the rush that is imperative to an existence beyond just surviving. That's the only reason why we are still obsessed with Sherlock Holmes, a detective born in the 1800s, Victorian England. He continues to enchant us with his singular personality and an incessant craving for the just perfect crime. What I am saying is that what the world truly needs is a great detective and a mystery that we can solve alongside him. Bhrigu Mahesh is very different from all the detectives that have gone before him. There came a time when I was drawing a blank and he, with the amazing powers of perception that he has, understood my plight and taking my hand in his, safely guided me through the maze. It was then that I knew that he had now a life of his own!

My passion for writing was coupled with a burning desire to keep the mundane at bay, and what better way than to dive headlong into an adventure with a detective that I adore? Readers, I now submit Bhrigu Mahesh for your inspection. If you happen to fall in love with him like I did, you can always kick Sutte from his side, implant your thrill-seeking selves, and embark on an adventure that I have crafted only and only for your pleasure.

P.S- Oh yes! I just remembered. I should duly inform my readers that this book has been inspired by a true incident. In the village of Senduwar, it was indeed raining gold and an article that I read about the phenomenon in 'The Times of India', two years ago, fascinated me so much that I decided to weave the net of my first mystery around this once-in-a-lifetime incident. I have exercised my poetic license in describing the beautiful village of Senduwar.

Nisha Singh
19-02-2016

PROLOGUE

For the past week, the clouds had been building up their strength, gradually darkening from a light grey to a bold black and as their dark canopy overshadowed the earth below, they had relieved themselves at the expense of the poor, defenceless population below. Their unwanted generosity had transformed the landscape of the little village. A day before, the mustard and the wheat crops were standing tall in the fields ready to be harvested, and on the very night, an unexpected torrential rainfall had flattened the crops to the ground. The fields that didn't have proper drainage stood water logged with the crops in their watery graves. The hustle and bustle of a busy agricultural village had come to a standstill, battling with the uncomfortable dip in temperature and unrelenting, unforgiving rains. No one dared come out of the security of their homes, feverishly praying and hoping that their humble abode won't give away leaving them at the mercy of the brutal weather. The village alleys were totally empty save for a dog or two that whined unhappily at the gloomy weather. The wind howled moodily and the boughs of trees swung lugubriously to its eerie tune. The small houses around were lit with spirit lamps the flicker of which proved how feeble their only source of comfort was. Dirt roads wound their way into and out of the fields, slushy and dangerously slippery, covered in a combination of dung and mud. The onslaught of this terrible weather had forced every life to withdraw but for her.

She had run for miles on the narrow dirt road that opened from the back of her room. Her family had been asleep but not before securing and locking her door firmly from outside. But, she had escaped through the ventilator, sustaining only minor bruises at the hip. But what were these bruises compared to the one that was inflicted on her heart and that, too, by her own kith and kin? As her feet touched the sloppy ground, she had run steadily, cautiously, without once looking back.

Her heart was beating wildly in her chest. She knew that they would find her but not before she was done with her work. Her feet hurt and the slippery road was no comfort but there was no time to stop. She ignored the weather, the whining, rabid dogs, the puddles of mud water, the chilly sword of winds cutting deep into her flesh . . . everything but her object. Her destination loomed closer but her feet didn't falter as she kept repeating to her—'Today, I sow the seed of their downfall. They will not escape. . . . They will pay. . . . They will pay. . .'

As her feet hit their destination, she kneeled and started digging a hole in the soft mud. Her eyes blazed with a ferocity that could outshine the fieriness of the sun. Her hands worked with a feverish, manic energy. At a distance, it looked as if an exceptionally passionate rabbit was digging a hole for its shelter. Finally, she looked at her handiwork with a slow, lunatic smile playing on her lips. It was a wonder how it transformed her pretty face, twisting and perverting its beauty to an extent past all recognition. After finishing her work, she took out a small bottle from the inside of her wet jacket and emptied the contents in her mouth. She smacked her lips with a relish, as if it was some delicious drink. The ferocity was gone, the anger was gone, and the fever was gone. She just stood still with the faint smile still lurking about her lips and eyes shining with the satisfaction of a job well done. She let herself go, swaying gently with the wind, her wet clothes sticking to her bones. A second later, she had hit the ground and as she lay there, she could feel the sound of the rain hitting her body go fainter and fainter with every passing second. Her eyes started to dim as if she were going to drift into a sleep after a long period of exhaustion. Yes, a long peaceful sleep from which she would never awaken.

CHAPTER 1

BHRIGU MAHESH

1

I was reposing in my chair that stood opposite the open window. Sun was sinking over the horizon and the last shimmer of red was finding its way into the small, sparsely furnished room. It felt warm and cool all at once. The cool air caressed my face with its gentle whispers and with every breath; I could get a lungful of the wonderful earthy smell that rises from the rain kissed ground. I couldn't have asked for more. The peace and quiet of the quaint little village was exactly the reason that I had coaxed Bhrigu to pay a visit to his long abandoned hometown to which he had reluctantly agreed. My thoughts were blank as is natural with one in a highest state of meditation. Something in the air, in the soil and in the very surroundings was enough to lull my senses into complete oblivion. But I discovered that like all good things, this heaven was also short-lived.

'Bhriguji! Are you sleeping at this time of the day?! Bhriguji!'

I was jolted out of my peaceful reverie and my heart pounded with the shock.

The old woman that stood facing me was around 70 years old. She had a shock of red hair, the inevitable result of vigorous application of mehndi. Her eyes were sunken deep in their sockets and the cheek bones were highly prominent. She was wearing a white sari with a dark red border. Although she was quite emaciated, the way she carried herself spoke of a rigid and inflexible mind. The hint of steel behind her cold eyes also hinted at passive aggression.

She looked at me and said with a sneer, 'Oh, It's you.' Her voice betrayed a mix of repulsion and irritation.

'Where is Bhriguji?'

'I don't know. He didn't tell me.' I replied casually and closed my eyes again, determined to ignore her prattle.

'You should have asked!' She croaked in her hoarse voice.

I continued with my noncooperation movement. This old woman was nothing but a burden to my friend and to the society she was a debit to. She could torture him into submission but I was made of sterner stuff.

I understood that she was far from being done. She stood there like the ghost of a sentinel, searing me with her blazing eyes. 'I want you to go to Vaidnath and bring the kerosene oil. We have none left.'

'Okay. I'll go after I have had my siesta,' I mumbled sleepily.

'That won't do. You go now.'

'I won't.'

She glared at me. 'My nephew was much disciplined when he was a boy. The air of the city and your influence has changed him in a bad way. I don't like it! I don't like it!' She stamped her foot in her anger and left muttering under her breath.

I couldn't believe the extent to which this woman could exercise evil. No doubt Bhrigu was so reluctant to visit her. He had abandoned his hometown for a decade just to stay clear of this woman. After leaving Nirja Masi, Bhrigu had come to Patna to complete his studies. He used to work the night shift at a K.P.O as a part time job and went to college in the morning. After graduating with a bachelor's degree in Psychology from Hindu College, he sat for the police exam and had passed it with flying colours at his very first attempt.

I was his neighbour in Patliputra where he had been allotted his government quarters. I first met him at the wedding of a common friend from the neighbourhood, a well–to–do paediatrician called Debashish Sengupta. He was standing with a short, stout, middle-aged man who kept talking to him animatedly. I noticed that the man looked much perplexed and his tale was probably that of woe. But I could clearly observe that even though Bhrigu was just an attentive listener, with a word of comfort to offer here and there, the man considerably got better in the spirit towards the end of the conversation and he was practically smiling when they went together to the food stall to try some of the dishes. He had an aura of unassailable peace that was so infectious that his presence alone was enough to make any burdened soul light again. As I continued to observe him, he struck me as a private person, timorous even, with a dignified carriage but somehow I felt that the thick crowd was making him unduly self-conscious. He kept looking towards the gate as if anxious to make a quick dash for it at the earliest possible but the code of etiquette held him back from any such attempt. I was drawn towards this taciturn, mysterious man like moth to a flame.

5

His face was long and narrow; oblong, as my eighth class mathematics teacher would describe it, with a straight nose and thin, sensitive lips. The most striking feature of his remained his round, kind, black eyes that were set deep in his forehead. They had a depth in them that I couldn't even begin to fathom. It was as if they penetrated your very soul and knew everything that you had stowed away even from yourself. Enchanted, I couldn't help introducing myself to his person and discovered that he was a soft-spoken man who mostly talked in a few syllables but his eyes seemed to speak volumes. No matter how much you tried to gain, the upper hand in any conversation by your knowledge and articulation, his gentle, nervous smile and the reassurance in those clear, bottomless eyes seemed almost always to get the upper hand. I knew then and there that this unusual man was hiding something very formidable behind his persona, and a week from then, it was proven that I was right.

It was a column in a leading English Newspaper carrying his picture and an article on him. It said that this man was Bhrigu Mahesh, a cop, and that he had come into the limelight by solving a sensational crime in which a minister of state, Rajshekhar Swami, had been accused of poisoning a young woman to death with whom he was having an illicit affair, within a month of his career. The article further stated that this success was extraordinary as the culprit owned to his crime with such lucidity that people were left puzzled as to whether he was confessing to a crime or narrating a desultory affair from everyday life. One visit from this officer was enough to bring about this result and that, too, without the use of any kind of force.

I started visiting him often. During my first visits, he timidly welcomed me with little enthusiasm and I could sense in his conduct an eagerness to get rid of me. He was reserved and did not participate much in the way of conversation. I could see that he was not a person who entertained any form of society and loved to live with himself and his occupation, whatever that may be. However, I was persistent in my effort to win him over, and ignoring his passive resistance, I continued to visit him. Our growing familiarity strengthened by a certain modicum of liking that he had developed towards me during our meetings and also helped to remove the obstacles of formalities and of his reserved nature. He was a man who loved to have a very analytical and research-oriented discussion on any number of topics from diverse walks of life, including the revolutionising field of investigative science. I was surprised and impressed with the insight and depth he brought to our conversations with his vast knowledge on an eclectic selection of subjects and unique, sometimes peculiar viewpoint of human nature. I felt on certain occasions that he talked about humans as if we were robots which worked on an inbuilt program that just needed to be run and the results analysed and recorded for further use. One fine day, he went ballistics on a philosopher. 'Why does everyone keep saying that human nature is so very complex and thus difficult to understand? To the philosopher who said this, I sharply beg to differ. They only say it because they don't know what and where to look.'

He didn't reveal much about his work, though, and I avoided the temptation of pressing him but my excitement was growing at the speed equal to that of our bonhomie.

In the course of our meetings, I discovered a little secret of his that left me surprised and impressed. Bhrigu Mahesh's vast knowledge had a toehold on my field as well. I, to my great surprise, accidentally discovered a remote cabinet in the far corner of his reading room, stocked with classics like Leo Tolstoy's *The Tale of Two Cities*, Prem Chand's *Gaban*, Alexnadre Dumas's *Black Tulip*, Victor Hugo's *The Hunchback of Notre Dame*, Fyodor Dostoyevsky's *The Idiot*, Anton Chekhov's '*The Cherry Orchard*' Oscar Wilde's '*Canterville Ghost*' and other world classics. It was a clear sign that this amazing man adored literature, too. Imageries thrilled him, metaphors excited him, similes made him smile, and lyrical prose enchanted him into sweet oblivion. Still, he hid this fact from me leaving me to conclude that the jibes that he constantly directed at me for being a literary man was the outcome of a small fire of jealousy that was continually stoked by his admiration for my talents and the frustration he felt for his total lack of it. I respected his secret and never bothered to cross question him on it, promising to myself that if fate willed, my gift would colour his master skill and his, mine. It was a mutually beneficial idea. Our gifts combined, complimented, and completed us, each filling the lacunae in other, fitting gracefully and seamlessly together.

I think I should mention another incident that would go a long way in understanding the sophisticated and exceptional brain of this intriguing man. I remember once barging in on him without announcing myself and I found him lying curled up in his couch, reading a copy of *Shree Shree 1007 Madhusudanacharya: Tale of a Psychic*. He was totally absorbed in his reading and did not even notice me come in. When I coughed gently to get his attention, he jolted out his reverie, panting hard 'Oh Sutte!' He replied, breathlessly, 'You gave me a fright!'

'Yeah. Sneaking up from behind is usually your forte. Glad to have returned the favour.' I replied with a grin, taking my seat on an oak chair. 'What are you reading?'

'Can't you read the bold heading on the frontispiece?'

I was expecting this answer. 'Yes, I saw. I didn't know you were into Psychics.'

'I am not.'

'Then why are you relishing a book written on one?'

'Because' he said, closing the biography after putting in a bookmark, 'The man and his situation interest me.'

'Why?'

'This man was a Jyotishacharya and an important figure in the Hanumat seva trust of the Akhil Bhartiya Brahmin Sabha but when his popularity grew beyond that of his religious peers and the money that poured into the trust because of his oratorical skills and a knack for hiding ignorance behind a natural flair for showmanship and theatrics, he decided it was now time to cut his losses by disengaging himself from the trust and running solo in the business. The only thing that he retained from his past was his title—Shri Shri 1007 Madhusudanacharya. In order to increase his income, he exploited his talent for flamboyant chicanery by turning into a clairvoyant. After a successful career of over twenty years as a psychic and medium for talking to the dead, he was to get awarded with the title of 'Guru, the divine one' for his pivotal roles in helping humanity find god, religion, peace, and happiness. You know what he did?'

'No.'

'He rejected the title saying that he wouldn't defraud his good work by hiding behind a dishonest profession anymore. In other words, the love that people showered upon him struck his conscience pretty badly and unheeding words of caution from his PR employees, he came clean.'

'That is odd. Crooks like him never change. I don't know what happened that caused the sudden arousal of his impotent conscience.'

'You didn't get the sarcasm, didn't you?' Bhrigu said with a faint smile lining the corners of his mouth. 'There was no conscience involved at all. This man, for all his ignorance, understood human nature. He wanted to test the faith of his followers in him and hence he took a calculated risk that made his position even unshakeable than before. In this way, he put a firm stop to all the bad publicity he had been receiving from the media and sceptics lately.' He took a pause packed with suspense and asked, 'Did you know what his followers did after this confession?'

'Why? They must have been shocked to say the least and then they would have left his side, cursing him loudly.'

'You are wrong, my man.' He replied with a smile. 'People flat out refused to believe him. They said he was getting a little senile in his old age. They are hell bent on giving him the title and are ready to go to any means to see to it that he accepts.'

'Really?'

'Yes. This episode hides a very significant lesson and on it lays the whole game plan of these esteemed, self-canonised *Gurus*.'

'And what would that be?'

'The desperate desire to believe, to hope, to dream, to love. When you lose someone you loved and when the last thing you are capable of doing is to let go of him or her, despite people telling you so; one seemingly empathetic person, however corrupt, holds your hand firmly, looks into your eyes and says that your loved one is still with you, you are so relieved and happy, the excruciating pain is gone only to be replaced with contentment that you would never even for a second believe that he may be lying. Be you the most reasonable and logical person on the planet, but when you are faced with such a crisis, you would always prefer to leave the cold hands of reason to join the warm ones of deceit. This is human nature. To hope is to live and anything that keeps this hope alive is welcome. Many of his followers, deep down, must be sceptics themselves, but they have buried that reasoning part of themselves because it interfered with their desperate desire to hope. This man like the rest of the *Gurus* was just a symbol of hope desperately crafted by the part of humanity struggling to jerk off the thick blankets of gloom. Even clairvoyants, who claim to have astonishing perceptive powers, ingenious ruses, and uncanny ability of insight that can easily fool a bystander into submission, fail to understand that they are there not because of their powers mimicking the supernatural but because of that bystander's desperate need for the psychic to possess those powers. He gives the psychic his powers and can take it away as soon as he is ready to combat the situation instead of hiding from it. And seeing this may never be as it is our primal instinct to fly instead of fight, the world of psychics, pundits, soothsayers, et al will continue to flourish.'

Again, I found myself looking at him with my mouth hanging half open in wonder. This is just a prototype of the conversations I used to have with him. He always analysed and dissected a controversial issue with such a surgical precision that I was speechless for a moment or two. I had never thought that the world of Psychology that is so vague with ill-defined boundaries could be explained almost as if it were an exact science. Had he gone a bit further in his lecture, he could have even made it into a law. A law not very unlike that of Physics which is rigid and not given to ugly exceptions. I said as much to him and he replied, half amused, 'Newton stated in the first law of motion that "for every action there is an equal and opposite reaction". Well, is it not true for human behaviour as well? Psychology looks like a pseudoscience, but let me assure you that if we are here for a hundred years more, it *will* be proven that it is as exact a science as any. At present, we just lack the proper tools to study or analyse the human mind. Once we do, psychology could become so exact a science that there would be a unit system for thoughts and dreams, emotions and feelings.'

'Are you trying to say,' I asked incredulously, 'that there could come a time when we would have machines to plumb the depths of a human mind, reaching its every corner, and producing a perfect report of what lies there?'

'It would depend on the sophistication of the machine but yes.'

I was now laughing aloud. 'Well, if I say it is over the top, it would be a gross understatement.'

He looked a little offended. 'I do it occasionally. Though my methods are manual I can assure you that they produce astounding results. In a very near future, I am sure that my researches would be used to write algorithms for computers and that would mean the same work in much less time. If we can program computers to do myriad jobs for us in much less time as compared to when we had to do it manually, why can't psychologists do the same?'

My mirth had left me now. Against my wish, I was finding myself bending towards his theory. 'You say that you can do it? That you can analyse a mind like you do a physical sample and run it like a program?'

'Yes.'

'Well, demonstrate it to me.'

'I will, my friend. God willing, I will,' he said with a smile.

He said this with such conviction that it ceased to sound like an impossible or fantastic theory. Who knew what future had in store for us? And the rate at which this world was getting mechanised, there could come a time when the mind would also go the same way. Bhrigu Mahesh was definitely a futuristic man in that respect. He had such tremendous powers of uncanny insight that he might as well be the first person to set this process into motion. If I believed what he had just said to me, he could have started it already.

Our camaraderie went from strength to strength and there was seldom a weekend when we didn't pay a visit to each other. After a year of our acquaintance though, I started to observe certain changes in him. He had become very despondent and looked as if he was grieving over something. His condition worsened with every passing day. When I could take no more of his gloom, I asked him, 'What's the matter? Why are you so upset nowadays?' At first, he was reluctant, but when I reassured him, he poured out his story to me. It was the very first time that he was discussing his professional life and its challenges with me.

After a long wait, I actually got a glimpse of how he worked. His methodology in dealing with the suspects was very scientific, to say the least. He used interrogation to study, research, and collect data that he would then feed in his brain for future reference. He was fine-tuning the abnormalities, anomalies, and traits of a vast number of personalities; so that when time arose he could sift through the cosmic data to come up with the one that matched with the person under study. I was witnessing, for the very first time in my life, such an analytic and objective way of studying something so subjective. He had not lied to me, after all.

I gathered from his account that he was an officer who applied his logical mind and good memory in apprehending the offenders of the law. His gift, as I already knew by now, was an innate ability to read personalities. Even from a very early age, he could understand the motivations of human beings way better than anyone else. He was very sensitive himself. This constant, effortless, and successful probing into the human psyche had given way to a strong feeling of empathy and an intense desire to help humanity. For this sole purpose in mind, he had thought of joining the police force. But, his ideal was soon shaken. He believed that what the crack of a whip couldn't do, a few, simple but efficient methods could.

'My findings, I should tell you, are based on experience and detailed research,' he explained. 'I have found that the bulk of convicts, which, for comparison's sake, I call the A-Type, constitutes of first-time offenders committing a crime in the grip of a very strong emotion or misunderstanding. This class is already weak, vulnerable, fearful, and almost at the verge of breaking down, approachable only by a show of compassion and understanding. The second type or B-Type is of the first- or second-time offenders who commit a felony either for their profit or due to strong, prejudicial beliefs. This group is tougher than the first one because they are in better possession of their faculties with an already thought out plan of action if any such contingency arises. This category could respond very well to a few psychological tricks that I have invented and applied by careful observation of criminal behaviour with astounding results. The last pool or the C-type comprises hardened criminals who survive and thrive by extorting, exploiting, and killing. Now, this is the class that is known to show some sort of compliance only when thoroughly whipped. What the system should do is to classify them into their respective categories and treat them accordingly. But the police force is apparently oblivious to this fact. Their treatment is same for a first- or second-time offender as it is for a history-sheeter. They beat the pulp out of anyone, sometimes even before they have any concrete evidence to support that the accused is actually guilty. Justice is impeded by such primitive, barbaric methods where logic and reason is always considered an ill affordable luxury. The policy of violence begets confession is surely and steadily bending the backbone of the criminal justice system and it is now a matter of time when it would eventually snap beyond all repair.' He sighed like a tired man. 'I feel like a freak when I see my colleagues laughing with derision as I try to apply my methods for getting speedy and elegant results. They joke that I behave more like a scientist and less like a police investigator and that the suspects are my test subjects. But I can hardly blame them. Hardened over the years by constantly trying to make their low pay, work with their mediocre brain and difficult job, my fellow officers have learnt to rely fully on the rule of the cane. It's the easiest way to vent their frustration and also requires minimal effort from the brain. Their undying faith in their muscle power is further strengthened by the fact that detailed investigation is a time and labour consuming process which is better left alone. If that was not enough, procedural bottlenecks and red tapes have given more power to my colleagues and have tied my hands even further. There is no freedom to work or to experiment. If I say that I am suffocating in this job, it would be a gross understatement. I had come here hoping to make lives better but instead have ended up as a puppet in the hands of the bureaucracy and a standing joke in the hardboiled police circle.'

I heard his dilemma and advised, 'Is there nothing you can do? Surely, there's got to be a solution.'

He must be pondering over a possible solution himself because at my next visit, he told me, 'I have decided that I can no longer serve a system that I can neither understand nor support. I have almost decided of leaving the job and turning into a private investigator. I believe that with my hands no longer tied down by obsolete protocols, lengthy procedures and draconian ways of investigation, I would be able to serve better.'

For me, it felt as if ordained by god. The arrangement that I had secretly prayed and hoped for was coming to fruition! I should mention that although I wrote a column of political satire for one of the leading English newspapers of India and simultaneously worked as an editor for an International Publishing house, the genre of detective fiction had always held a fascination for me. It was a hobby that I had acquired while still on the threshold of adolescence which had only matured with time. I was wonderstruck by the observational genius of Sherlock Holmes, bold over by the logical marvel of Dupin, totally mesmerised by the insight of Father Brown, astounded by the energy of Monsieur Lecoq, and stupefied by the attention to the microscopic detail of Dr Thorndyke. Inspired by these maestros of deduction, I unsuccessfully tried my hand at writing some of my own but it didn't take long for me to realise that I totally lacked the acuity and insight that a true detective takes for granted. After having this epiphany, I teetered on the edge of giving my endeavours up when this man came along. That lucky day, when I first met him, I wasn't even aware that my subconscious had already registered that I had finally found my inspiration. This taciturn, highly sensitive man of amazing calibre who wanted to serve humanity and also to learn from it to help aid his researches, the scope of which I still didn't know, was now my protagonist and I felt honoured indeed to serve him on his mission by writing the memoirs of our experiences together, where Bhrigu worked in the full capacity of an investigator and I (as he loved to say and I let him humour himself because I well knew about his secret fascination with anything that sounded even remotely literary), his scribe.

Bhrigu's stint with the Patna police and few of his high profile successes had made him a sort of celebrity in detective circles and as soon as word spread of him turning into a private investigator, requests started pouring from every corner of the country, imploring him to look into this matter or that. His reputation grew to such an extent that when someone was in a fixture, they contacted him instead of money guzzling lawyers or police officers suffering from the acute form of procrastination.

After leaving his five-year-old job, Bhrigu had yearned to visit his homeland, Senduwar, in Rohtas District of Bihar. The crippling fear of Nirja Masi had been a deterrent in fulfilling his simple wish. He vividly remembered the days from his childhood when the woman had ruled over him with an iron fist. The only working relationship that they shared was that of a master and slave. The slave had finally run away from his master in a wild shot at freedom, vowing never to return again.

On the fifth of June, 2010, we arrived at the Sasaram Railway station and took a Tempo to Senduwar. Bhrigu had plucked the courage to return back after I advised him to face his troubles squarely and get done with it. Fears tend to become terrible phobias if left to fester. He had to chin up and face the woman boldly, never letting her bullying affect him again. The trick had worked like a miracle. The inexorable torments of the woman were, if not destroyed, now well on a leash.

It's a popular adage that when someone you talk of materialises before you, he or she would have a long life. I don't know if there is a scientific explanation behind this phenomenon, but it's a saying, just the same. So, without realising that he had just earned himself a long life, Bhrigu came traipsing in. He was wearing a green and white Kurta-Payjama, and in his left hand, he held the handle of a battered-looking umbrella.

'Oh! Here you are!' I beamed. 'What took you so long?'

He took a stool and lapsed into it with relief. 'It's been a long day. It took hours to find a recharge shop.'

'Did you meet your friend?'

'No. He has shifted to Delhi. I should have known. I wasn't the only one who wanted a new and better life. How was your day?'

'Minus your relative, it was very pleasant indeed.'

'Hah! She got under your skin, didn't she?' he said with a chuckle. 'Don't say I didn't warn you before.'

'She tried hard, no doubt, but I resisted her firmly,' I said with certain pride.

He smiled. 'Sutte, I met an old woman today.'

After a thought, he added, 'She will be coming here in the evening with what she claims to be her tale of woe. The woman is beside herself with grief. I felt I should hear what she has to say.'

This surprised me a little. It was a wonder how positive strangers divulged their inmost secrets and unspoken fears to this man without the slightest hesitation. I remembered how I was drawn towards him the moment I noticed him in the crowd. He looked ordinary with nothing even remotely remarkable about his personality. Yes, he was in the habit of wearing Kurta Pajama only and that, too, in myriad combinations of colour, but that could hardly qualify as a plausible explanation for his gift. The closest I could get in the way of finding an answer to this unique ability of his was by observing him when he was in conversation with a troubled soul. His eyes would shine with the brilliance of compassion and the few words of commiseration, offered with a reassuring smile, was enough for anyone to trust him and his judgment more than any passionate rhetorical.

'Where did you meet her?' I asked with unmasked curiosity.

'At my friend's house. She lives there now. I invited her over to our place, tomorrow morning.'

'That's all right,' I replied. 'Our plans for tomorrow stands corrected then.'

CHAPTER 2

THE MYSTERY

2

A hint of humidity in the air, post the rains, had significantly lowered the pleasant cool of the day before. Electricity went off early in the morning adding to our discomfiture. Although, I was an early riser, I felt I could have added a couple of hours to my siesta if the fan was still working. To my surprise, I found that Bhrigu had already arisen. I found him sitting on the porch outside, fanning himself with a hand fan.

'Wow!' I said, yawning. 'You woke up early.'

'Yeah, couldn't sleep last night.'

'Why? Let me guess, the heat or mosquitoes?'

'Nightmares'

'Nightmares?'

'Yes.'

I waited for him to explain but he continued fanning himself, staring at the wicket gate. 'Well, what nightmare?'

He sighed. 'I slept in this house after almost a decade. Let just say, some not so good memories paid me a visit.'

I could detect a dull pain in his voice. 'It will be all right. Tomorrow will be better, I'm sure.'

He didn't reply but kept staring at the gate. I followed his gaze to locate the object of his interest. Besides the dilapidated wooden carcass of the gate, a squirrel sitting atop the boundary that ran along it, and a few wild shrubs scattered about, I could find nothing of interest.

'What are you staring at?'

'I am expecting her any instant,' he replied dully.

I was about to coax him into getting inside, when an old woman sneaked up to the gate and struggled to open it. Bhrigu wasted no time in running to her help. He held her right hand and led her to the house.

She was a small, frail woman somewhere between 60 to 65 years old. Her slight stoop and shuffling gait made her look far older than she already was. Double-rimmed spectacles sat on her nose, completely obscuring her eyes with the powerful lenses. Her skin was racked with wrinkles and she was in the habit of smacking her lips continuously. Her unsteady walk was a proof of arthritis as she carried herself on a stout, wooden stick.

We seated her on a chair and took our positions on a stool, opposite her. She shifted in her chair awkwardly.

'Amma, please tell us your story. I promise that we will help you to the best of our abilities,' Bhrigu said sincerely.

She was silent and looked at me instead. 'This is my friend, Sutte,' Bhrigu explained. 'He is just like me. You have no need to fear him.'

I smiled and tried to make her comfortable.

She relaxed visibly and, after clumsily fixing her sari over her head by clammy fingers, began—'My name is Jayanti Devi. I . . . I am the widow of Jankhelawan. He was a teacher in the government school here. About thirty-five years ago he died of kidney failure. I had an only son, Malthu. It is about him that I want to talk about.'

'Yes? Please continue. What happened to your son?' Bhrigu coaxed.

A shadow darkened her features and her face muscles twitched with spasms. Her breathing had become a trifle laboured, too. 'I . . . I haven't told anyone. I . . . I was very scared.'

I offered her a glass of water which she gulped down readily.

'Please take as much time as you want. Relax, and when you feel better, we can talk,' said Bhrigu.

She steadied herself and began again. 'My son, Malthu. He . . . he died five years ago. But . . . but it wasn't a natural death, or an accident. I know that.' She stopped to take a breath and said in a tortured voice, heavy with anguish and horror, 'I think . . . I think my son was killed.'

There was a pregnant silence in the room, her last words still reverberating in the air. When the atmosphere cleared, Bhrigu broke the uncomfortable silence. 'Why do you think so?'

She clasped and unclasped her long, bony fingers in sheer nervousness. 'Even after my husband died, his pension afforded enough for me and my child. Also, there are not too many expenses in the village and one manages just fine. Malthu was the apple of my eye. I loved him devotedly and the sole purpose of my existence was to keep him happy and well. You see, Malthu wasn't like normal people. He . . . even at the age of 19, he was still an 8-year-old child at heart. He couldn't study beyond class three as after failing for three consecutive years; the headmaster expelled him saying that what my son really needed was a special school. I pleaded to him and reasoned that if not anything, as the son of a very respected and beloved teacher of the school, that was my late husband, he should be allowed to continue his studies. But the headmaster was adamant and I had to accept my son's fate as it was. My son was such a good person. Was it his fault that he was so innocent? If anything, it was a gift. He was pure of heart and faultless.'

'But why would anyone kill him?' I asked with some impatience.

'For that, I will have to tell you about a legend from this village.'

'Legend?' Bhrigu ejaculated 'What legend?'

A vague, misty look crept into the woman's eyes. Her face relaxed as the years of past unrolled before her. I could clearly see that she was quite fond of telling colourful stories or folklore as is the custom with old village women who have self-appointed themselves as the unofficial authority on the subject. I had a doubt if the following narrative had anything to do with her son. Still, we listened attentively, careful not to aggravate the pain she already felt by our impatience. 'Our village has a legend for a witch, the witch of Senduwar. She was a woman who walked over the soil of this very village some two hundred years ago. She was very well versed in the, what is called "black magic of the herbs". It is said that there are some herbs, special herbs that are found only in certain obscure parts of the village. They have a rather hypnotic effect on people. Jiyashree, that was the witch's name, was skilled in the knowledge about these herbs. She collected them and, after maceration, extracted the potent drug that they contained. She then made a concoction and packed it in several bottles. She used the contents of these bottles on her preys or victims. It is said that one drop of this brew could send a person in to a temporarily induced coma where his own consciousness was destroyed and a new one was created; the one that listened only to the witch. The people under its effect were now her slaves who existed to do her bidding. The tales of her powerful hypnotic potion spread like wildfire throughout the area. Most of the people were outraged and wanted to put a stop to her illicit activities. But, there were some wealthy men who found her evil concoction very appealing. You see, a person under its influence would do anything for his master. The drug could be used for extorting money, executing amorous plans without a hitch, passing an exam, or virtually anything. They secretly started buying the stuff and slowly its black market widened. Jiyashree soon became one of the wealthiest persons the town, let alone the village, had ever seen. After all, it was only she who knew how to prepare the drug. No one shared this knowledge.' She took another sip from the glass and continued. 'A total anarchy gave way to this indiscriminate use of the drug. Sons used it on fathers, fathers on sons, wives on husbands, husbands on wives, students on teachers, farmers on landowners, so on and so forth, each to achieve his or her own selfish end. The drug's effect was reversible. It lasted only for a day but was enough to change one's fortunes in that duration. Now, seeing utter chaos and ruin of human decency and morality and everything that our *shastras* hold dear, a group of elders held a meeting and it was decided that in order to save their town, they had only one option. Jiyashree had to be killed.'

'But what has this fairy tale got to do with your son?' I asked with visible frustration.

'Everything. Please listen to me,' she said and coughed before beginning her narrative again. 'Jiyashree got the wind of the news and went underground. She, despite her efforts, couldn't hold her pursuers for long. Someone tipped them off about her location and they at last captured her. She was then killed in a manner befitting a witch. With much fanfare and the whole village gathered there to witness the execution, Jiyashree was bound to a tree and then set on fire. Her anguished cries were heard all over the village reverberating and then dying somewhere deep in the jungle beyond. The area where she was burned was then barricaded. People were scared of her in her life so were frightened more so in her death. No one visited the place where she was killed. Over the years, a rumour spread that her spirit haunts that place. So, the region surrounding it was totally abandoned and not a soul lurked there.' She stopped to clear her throat. 'But six years back, few of the younger friends of my son dared him to go to the abandoned land. As he was very innocent, he didn't understand the full implication of this challenge. He wandered to the heart of the strip and returned with a smile. He didn't tell his friends, but he had found two gold coins embedded in the ground there, fearful that they would take them for their own.'

She stopped to collect her breath. 'But he told me. I took the coin to a *Seth* and tried to get a good sum for it. He almost cried with amazement and sheer joy claiming that they were no ordinary coins that are pressed in mints but very old gold *asharphis*. I got a fat sum for it but he forced me to explain how they had come into my possession. Already bursting with joy, I told him all. I don't know how it happened, but the news spread like wild fire. The greed for wealth defeated a century-old fear; a fear that had already weakened over the years. It was a gold rush as everyone hurried to the land to find more of those golden nuggets.'

She was silent as if wrestling with strong emotions. We let her collect herself before narrating what was probably the most tragic part of the tale.

'It was a week after the golden fever that had gripped almost everyone in the village that the worst happened. My son was found dead near a well that stands a little way from my house. The villagers said he was killed by Jiyashree who punished him for disturbing her turf. The rumour spread to such an extent that the villagers never dared to enter that area again, afraid that the same fate would be meted out to them.'

'You don't believe in the rumour?' Asked Bhrigu.

'Of course not. My husband used to say that one had no right to support or encourage anything that couldn't be backed by valid reason. I believe in him and his philosophy,' she said proudly.

'How exactly did he die? I mean, did you have a post-mortem?'

'Yes. I couldn't rest without knowing the reason for his sudden death. The report said that he had broken his neck in an accidental fall. There was nothing to hint at a suspicion. But a mother's instincts are very strong and I somehow know that there is foul play behind it. I am certain of it. The police didn't show any interest in the matter, and after being stalled, it was dropped altogether. I beg you to help me, son. I feel that you can help me. I want to be sure about my son's death. I have to know or else there will be no peace for me in this life or after.'

She looked pathetic and careworn. My heart went out to the poor woman who had suffered so much. It was the work of an instant and Bhrigu was on his knees. He firmly held her trembling hand and looked into her sad eyes earnestly.

'Amma, you are no longer alone now,' he said with a sincerity that is hard to describe, 'and your matter is in safe hands.'

3

After Jayanti Devi left, Bhrigu sprawled on the room's only divan. He used his elbows to raise himself on the cushions and started playing with his knuckles, as was his habit when thinking over the odds and ends of a new mystery.

'A typical case of legend tripping,' he said, tapping his knuckles. 'Sutte, why do you think people are so drawn towards the forbidden or tabooed?'

I thought for a while and then observed 'Because such things often hold the greatest fascination for adventurers, young and old alike.'

'But why?'

'Adrenaline rush is what I would prefer to call it. It gives them a high and they enjoy it.'

He made a clucking sound with his tongue and said, 'Don't you think it's sad that there are people so deprived of true joy in their lives that they have to seek such cheap thrills? Pathetic is what I would prefer to call it.'

I looked at him with what would have amounted to a bemused expression on my face. He had such a unique angle of viewing things around him that most often than not he would leave me reeling with wonder at his tremendous hindsight. This time though, I didn't want to fall in with his observation so easily.

'You can say that, of course,' I said. 'But is it such a bad thing to be censured? After all, there are many ways in which people find amusement. And let me tell you that sometimes they are way weirder and dangerous than legend tripping, too.'

His reply was quick and curt. 'More pathetic still.' And after a thought, he added, 'I agree with you on the point that one should not censure a little enjoyment but the ways in which that enjoyment is procured.'

This answer baffled me still. 'I am sorry but I am not following you.'

'No form of entertainment should be allowed that harms a good man in even the slightest possible way. It is not worth it. Human lives are worth more than merely succumbing to popular amusements.'

I sat there absorbing the words he had said so passionately and suddenly the humorous side of it struck me so sharply that a chuckle escaped me even before I had the time to smother it.

'What?!' He bounded at me in sharp retort.

'Nothing,' I said between the fits of laughter 'If . . . if you have had your way then . . . then people would still be dying but this time killed by boredom. Not everyone has a unique gift like yours to keep them occupied, you know.'

'Why don't you reserve your witty cracks for that weekly column of yours?' he said, deeply offended. 'I'll see how it tickles your funny bone when I fire you from the post of my scribe.'

This time I reeled and the light of mirth dancing in my eyes was extinguished as if on a switch. 'It was just a joke, you know. Nothing serious.'

He looked at me with an expression that spoke of nothing but the collective wrath of the titans and as I braced myself for what was to come, he burst out laughing. 'I know how to push your buttons, don't I? Who's the wise guy now? Just look at your face!'

It was my turn now to feel indignant. 'I knew all along that yours was an empty threat. You would never do a thing like that. I know you cherish my company.'

'Really?'

'Yes.'

'Wanna bet on it?'

'I am not a person who encourages betting. So thanks, but no.'

'Ha!' He cried and I knew that the syllable was nothing but the ejaculation of a victor.

Silence prevailed for a space as I groped for ways to get back at him when he said suddenly 'Your hypothesis on this case, please.'

I should mention that whenever we were on a case, he made it a point to know what possible theories I had formed regarding it. I often wondered the reason behind this whim of his and could come up with one or two explanations. First, he really thought much about my intelligence as a puzzle buster or he just wanted to prove the superiority of his acumen for deduction over mine. If one went by experience, the latter would qualify as the correct answer.

Well, whatever the reason, I loved to exercise my brain and grabbed every opportunity that he threw my way.

'Well, unlike some of your cases, this one was clear from the very beginning,' I said with confidence. 'There was someone who wanted to have all the ancient treasure for himself. He saw a golden opportunity after Malthu's death and conspired to turn this tragedy into his own benefit. He circulated the rumour and stood to gain all the wealth.'

'So you believe that Malthu's death was accidental?'

'Why, yes. Don't you?'

'That's debatable,' he said, now gently tapping his knuckles. 'There is one flaw in your theory that you have overlooked'

I started. 'Flaw? What flaw?'

'If you recall, Javanti Devi said that the coins were 'embedded'. Don't you know that ancient artefacts are excavated? They have machines for that sort of thing. Antiquities are dug up through efforts and resource. You don't find them casually lying around for you to pick and pocket.'

I was frankly confused. 'How can you account for it, then? Do you want to say that the coins were counterfeit? That they were not genuine?'

'No. I am not saying that. Remember, Jayanti Devi took them to an expert. If they weren't genuine, he would know for sure.'

'Then?' I asked 'Please tell me clearly whatever you are implying.'

He was lost in his thoughts for a moment. 'We are clear on only one point at the moment,' he said. 'The coins are a part of an old treasure but they weren't discovered where they were found.'

'So?' I asked with a hint of exasperation. 'Why is this so important? Should you not concentrate on the bigger problem? A man is dead and we have to investigate it. Why do you care for trivial details that have no bearing on the case!?'

'Trivial?' He almost exploded. 'There is no such thing as important or trivial. Every detail is important. Of all the people, you should know that. Haven't you read your fair share of detective stories? The fictional detectives have a good point when they say it. If not all, this observation has profound practical applications. And again, if we have to look into the matter, we better be thorough or else we'll leave room for doubt.'

'All right,' I conceded. 'I don't see myself agreeing with you on this but you are my protagonist. According to the rules, you investigate and I follow.'

He laughed heartily. 'Sometimes I forget that I am your hero,' he said with a chuckle.

'Protagonist,' I corrected.

'Or hero,' he riposted.

I was about to get ready for a long debate when he said, 'My battery's dead. Will you Google the legend of this witch for me? Let's see what it has to say.'

I flicked my cell phone and, after typing 'The Legend of the Witch of Senduwar', waited in anticipation for the page to load. There were a few headings and I clicked the one at the topmost. It mentioned the details much the same as the woman had narrated before. However, there were inputs from a few anthropologists and historians who had researched the subject thoroughly. They had come up with possible reasons for the existence of such a legend, the rich history behind it and the strong forces of superstition that had led it to become almost a reality for the inhabitants of the village. I read a paragraph from an online article from a prestigious national newspaper that had been posted a couple of years ago—

'Sometimes when truth is buried under the weight of years it becomes distorted. Sometimes the diversions from the truth are so marked that they take up the mantle of the supernatural and turn into a legend. Says Dr Chandrika Mahendra, head, department of anthropology, Delhi University. "The Witch of Senduwar, Jiyashree, must originally have been a woman well versed in pharmacognosy—the science of plants and its medicinal properties. Her talents would have been so immense as to exceed the development of science during that period. Her gift must have been misread as great evil by people who could neither understand it nor offer an explanation for it. The things that we cannot understand invoke the greatest fear. This fear soon escalated to such an extent that it took the form of hatred for the woman, who they thought to be the worshipper of black magic. Hence, in order to get rid of the constant dread under which they lived, they decided to finish it once and for all by killing the woman. This incident warped with time to an extent that it has now become a legend. It is pathetic that even after such an advancement in science, the tragic, superstitious part of the story was preserved whereas the truth was obliterated. To search the reason for this, we visited the village and found that our analysis and fears were realised. Owning to the low literacy rate and utter failure of the government agencies to extend proper education to the inhabitants, the village has become a breeding ground for such ridiculous dogmas." Another scientist at NABARD, Dr Rishi Kelkar, confirmed that. . .'

'Here they have mentioned a set of reasons that account for the pathetic state of affairs of this village,' I concluded.

'Isn't it the same story over and over again?' Bhrigu said with a touch of regret colouring his voice. 'Senduwar came under review because of this strong and preposterous belief that the villagers have in their local witch. If they could only find the time to reach each and every village or hamlet of the country, save a few of them, the rest would be telling the exact same story. No proper drinking water, inadequate electricity, nonexistence of functioning *panchayats*, no proper healthcare system, exploitation of farmers, no sustainable jobs, so on and so forth.'

His line of thinking had diverted into a totally different stream of thought that he soon checked.

'Well, I have avowed that I will do my job to the best of my abilities. The poor woman's state was so wretched. I would love to be the person who brought peace back into her life. For that, it is very necessary that she should find closure about what really happened to her son.' He said, 'Try to get a good night's sleep today. Tomorrow, we are going to pay a visit to this famous ground that has been a source not only of unaccounted wealth but also of a woman's unaccountable grief.'

CHAPTER 3

THE INVESTIGATION

4

Sometimes, I wondered whether he was not only a gifted sleuth but also, a sort of social worker who worked for the underprivileged in his own way. I have observed that, from the loads of emails and letters of requests pouring in, some from very wealthy and powerful people, he preferred to pick those who couldn't afford the costs of a wealthy lawyers or the expense of a costly private investigator. Only once in a while, when his resources depleted, he took over a rich person, one who could adequately fill his coffers and enable him further to help those in need.

Having been born and brought up in a family of wealthy entrepreneurs who moved from city to city, promoting and adding to their ever-growing business of 'Sutte Rubber Tires and Spare parts', I could never get an opportunity to visit a town, let alone a village. For my parents, business was life and they seldom deviated from topics other than 'Don't you think this is the best time to buy such and such stock?' or 'Our profits will increase twofold if we amalgamate with the

Bharat Automobile parts. There business is shooting high!' My life's goal had been decided even before I was born. I had to be another cog in the machinery that ran 'Sutte Tires and Spare parts'. But to the chagrin of my parents, and to my immense relief, I wasn't blessed with the loss-gain-oriented pragmatic mind that is imperative for a person who wants to make big in business. I never longed for either a high-end entrepreneurial line or the attractions of a tantalising city life. Growing up, most of my time was spent either buried under books or lying on my roof, trying to make out the dim stars hidden under the thick blanket of smog. At school, I had only a couple of like-minded friends who shared my hobbies and as a protection from the bullies; we formed a tight group thinking it to act like an impregnable fortress against our enemies, faithfully relying on the adage that 'there is strength in unity' and realising dismally that proverbs could sometimes be grossly misleading. I subsequently graduated from a prestigious university with honours in English literature and went on to get my PhD in the same subject. My astounding performance (and a little push from an influential friend of my father's who was also one of the trustees of the said university, I should add) I got the position of a reader there. Soon though, I reluctantly arrived at the conclusion that what I had expected to be my dream job had insidiously turned into a nightmare as after teaching for a couple of years, the inexorable routine of my work that always followed a rigid line, threatened to destroy the unpredictability of my life and hence the excitement that comes with it. To cut a long story short, my work had stagnated and so had my life. As I heard myself lugubriously repeating the same lines from the same poet for a hundredth time, realisation struck that I had reached the end of my tether. I resigned from the job (much to the chagrin of my father and his friend) and, after struggling for a year, landed the job of an assistant editor at a publishing house, working simultaneously with the local paper in the capacity of a satirist. Although I was still not fully satisfied with this job as well and secretly yearned for the ever eluding excitement for novelty, I chanced upon Bhrigu one fateful day and my world went upside down. Old passions resurfaced with a chance to satisfy them to the full. I had at last found the spicy ingredient, the missing element, in the broth of my life that would now give it the flavour it so sorely lacked.

I remember, when I was young, my father was always in the annoying habit of teasing me by saying that I was a long lost soul of some ancestor who must have been a poet. And true enough, I was rather drawn towards culture, ethnicity, festivals, and traditions that could never be found in the cosmopolitan climate of a great city. The roots almost invariably led us to the countryside. However, the villages may lack in the glamour and easy, comfort-ridden life that the cities take for granted, the cities could never provide an adequate compensation for the rich mores, painstakingly preserved by the indigenous. I longed to be on the other side of this cultural divide; free at last to explore my roots and to feel, for once, the pride and joy of being a true Indian. I longed to experience the joys of nature that inspired great poets like Keats to write such beautiful poetry. So, one could imagine my joy as I prepared myself for such a visit. This was the very first time, after our arrival at Senduwar that I was about to tour the village and to my good fortune, our sojourn was also going to herald the beginning of what could amount to a remarkable adventure.

The beautiful village of Senduwar is located in the south-central Bihar's Rohtas district. It sits in the lap of Kaimur hills that encloses it like an impregnable fortress. Nature has tried its best to help the residents forget the lack of basic amenities by providing them with its gifts instead. It's verdant as far as the eyes can see. The immensely fertile flood plains have given birth to foliage as abundant as it is diverse. The lush forests claiming the hills add to this beautiful landscape of green. It is akin to looking at this world through a green filter. The small but colourful houses that are nestled comfortably in these foothills along with the broken, meandering dirt roads provide an insignificant break to this overpowering, all encompassing hue.

The human race living here has succeeded in existing harmoniously with nature in its raw, rugged form. But there is an expanse of land just outside the fields and inside the boundary of the foot hills where this coexistence ends. It's a desolate, abandoned stretch of land that borders the hills and as it is under the sole control of nature, the complete lack of human touch also becomes apparent. There is no civilisation as far as the eyes can see but only a long stretch of gloomy flood plain of which the controversial area forms a part. As one moves a little inside this area, one will meet a dust laden board, with its stem thrust deep into the soft ground which says 'Jiyashree's Garden'. Once upon a time in history, roughly two hundred years ago, this region had prospered under Jiyashree as a natural botanical garden were she laboured hard day and night busily collecting and classifying her alleged magical herbs. It was here that Bhrigu and I stopped at last, weighing our chances of stepping foot on the unholy ground that had somehow been the source of a woman's tragedy. If the past had stayed past, the region would have remained the picture of reckless abandon that it was but when it started to threaten the present, it had to be disturbed from its long sleep.

'It looks as if no one has come here in ages.' I observed.

'With good reason,' he replied grimly.

Slowly and surreptitiously, we stepped foot on the no man's land and cautiously moved forward. The alluvial soil felt damp and soft under my feet. It had rained heavily for the past week and hence the ground was still wet. The fresh, earthy smell that emanated from the damp top soil was intoxicating and overpowering. It was little after one in the afternoon, but the thick copse of trees towards the foothills totally obliterated the sun, leaving it dark and dismal. A solitary ray of sun would peek through the trees now and then to offer a weak respite from the dark, lighting the ground for a moment. We were moving about slowly, eyes trained on the ground.

'We will have to scan the earth carefully,' Bhrigu said. 'I am not a big fan of sloppy work. So, I have a plan. We will break the ground in two halves. This half is yours and this, mine.'

I nodded to show my agreement. There was something heavy and depressing about the place that made speech of any kind almost impossible. My heart was heavy as if weighed down by a stone and my instincts were telling me to leave the place alone. Still, ignoring the unreasonable dread, I put myself to work.

Bhrigu, too, had relapsed into total silence. I could sense by his grim expression that he, too, shared my thoughts in silence. We hadn't expected it to be this dark during the day and hence we were compelled to use the feeble light from our cell phones to look around. It was a mighty difficult task and my eyes, behind my spectacles, had started to water. Still, I was doing my best not to leave any square inch of the ground unexplored as I am a perfectionist (at least in the presence of Bhrigu) and there is nothing in the world that could impede me while I was at my job.

'Did you find anything?' Asked Bhrigu, his voice coming somewhere from the far side.

'I am still searching,' I replied. 'But I think there's not much to see. It's just a desolate part of the flood plain and nothing else.'

'I think you're right,' he said with a note of dismay. 'There is seriously nothing here. No sound of man or beast. For the last half hour, all I could hear was the shuffling of two pairs of nervous feet.'

'Well, yes . . . Wait! What was that?' It so happened that a streak of sun light, finding a gap in a tree, had struck the land at the extreme left corner and instead of revealing a solid piece of earth, had kindled it with a dazzling fire.

'The light hit something!' Bhrigu shrieked. We ran towards the source of brilliance and eagerly frisked the surface with our hands. I got hold of an object that was half buried in the ground there and with some effort I successfully pulled it out from its shallow grave. We stared at it together.

'Oh my god!' My friend gasped.

I was the first to regain my voice from the shock. 'Oh heavens! It's a corner of a gorgeous ruby necklace!'

5

'How did this necklace get here?' I gasped 'It makes no sense.'

'Embedded in the soil just like the golden nuggets that Malthu found six years ago,' Bhrigu said mechanically.

'What's happening? Who is the maniac who is going about burying priceless ornaments and jewels?'

I could see that the gears behind Bhrigu's brain were churning. I too tried to make some sense of the matter but realised soon that it was a futile attempt that was sure to yield no result. How did this new discovery figure in the already complicated mystery? Was it in any way connected with the death of Malthu? Was this a sort of scrambled puzzle with many of its pieces still missing? First, the desolate and pathetic terrain with an old legend haunting it, then the discovery of the gold coins, probably very old; the subsequent gold rush, the mysterious death of Malthu, and now this buried corner of a necklace. Were these events isolated or connected in some sinister way?

They built a legend and somehow laid the groundwork for a great tragedy. I had a foreboding that if this mystery wasn't cleared up soon, the stage would churn up graver tragedies still.

'I don't think that this is the handiwork of any person,' said Bhrigu. 'The ornament doesn't look planted at all. Had we not known better, we could have well mistaken it for waste, littered on the ground.'

'So what should we do now? Search more thoroughly?'

'And risk getting our fingerprints all over what could amount to potential evidence? No. We will get some concrete information first and then if it is required, we'll come back wearing a good pair of gloves and get on with the soil frisking. Not until then.'

'How will we get the required information then?'

Bhrigu thought for a space, staring blankly at the glittering piece of necklace in his hands. 'I know the *sarpanch* of this village. He is the fourth-generation head of *panchayat* from his family. I am sure that he would know, if not all, at least something about the golden rush, and who knows, also the reason for littered treasure?'

I nodded in agreement. Bhrigu wrapped the necklace in a tissue paper (he had good foresight to bring it along) with as little contact of his fingertips as possible and pocketed it in his Kurta. We were now unofficially the custodians of the exquisite artefact.

It was a little before sundown that we arrived at Bhrigu's house. Nirja Masi had gone to attend a *Ramayana katha* in the neighbourhood and was probably still there. The shrill chants from the holy scripture of Hindus, *Ramayana*, rented the air, making any kind of conversation impossible. The *kirtan* was an overnight affair and would end twenty-four hours from the moment it began.

'You know,' said Bhrigu as he unlocked the door and gained entry inside the house, 'these *kirtans* bring back not so good memories.'

'Really?'

'Yes. When I was a boy, Nirja Masi forced me to attend them. I would sit with her from morning till dusk; my hands clapped on my ears, waiting for the onslaught to get over. I could never understand how people could find peace in such a din.'

'I think they try to tune the frequency of their inner clamour to that of the outside. That way they experience an illusion of peace,' I reflected.

'You think so? Well, that's an interesting point of view,' he said. 'I never considered it that way before.'

'It only just occurred to me. How else can we justify the pleasure that people take in such a noise?'

'Because they have nothing better to do? Because there are very few sources of entertainment here? I recall that the people, Masi including, were driven to such functions more by the lure of exchanging local gossip than by any true religious zeal. Even the *pundits* shrieked mechanically, with their eyes greedily hovering over the gift and money they would receive at the end of the ceremony. It's a cover-up, I think. Nothing more.'

'Well, you sound bitter.'

'Well, truth is bitter, don't you know?'

I conceded. Obviously, the matter touched some very sensitive points in him that were better left untouched. We settled for a humble but healthy meal of rice, a bowl of lentils, and some bean curry. I had forgotten how hungry I was. We took our meals in absolute silence (minus the noise from the loudspeakers without) and called it a night. Nirja Masi had a separate room at the back of the house which she had locked before going out. It was all for the best as we wouldn't have to worry about letting her in.

The next morning, after having a simple breakfast of some mango chutney, rotis, and curd, we left to see the Village *sarpanch*. His name was Chaudhary Manendra Singh, and as Bhrigu had mentioned earlier, he was the fifth-generation *sarpanch* from his family. It was a long and difficult walk up a gently sloping, narrow, dirt road and almost an hour later, we arrived at a rambling house topped by a red, corrugated roof. The compound in which the house sat was surrounded by a high, brick boundary with a gate that led to an expansive courtyard. There was a shed in the far side of this courtyard where a couple of buffaloes were tied to their post, chewing cud languidly. We inquired for the *sarpanch* from the servant who had opened the gate to usher us in. He showed us to one of the plastic chairs that were arranged in a semi-circle and retreated to call on his master, providing us with the time to observe our surroundings. It was a very quiet and peaceful place. Apart from the mowing of the buffaloes, the chirping of the house sparrows, and the slow rhythmic vibrations of an out-of-sight flour mill in action, there was no other sound to be heard.

It was sometime when we saw the *sarpanch* striding towards us. He was a big, strong man with a resplendent moustache and a grey-green turban adorned his head. Bhrigu remembered how all the *sarpanchas* from this family had always worn this turban as a symbol of pride and authority. The man had dark, brooding eyes and a masterful look that could make a frail hearted man, tremble with awe and respect.

'Yes?' he said in a deep baritone that perfectly complimented his personality. 'What can I do for you, Hmmm?'

Bhrigu noticed that the man had a slight lisp and a habit of adding *hmmm* after every sentence.

After the introductions were over and we had paid our respects, Bhrigu ventured to ask his questions; he did so with a slight tremor in his voice which developed whenever he was making his acquaintance with a new person. In the throes of an investigation, he had to interact with many a people but after an initial hesitation, he overcame it quickly and very beautifully indeed to master every social situation and handle the suspects involved with ease and tact of a man of the world. Let those same people bother him otherwise and he would gladly shut the door in their faces and call it a night. 'Sir,' he said. 'We wanted to talk to you about a matter that I am investigating.'

Manendra Singh's bushy eyebrows shot up. 'Investigating? How do you mean?'

'I am a private investigator. Well, my client has requested for discretion so I cannot comment on the case. Nevertheless, I would be highly obliged if you could help us in answering some very important questions.'

'Does it in any way involve me, hmmm?' He asked a trifle suspiciously.

'Not in the least, I assure you. We only wanted some answers to our questions that only you could provide.'

'I don't know the basis for your reasoning but . . . what is your question?'

Without wasting a moment, Bhrigu produced the triangular corner of the ruby necklace from his pocket and uncovered it carefully. 'We found this necklace at the isolated patch of the floodplain the natives call 'The Haunted Garden'. We want to know if you know anything about how it got there and also about the golden rush that happened five years ago.'

A procession of expressions marched across the Sarpanch's countenance. The first and the only one that I could decipher was that of shock and recognition. 'Did . . . did you go to that unholy ground?!' I noticed that in his jolted state of mind, he had forgotten to suffix his sentence with his signature *hmmm*.

'Yes. We did. So, you really do know something,' said Bhrigu and fixed the man's startled gaze with his own. 'Sir, what's all this about? Whatever you know, please, tell me all. I assure you that a woman's peace lies on your cooperation.'

6

'You shouldn't have gone there,' he said in a choked voice. Had I not seen with my own eyes, I could never have believed that a man such as himself could be capable of quivering like a leaf. I could see that he was also breaking sweat as he removed a handkerchief from the pocket of his Kurta and wiped his brow nervously.

'Why are you so agitated? Surely, a rational man such as yourself mustn't believe in such fairy tales as are evolved round this gifted botanist,' I couldn't help but remark.

'What? Gifted botanist? Who?' Asked the *sarpanch*. Surprise masked his fear for a moment.

'Jiyashree. In colloquial language, she is also known as "The Witch of Senduwar". I object to using such a pejorative name,' I replied

'Oh, so you know an awful lot about the legend already.'

'Yes,' said Bhrigu. 'Please, we want to know everything that even remotely concerns the legend and also, as I said before, the golden rush. If you don't know I should tell you that the frenzy that followed killed an innocent person.'

With visible effort, the Sarpanch got control over his senses. He said in a low, hoarse voice that shook ever so slightly, 'I still don't know the reason that so forced you to visit the land of the damned. It bodes nothing but evil.' He took a breath and said again, 'But if a poor woman's peace hangs in the balance, I'm sure your reasoning must be airtight. Still, I don't think I understand exactly what you mean by your expression—"Gold rush"'

Bhrigu explained it in detail to jog the other's memory.

'Oh! We called it the hunt. And the answer to your question is easy.'

'Easy?' We both asked, surprised.

'Yes. When you have strong connections, it's not difficult to get to the truth, hmm.'

'We had expected as much. You are definitely the most influential man in the village,' said Bhrigu.

'The second most influential, hmm. Ghanshyam Singh, the man who owns the sugar mill and several hectares of land is the most prosperous and powerful man of this village. His forefathers had a grand fiefdom once but although much of it was squandered, he still has quite a fortune left. He is a friend of mine and the bonhomie between our families goes back five generations, hmm. Well. . .' He stopped and gathered his thoughts for a space. 'For the matter at hand, I clearly remember that a team from the Archaeological Survey of India and the Banaras Hindu University had visited this village about two decades ago. The team was led by a man from the B.H.U. department of ancient history, whose name I forget. They carried out excavations in two phases from 1986 to 1987 and again from 1989 to 1990. Necklaces made of precious stones such as harit mani, suryakanta mani, and panna besides earthen pots and hunting tools made of bones were recovered from the village, hmm. The team spent almost nine months in two phases to carry out the excavation. However, the excavation was stopped midway for reasons best known to the team. My source said that the articles recovered during the excavation have been kept at the Archaeological Survey of India's Varanasi-based museum.'

'But the precious bits and pieces of the treasure are strewn all over the ground. They sure weren't excavated!?'

'I was coming to that,' said the man. 'The garden is not the original excavation site.'

'I thought as much,' said Bhrigu.

'What do you mean?' I asked, baffled.

'A large mound above the village of Senduwar is a rich archaeological site. Over the centuries, there have been a lot of prosperous settlements in the region. This is where the archaeologist team came to excavate. The excavations must have loosened the soil and the rainwater seeping through the excavated pits must be washing away nuggets of gold and precious metals buried underground to the damned land, hmm. As is evident from this piece of necklace, the process continues.'

'I see,' said Bhrigu, absorbing the information. His face was clouded over and I knew that something was puzzling him. 'Do you know anything about the first batch of villagers who arrived at the hunt site?'

The man knitted his brows and frowned with concentration. 'I remember that a young lad, he was sort of an imbecile, I'm given to know, first discovered some pieces of gold. The poor boy died of an accident thereafter. He. . .' he stopped in mid sentence as a light of understanding dawned upon him. 'Has your investigation got something to do with him?' He answered the question himself: 'Sure it must be. I know for sure that during the hunt, no one other than this young man was hurt. This village is small and every word gets finally around. Do you think that there was foul play involved, hmm?'

'We cannot divulge further information, sir, but we cannot refute you either.'

'Oh,' said the Sarpanch and eased a little into his seat. He looked at us with eyes sparkling with the anticipation of what was to come. 'The matter definitely stands corrected now. If I say that the man's relatives were the ones who enjoyed the spoils of the excavation most, even before the village heard a word of it, what would you say, hmm?'

'Malthu's relatives? But Jayanti Devi said nothing about it!' I ejaculated in my surprise and regretted my lapse at once.

'Ah! Malthu. Yes. I remember now that this was his name. So, my doubts were well founded, hmm. It is indeed about him that you are investigating.'

'Do you know about these relatives?' Asked Bhrigu.

'No. I am sorry I can't help you there. I just heard that they were the ones who laid the foundation for the gold hunt.'

At this point, Bhrigu and I exchanged a startled look.

So Jayanti Devi had lied to us. It was not the gold peddler but her own relatives whose actions had caused the precious discovery of the treasure become general knowledge. But why? Did she suspect something about their possible involvement? Was this the reason she came to us for help? Why, then, did she hide the most important piece of information?

'How can you know this for sure?' Bhrigu asked.

'My old servant told me. He, too, had gone to the site to try his luck.'

'Can you give me his name and address?'

'I can't. He died a year ago from T.B.'

'Any family?'

'No. He was an orphan. My father took him in when he was a child.'

'I see,' said Bhrigu as we rose to leave. 'Thank you, sir. You have indeed helped us a lot.'

'And I will continue to do so. I am here at your service if you need my assistance again. He was a dear kid. If someone hurt him on purpose, he ought to get his just desserts.'

'Just one more question,' said I. 'I am sorry if I am outspoken, but I really want to know the reason for your irrational fear. You sure don't believe in the witch. Why then are you so frightened of her legend?'

The *sarpanch* took in a deep breath and said, 'I cannot explain it on logic alone.' He said slowly, 'It's just a feeling that has been cultivated in my pedigree through the ages and I guess I, too, have learned to share this fear. That is all I can say in my defence.'

'Well, thank you again,' said Bhrigu, and we were on our way home with my mind buzzing with a thousand questions.

7

'Why did Jayanti Devi lie to us?' I asked, trying to squeeze myself into the narrow seat of the *Parivahan* bus. Even after occupying three-fourth of it, I was still finding it difficult to fit in the cramped space. My friend on the other hand had easily slipped into a strip of the seat and was abstractedly looking out the window at the slowly darkening landscape that whizzed past us.

The bus was packed to capacity and many of the villagers, not lucky enough to get seats, were perched precariously by clutching the metal bar affixed to the roof of the bus. I figured them out to be workers returning home after a hard day's work at the only functioning sugar mill of the village.

'What I tell you now can only amount to conjectures,' said Bhrigu. I could scarcely make out his features in the dim, yellow light of the bulb. 'Let's not get into this tempting habit. The lesser we involve ourselves in guesswork, the better it is.'

'How about an intelligent guess? I have seen you advocating the use of one.'

'This won't be a case of the aforementioned. Intelligent guesses are based on solid facts that start you off in the right direction. We just extrapolate the events further and get to the final result. A wild guess, on the other hand, is pure conjecture and more often than not lead the investigation completely astray. We should avoid it at all cost. Tomorrow I shall go to meet Jayanti Devi and hear it from the horse's mouth. I will tell her squarely that if she wants her case to be investigated thoroughly, she'll have to be forthcoming with us or else we drop the matter then and there.'

I could see that he was not in a very genial mood right now. Jayanti Devi's betrayal must have forced him into thinking that he had failed in winning her complete trust and by what I knew of him that must have stung deeply.

'You didn't ask an important question, though,' he said with a hint of disappointment.

'Important question? What's that?'

'You remember your own theory that someone exploited Malthu's death by circulating the rumour and thus stood to gain all the wealth? Do you remember?'

'It was my theory so I do remember,' I said, a trifle hurt.

'Don't you see that your theory has been smashed to pieces?'

I was baffled. 'How?'

He looked at me curiously and I could feel that he was just a little piqued. 'You surprise me sometimes! Think hard!'

I mulled over it for a few minutes but gave it up. 'Please. I am very tired as it is and in no mood to play brain games. Do tell me.'

He exhaled as if coming to terms with my laxity and said, 'Okay. You said that this was a scheme of a conniving person to have the gold for his own. But the gold and the jewels were never taken. They are still collecting on the flood plain in total neglect. No one claimed them. So, your theory has been reduced to dust.'

'You're right! Oh god! How couldn't I see it?' I exclaimed, clutching his hand in excitement. 'But that includes another question. Why, then, was Malthu killed at all?'

'Now, that is a good question,' he said sombrely.

We spent the rest of the journey in silence, each occupied with his own thoughts. The bus dropped us at the station and we covered the rest of the distance on foot. Nirja Masi was already asleep in her room when we arrived. We took our simple meal and retired to the roof for the night. Tired from the long journey, I fell asleep almost at once, but not before thinking what tomorrow might bring for us.

CHAPTER 4

THE SUSPECTS

8

It was raining hard the next day and I was positive that we would have to spend the rest of the day trapped in the house with a man eater. Nirja Masi was in her prayer room and before she could pounce on us, I implored to my friend, 'Let's not change our schedule.'

'Scared of her?'

'I am not scared of anything,' I said, indignant. 'I just want to avoid her nag.'

'Well, your reason is sound enough. Let me tell you, my friend, that I have no intention to stay here, too, and await my destruction. What are umbrellas for? We will make good use of them.'

To our immense relief, the strong rains had reduced to a drizzle and our umbrellas managed quite well in securing us from getting soaked. The journey was a difficult one and the rain had done everything in its capacity to complicate matters further. Any foot hold on the slippery, slushy dirt road was proving to be a difficult technical manoeuvre that required great skill and control. Bhrigu's lithe body and nimble footfalls enabled him to glide over the surface, leaving me to struggle to keep pace with him.

'Can you not slow down a notch?' I panted

He didn't reply and continued to sprint down the road. After moves that could give Fred Astaire a run for his money, we arrived at a cluster of mud houses situated near an abandoned playground. There was only one *pakka* house in their midst and I knew that this must belong to the woman Jayanti Devi.

We took shelter in the dry balcony as Bhrigu firmly knocked at the door.

'Who's there?' A weak voice sounded from within.

'Amma, it's me, Bhrigu. Please open the door.'

We waited for a full five minutes when the door opened slowly, framing a woman in it. She looked at us with evident surprise. 'Beta, you?' she said 'Why did you come here in this awful weather?'

'Will you not invite us in?'

'Come in, come in,' she said pleasantly and struggled to tidy the room for our benefit. I could see that the room was almost empty save a plastic chair, a wooden bed, a low table where a heavy book of Holy Scriptures was kept, and a built-in cupboard that sported a messy collection of jaded, light-coloured saris.

'I have only one chair,' she said in a voice so thick with helpless regret that I could not help but feel deep pity for the gentle, soft-spoken old woman. She provided such a pleasant contrast to the ring master, Nirja Devi.

'I will sit on the bed with you,' I offered politely.

Jayanti Devi brought us two glasses of lemonade which we drank thankfully. It went a long way in easing the pain that our limbs had suffered in making the arduous journey.

'Amma,' said Bhrigu getting to the matter at once. 'I think that you have not been forthcoming with us.'

'What do you mean?' she asked, surprised.

'Is it not true that your relatives were the ones who started the gold rush? Why did you not tell us before?'

It was the second time for our humble client to look surprised. 'Who . . . who told you this?' she gasped.

'Amma, we are investigators. It is our job to know. Now, if you are in fear of your relatives, you need to tell me now. You have to be completely honest with me or else we'll have to leave your case.'

Jayanti Devi looked at the point of breaking down. The shadow that we had witnessed before darkened her features again. She broke in a cold sweat and stammered incoherently.

'I . . . I . . . don't know . . . I was afraid . . . I. . .'

We waited for her nervousness to subside and gave her time to collect herself. She began again, 'I wanted to tell you beta, but I was so afraid. When I was relating my tragedy to you, I thought that I heard someone shift outside the window. I thought . . . I thought that Mutukul . . . he had followed me again. I shut myself then and didn't say anything, lest he hears and make things difficult for me.'

'Mutukul? Who's he?'

'The younger brother of my husband.'

'Why are you so afraid of him?'

'Because . . . because . . . he is a very rough man. I never got along with him. He wants to usurp whatever pension I get. He is very bad. Very avaricious. Very vile.'

The rain had gathered force and was now unrelenting in its strength. Jayanti Devi rushed to close one of the windows that had come loose due to the sudden pressure. She came back and, after wiping off her face, sat on the bed beside me, looking at Bhrigu intently.

'Why did you think that he followed you?' I asked

'My next question, exactly,' said Bhrigu

'He always follows me. He is such a nosy fellow. Always interested in other people's business, especially mine. When my husband was alive, he fought with him often, demanding this and that. You see, my husband had been a father figure to his other siblings as his parents died an early death. He worked hard for them and loved Mutukal like his own son. Jankhelawan thought that Mutukal would grow to become his support and strength but his misfortune that the boy became spoilt and somehow got into his head that it was my husband's duty to care for him. Even after we got him married, he continued to feel that he was the rightful heir to everything that Jankhelawan owned. That is why he thinks that it is his right to receive a share of his brother's pension, too. The brat. Always bothers me and follows me about, trying to ascertain the alleged wealth Jankhelawan left me.'

'Your husband has other siblings, too?'

'Yes. They are four brothers in all. Jankhelawan, Mutukal, Ramavatar, and Bali. Ramavatar was a soldier in a regiment of the Indian Army and achieved martyrdom in the Kargil War. He is survived by his widow, Indumati, who remarried a month after my boy died. She lives with his second husband's family now. A pure harlot, that. Must be taking great advantage of Ramavatar's long absences by courting men and inviting them to her house. She never stopped dressing in fineries even after her husband died. I never cared much for her or her coquettish manners. The youngest is Bali and he is a sugar mill worker. After Malthu died, he was the one who took care of me.'

'Who?' I asked, a trifle confused.

'Bali, the one who works at the sugar mill.'

Bhrigu was silent for a while. He was looking at the woman in a marked manner, as if trying to read her like an open book. I could clearly see that he was still simmering with the latent hurt that Jayanti Devi's initial reticence had caused.

'Amma, you are not holding anything back, now. Are you?' he asked.

'No beta. I swear to Bajrang Bali. I am not hiding anything.'

'Very good. I expect the same frankness from you in reply to my next question.'

Jayanti Devi nodded her approval.

'I want you to answer me in one syllable only. Yes or no. Alright?'

The old woman looked confused but nodded nonetheless.

'Do you suspect the involvement of any of your relatives in Malthu's death?'

I had already anticipated his question but not the expression of Jayanti Devi that greeted this query. Instead of shock, surprise, or intimidation of any sort, she registered total surrender. As Bhrigu had expected, she replied in one word: 'Yes.'

'Was this the reason behind your suspicion that your son was not killed in an unfortunate accident but was murdered?'

'Yes.'

'But what would be their motive in doing so? Even Mutukal would gain nothing by killing your son. Why do you believe this so strongly?'

Jayanti Devi looked at her calloused fingers, collecting and marshalling her thoughts, then she said in a dull voice, 'When Malthu discovered the gold coins, the innocent boy ran off to show them to his uncle, Mutukul. He didn't care who was who and how was who. His heart was too simple and pure for such discrimination. On being asked, he even showed them the piece of land where he had found the coins. They took him with them to show them the ropes and help them locate more treasure. It was always 'Where's Malthu?' 'Malthu, come with me.' And then in the middle of the frenzy, one hears that one's little boy is no more! Except Bali, no one even cared to come and sympathise with me! I knew then and there that something was wrong. My gut instinct was too strong for it. These people, blinded by their greed, had done something to my Malthu which had caused his death. They are somehow responsible, that I know.'

'But Bali is in the clear? Is it not so?'

'Yes. Of course. He is the only one dear to me. He wasn't that involved in the gold hunt, too. When Malthu died, he took great care of me. Before coming here, I lived in a small dilapidated cottage, one of the many, littered around the railway line. He relocated me to this place. Whatever furniture that you see here was also bought by him. In my difficult times, he was the only comfort.'

'Still, Amma, if we are investigating, it should be thorough. Bali is one of your relatives and so he comes under the probe, too.'

Jayanti Devi nodded reluctantly and said, 'As you say.'

'This woman, Indumati, was she. . .?'

'Oh no!' Jayanti Devi shouted even before the question was over. 'The queen wouldn't do this herself! She is too proud to soil her dainty little hands doing menial labour! She sent her lover instead, who is now her husband, to go hunting for her.'

'What's her husband's name?'

'He goes by the name of "Amrood". I don't know why? I doubt if that's his real name. I know nothing else about him. As I said I don't care for the cheap woman or her life.'

'H'm,' said Bhrigu, frowning in an effort to sort all the information in his brain. 'One last question. Do you think that Mutukal or one of your relatives circulated the rumour for Jiyashree?'

I could clearly see that she was struggling to find an answer. 'I don't know.' She said at last, 'The rumour just lifted like a fog from nowhere and eclipsed everyone. So many people were endorsing it all at once that it's very difficult to locate the original source. I am afraid you will have to find that out for yourself. But Mutukal is capable of anything, absolutely anything, I tell you.'

I could see through the half-open door that the pattering rain had again subsided into a gentle drizzle, but the wind had gained in ferocity and speed. I suspected whether the rainfall wasn't to be followed by an ill-timed storm.

'Amma, I have a plan. I will surely investigate matters to the best of my abilities, but for maximum cooperation from your relatives, it will be very important that we go in the cover of disguise. Unsuspecting people have their guards down and so they are much forthcoming. Also, remember that this is a private investigation. They are not bound by law to comply. Hence, we will have to keep this matter under wraps and approach it very cautiously.'

'As you say, beta,' replied Jayanti Devi. 'I have full confidence in you.'

Bhrigu's lips broke into a smile. I knew that he had longed all along to hear these precious words. His client's unfaltering trust in him inspired him to work hard in order to get to the truth.

'Very well, then,' he said brightly and explained to us in minute detail, the plan of action that we were about to pursue. He requested Jayanti Devi to inform her relatives about our imminent arrival so that they are well prepared for our visit.

'Let's stir the murky waters. I assure you, Amma, that if there's anything hiding in their depths, I'll find and bring it to the shore and the criminals to justice.'

9

Mutukal Kumar

I thank the benevolence of heaven for holding the rain as we headed home and to my joy, our belated good fortune also sent us a rickshaw that deposited us in front of our house. After a quick lunch (under the suspicious and querulous eyes of Nirja Masi, I should add), we assembled in Bhrigu's room to discuss the matters further.

'What do you think?' I said, relaxing on the bed. 'I am almost certain that the evil Mutukal must have had something or the other to do with the matter.'

'Again, the wild hypothesising that has become an irksome habit of yours. What are your justifications for this insinuation?'

'The honest word of a dear old lady.'

He looked at me for the umpteenth time in utter disbelief and disappointment. 'If our legal system worked on honest words of dear old ladies, every other person would be finding a seat in jail.'

'But . . . don't you believe she's telling the truth? You can read people, can't you? Come now, man! This is no time for modesty!'

'You know, more often than not, you're quite a handful for me,' he said, glaring at me with mock anger. 'And please. What do you mean by "read people"? How can you simplify my work with such a common expression? I don't *read people*, I decipher them. But let me tell you that the convictions I got weren't only because of this expertise of mine. It helped a great deal but I worked hard to secure concrete evidence to validate it.'

'Let's not consider evidence for once,' I said, a little excited. 'Tell me, by face value, sorry, by *deciphering the woman. . .*' And I said it nice and slow to pacify him, '. . .your views on Jayanti Devi's suspicions.'

He had taken a seat on his favourite reclining chair and a chewing gum was already working itself in his mouth. He said between his preoccupations, 'I can't say anything for a certainty before meeting this Mutukal character, but on Amma's story alone, it looks like a . . . like a . . . an exaggerated suspicion.'

'Exaggerated suspicion, eh?' I said, feeling a shade uncomfortable over the awkwardness of the phrase. This was not the first time that my friend, in his literally escapades, had produced an expression so unorthodox. Apparently, my discomfiture didn't go unnoticed.

'You are giving me the look again,' he said irritably. 'Go on, say it for me.'

I thought for a while and suggested what came to me best. 'A paranoia stemming from deep dislike or distrust?'

'Close. Very close,' he replied with a slow smile. 'You know, sometimes I wish I was as articulate as you.'

'Your ideas are articulate.'

He looked at me with an intensity that completely befuddled me.

'What?' I asked

'When I read your first chronicle of our first case together, I was right in thinking that you have managed a seemingly impossible feat.'

'What?' I asked again.

'Of expressing me in ways I could never have done. Sometimes, I feel like we were divined to come together. You have brought art into the cold, calculating world of investigations and to my life.'

'I appreciate your admiration,' I said, deeply humbled. I refrained from bringing to his notice that he had just professed his love for literature, the one thing that he had resolutely denied from the very first. 'But let me tell you that your methods of deduction, especially the ways in which you connect with your suspects, are nothing short of poetry.'

He looked at me a second time with an unabashed and unmasked admiration and I, sensing that he could go on a rampage of gratitude any second, swiftly endeavoured to steer the conversation away from the topic of mutual appreciation. 'Has this also got something to do with old age senility? Most people in their advanced ages tend to become paranoid about everything.'

'No,' he replied resolutely. 'It's nothing of the kind.'

'How can you be so sure?'

'By simple observation. Did you notice the built-in cupboard in which her clothes were kept?'

'Yes.'

'So did you notice anything?'

'She had kept her saris there.'

'Yes, but did you not observe the order in which the saris were kept? Every single one of them was expertly pressed and arranged in neat bundles of similar hues. The shade of blues where stacked together, reds came next, yellows, then so on. If her mind is fit enough for such intricate colour cataloguing, do you really think it's senile?'

'You are right. Damn. Why do I always miss such details?!'

He cocked an eyebrow at me and began. 'You see, the inference is easy if you keep your senses, and not your tongue, alive and active. Therein lies your problem. Tomorrow, we will meet this Mutukul kumar. Enjoy the weather for the remainder of the day as I will on the porch,' said he and left the room, leaving me to enjoy a delicious nap after yet another long and physically exhausting day. In the evenings, we rehearsed the roles that we had to assume for our suspect's benefit. I was Shekhar and Bhrigu was Deb, distant relations of Jayanti Devi. In order to enlist their full support, Bhrigu had come up with a master plan. Jayanti Devi had told us that her relatives were hard up people, struggling to make ends meet and hence it was decided that we would exploit this weakness of theirs to our advantage. Deb and Shekhar would be well-to-do men in the flourishing business of a local brand of Pan Masala called '*Maza*' who have come to Senduwar to set up a branch of their business. We, thus, wanted to employ a familiar man who could be trusted to manage the business here. Jayanti Devi had suggested the name of her relatives and so we had come to interview them. The one found suitable would be asked to take up the charge at once.

The next day dawned bright, fresh, and cool. The rainfall had finally succeeded in mitigating the unbearably humid days of last week and I was thankful to the gods for sparing me the difficult journey of the day before. By 10.30 in the morning, we were off to see Mutukal Kumar. He lived near the local post office in a small two-room house very much like that of Jayanti Devi's. A cow and her calf were tied to the post at the very entrance of the house and a fairly obese woman was squatting on the floor, collecting the heaps of cow dung in a huge straw basket. Having lived in cities all my life, I had never come across such a display of cow dung ever in my life. The stench was proving to be a little too much for my sensitive olfactory lobes, but I still worked hard in putting up a gallant show of sangfroid. My friend, on the other hand, stood as comfortably as he was standing in the Garden of Eden. He looked at me and smiled significantly as I laboured hard not to grimace any second. Engrossed in her work, the woman paid little attention to us as we approached her and hadn't Bhrigu coughed respectfully, she would have went on with her not-so-pleasant work with not a care in the world. She looked up from her vantage point and asked brusquely, 'What do you want?'

I noticed that she had a florid face with fat, bulging cheeks; small, rude eyes; and thick lips. To conclude, she was an ugly woman by all accepted standards and the belligerent, hateful look that she was giving us generously, didn't help much to improve matters further.

'I wanted to meet with Mutukal Kumar,' Bhrigu said politely.

'Why? Who are you?' she asked in her harsh, grating voice. I noticed that the woman was eyeing us with evident distrust and a modicum of alarm as well.

Bhrigu told her our fake names that we had decided the day before. 'I am Deb and this is my friend Shekhar. We are the distant relations of Jayanti Devi. I hope she told you about us?'

The woman's face relaxed visibly. The distrust, the apprehension, and the alarm all faded off to be replaced by something very close to affability.

'Oh! You people have come earlier than we expected,' she said and stood up in haste, pinning her pallu to her head with, to my chagrin, her dirty, dung-smeared hands.

'Come in, come in. Why do you stand here?'

She led us into a small sitting room with a small TV, three wooden chairs, and a folding bed. A huge calendar with a colourful photo of Ganapati was pinned just above the TV. The room was very untidy and an assortment of clothes were scattered about on the bed. I could find cobwebs nearly everywhere that the eyes looked. The chairs were dusty, too, and in ordinary circumstances, I would have bolted out the way I came but the exigent state of affairs forced me to look contrary to the way I felt inside. No sooner had we settled in when the woman shouted at the top of her lungs—

'Meena Kumari! Bring in two cups of tea! Quick!'

'No need for formalities, madam, please,' Bhrigu said

'Why formality, Bhaiji? This is your own house as we are your own. Is it not?' she asked in a pitch that sabotaged my poor eardrum.

'Yes, yes of course.'

She took a stool and sat in front of us. 'Bhaiji, at first I thought that you were one of those people who badger us for money. They don't understand that if we had some, wouldn't we give them?'

'You lend money?' I asked, very much surprised.

'No, no,' she replied with a smug, skin-crawling smile. 'He borrowed some. He works hard on that silly secondhand books shop of his but after the advent of the 'New Book Dealer' our profits dwindled. Afzal Mia, the proprietor of the shop, knows an agent in the town who supplies him with all the books that the children need. No one comes to our shop anymore. But. . .' she added with a deadly flattering look, 'you have come as our saviours. He is a very hard worker. You won't find anyone more suitable for the job.'

'Yes. But where is your husband?'

'He is on the shop. It's located outside the primary school where Bhaisaab, that is, Jayanti Didi's husband used to teach. It was he who had come up with the idea of the shop and contributed to the effort as well. But . . . the things that are doomed to fail . . . fail. And Jayanti Didi. . .' She held her tongue barely in check, regretting her lapse at once.

'Yes? Jayanti Devi what?' Bhrigu inquired.

'Oh! Nothing. Didi was very helpful also. That's all.'

I could clearly see that the woman had meant to say something spiteful, but realising at the split second that this favour had come because of her sister-in-law, she had to chew her own words.

Just then, a girl in her early twenties entered with a tray laden with biscuits and two cups of tea. She was on the heavy side, too, but the long, pleated hair and clear complexion compromised it significantly. Her eyes were larger than her mother's, a slightly flat nose, and full lips. All in all a rather good-looking girl. As she raised her eyes to take us in, I could sense a shrewdness, way beyond her years. Her face and expression looked way mature than her age and there was a raw sensuality in the way she moved with her voluptuous figure and also in the slight nervousness well discernible in her clear-cut features 'Amma, Chai,' she said in a deep, husky voice and left the room hastily.

'Meena Kumari!' cried her mother at her retreating figure. 'Tell Vinod to go and call his father. Tell him that our guests have come.'

The girl nodded and left. Absentmindedly, I followed her with my gaze, wondering as to how a daughter of such a frumpy woman could turn out to be so nubile and, well, attractive. Bhrigu caught my eye at this moment and his eyebrows arched meaningfully. Embarrassed, I looked away at once but not before being conscious of the fact that he was smiling and that to, to my immense discomfort, quite mischievously.

It must have been not more than ten minutes when the door was pushed open and the boy, Vinod, entered followed by a man with the built and bearing of a wrestler.

He looked at us with a strange combination of respect and defiance, folded his hands in greeting, and said, 'Namaste.'

'Namste,' we returned.

'I am sorry that you had to wait for me, I am. But one has to work when one has a big fat family to feed, you know.' Only when he started to shake with peals of laughter did I understand that this comment was meant to be a weak attempt at a joke. To be polite, we laughed awkwardly.

'Has Sumati asked you for Chai?' he asked in the same squeaky voice of his, very at odds to his massive personality. Then, after eyeing the tea cups before us, answered the question himself. 'Oh! I see she has!' And he was off to another annoying round of cackle. It didn't take me long to understand that this man was suffering from a variant of humour that did not arise from an external stimulus. It's just an uncontrollable emotion, for some men when in a judicious mood, to laugh at just about anything, however unfunny or commonplace the object of amusement might be.

'Mr Mutukal Kumar,' began Bhrigu. 'I don't have much time at my disposal. I would like to get started with the interview.'

The light of zest that was still shining in the depths of his big, bloodshot eyes, vanished in a moment. With his broad shoulders, drooping ever so slightly, I could not help but find in him a resemblance to a candidate who is about to face a particularly tough one from the H.R. executive who is out to do business.

'Ask me anything. I am up to the job, I swear.' Mutukul Kumar said meekly.

'Well, we will decide that after the interview's over,' Bhrigu said, drawing himself to his full height in order to scare his unsuspecting suspect further. I must say, he was doing a pretty good job at it.

'What are your qualifications?'

'Metric pass, no, fail, no! Pass.'

'Pass or fail? Reply truthfully.'

'F . . . fail.'

'What kind of jobs have you done till now?'

'Jobs?' he said, swallowing a lump. 'Well, that's an easy one. Currently, I am working in a book depot, I tell you. Before that, I was working as a clerk in this here post office. Even before that, when I was a lad, I used to work as a farmhand of Raghubir. He looked after one of the many farms of Ghanshyam Singh's father. I was very good and skilled at all my jobs, I tell you. Worked hard, very hard. I will be very good for your business.'

'Of course. Of course. Now, this was your professional life. It's now time to shed some light on your personal one.'

'What has my personal life got to do with all?' he asked with a touch of temper.

'Well, don't you know that an employer has to know about the family background of the candidate as well? In order to know if he can be trustworthy.'

'Oh that?' he said and simpered like a girl. 'Okay, y'all. Go on.'

I noticed that his wife, Sumati, was watching the entire episode, half concealed behind a curtain of the door to one of the rooms. I half chuckled at the thought that the woman was overambitious enough to actually think that a curtain of standard measure could successfully hide something of her size.

'Please tell me about your family members. All of them, mind you,' Bhrigu was asking now.

'Let me see. Now there is Jayanti Bhabhi as you know, you see,' he said with a slight frown of concentration. 'And then come my brothers. The elder one, Jankhelawan Bhai ji was a government school teacher. He is the one who got me the job at the depot, don't you know? My other brothers are Ramavatar and Surat. Ramavatar died in the Karwil war.'

'Please,' I said, trifle heatedly at the man's disrespect and ignorance. 'It's the Kargil War.'

'But I said that.'

'No, you said. . .'

I halted in my argument when Bhrigu raised a palm. 'Not now, Sutte,' he whispered.

I took his advice but couldn't stop myself from glaring at the man quite unabashedly. He had deeply hurt my patriotic sentiments.

'Go on please,' Bhrigu urged him on.

'Next is Bali, the youngest who works at the sugar mill. Now come the wife. You have met mine, Sumati. Ramavatar's widow's name is Indumati, and Bali is not married. I have two children, Meena Kumari and this here Vinod. I had another son too, but he died of jaundice when he was only but 9. Ramavatar and Bali have no children.'

I noticed that he hadn't mentioned Malthu at all. Was this the murderer's guilt? I tried to study his countenance with interest but apart from the smell of a simple brute, I could detect nothing.

'Did you not have a cousin by the name of Malthu? Jayanti Devi's son?' Bhrigu asked.

The man was slightly taken aback but composed himself at once. 'Oh him? He died in an accident. Good thing for him. No good, was he, I tell you. A poor fool, yes, that's what he was.'

'A fool eh?' said Bhrigu, cocking an eyebrow at him. 'You didn't consider him that big a fool when you enlisted his help to find the good old treasure, didn't you?'

He sprung the question at him with such a chilling suddenness that Mutukal Kumar almost fell from his seat. I observed his wife, too, taking a step or two in our direction, as if to save her husband from the unexpected onslaught. She held herself in check by sheer force of will.

'I . . . I . . . what are you talking about? What treasure?' he gasped and sputtered. 'Who told you about such a farce?'

'It's no farce, Mr Kumar. Before interviewing our potential recruits, we go through their background checks. Now, tell me, is it not true?'

'Who told you this? Jayanti Bhabhi? And what has this to do with the interview?'

'It was just a casual question, that's all,' Bhrigu replied in a relaxed tone. 'Why have you got all worked up?'

'I was just a little shocked is all. Even if I did use the boy's help, I didn't do nothing illegal. You have no reason to count that against me.'

Bhrigu smiled genially. 'But why do you think that I would count that against you? Do you think I should? Why?'

At this juncture, the wife stepped into the room with heavy footfalls and said heatedly. 'He has nothing to hide, Bhaiji. But he will sweat if you act less like interviewers and more like police. Why is this question so important at all, say?'

'You people are making it important. Not I. I was just asking a casual question, like I said.'

'Yes, he took the help of that boy and who wouldn't? We have to work so hard to keep our head above the flood of debt. A few gold coins would have meant the end of all our woes.'

'Were you successful?' he added 'See, I am just very interested in these antiques and hidden treasures. That's why I am asking such questions. Nothing personal. Raw curiosity.'

The wife's contorted expressions relaxed on hearing this. Mutukal, too, was now completely himself. He was simpering even more than before, igniting in me a feeling to break his jaw in one swift motion of the fist. He was a man who could easily get on the nerves of even very mellow a people like me. His wife sprawled comfortably on the floor and lapsed into a chatty mood 'Are Bhaiji, we searched for two days but found nothing. The boy died at the hands of *her* on the third. Who would then even think of disturbing her land again? We never once went in that direction again.'

'Yes, we were lucky that *she* spared us!' said Mutukal. 'The boy's death was a warning for us folks to stay the hell away from the place or else we was witch food!' He was now laughing hard, banging his fat fists on his knees. A smothering look from his wife was all that was needed to bring him back to normalcy.

'Jayanti Bhabhi has horded the gold coins.' The wife said. 'She says that she won't sell them because they are too precious for her. The boy lost his life over them, she says. I call it foolishness, that's all. If she didn't want to use them, she should have given us instead. After all, my husband here is her own brother-in-law. Hain na Bhaiji?'

'Right,' Bhrigu replied, getting up. 'The interview's over now. I will tell you the results after a few days.'

They greeted us with a mechanical affability and we left the house in a hurry. My heart had turned to lead in the presence of such a callous, apathetic people who cared nothing for anyone but themselves alone. I was very glad to be out in the open air again. We took a rickshaw and were back at the house in the work of a moment.

10

INDUMATI

'Mutukal Kumar is one of those brutes who are a terror to all, but there is always one person who controls them with a remote.'

'You are talking about his wife, Sumati?'

'Who else? Didn't you see the clear distinction between the master and the slave in that house?'

I nodded in approval. 'He is a ruffian but like many hot-headed oafs like him, he has no brain to claim as his own.'

'Exactly. As soon as that woman stepped into my view, I knew that she was the only force in that family to reckon with. A couple can never survive together if both are equally controlling. One has always to back down to make room for the other. That's a rule and this family was no exception to it.'

Unable to contain my curiosity, I jumped the question on him. I knew he resented this urgency on my part and always advised me to be watchful and patient but I could never really bring myself to it. Almost always, curiosity got the better of me and my pride.

'So?'

'So what?'

'What do you think about Mutukal Kumar?'

He made a wry face in my direction. 'Not again!' he cried.

'Come now. Don't be so pompous. Tell me prima facie what do you think?'

'You have spoilt yourself, dragging me to the pit as well. This is not a good investigating practice! We shouldn't speculate before we have done a complete and thorough investigation and firmly hold all the threads of the case in hand. It is then that . . . that. . .' he struggled for the appropriate expression and came up with something almost as good as mine. '. . .we can unravel the difficult knots and see the beauty of truth within. You, on the other hand, try to make me guess the threads that are still in the air! I won't indulge you anymore.'

'But you must have formed some opinion! That is what your talent is!' I cried in sheer desperation.

'Yes. But I won't corrupt my findings by voicing them out loud prematurely and risk you adulterating them with your own guesses.' Was his stock answer.

'Okay' I replied with some heat and was about to retreat from the room when he said, 'But I can give you some peripheral details, though'

'Like what?'

'Like you are attracted to their daughter Meena Kumari,' he replied with the smile of an imp.

I glared at him with eyes spitting fire and then stomped out of the room, swearing never to bother with him or his cases again and sensing almost at once the hollowness behind my empty oath. Curse this curiosity!

It was five o'clock in the evening that we headed out to meet Indumati. As expected, Bhrigu did not leave a stone unturned to saddle me with the knowledge that I had gone back on my own promise of never working with him again in less than three hours. He joked that this was the shortest possible time of renege that he had ever seen in his life. I, as always, knew that when he was in one of his light moments, the best course of action to be followed was to ignore him thoroughly. As a gentle fire dies if not stoked, his gay humour would suffocate if left unattended.

Indumati's new family lived on the borders of Senduwar and Dharampura. It was a journey of little over five hours and we took the services of a jeep to take us to our destination. I felt nauseous as the driver manoeuvred his jeep through the busy market area, but as soon as we were out of the village, the roads grew broader and finally our ride became smooth. I was enjoying the passing fields of wheat and mustard and the heavy canopy of trees that hung over us like a guarding patrician. Bhrigu, on the other hand, was busy going through the questionnaire that he had prepared for his next suspect.

'Stop it now. You are missing the view,' I said.

'I have been subjected to these views so often that an immunity has developed in me against their charm,' he said with his eyes still trained on the paper. 'Besides, the sequence of questions is very important. You introduce one before the other, the response would never come that you had always hoped for. It's a delicate method and one has to be well versed in it.'

'You make it sound like a science.'

'Well, it is.'

'And Mutukal? Did you prepare his questionnaire too?'

'Damn right I did. You could never underrate the importance of proper interrogation. It's a very technical affair.'

'Technical?' I said, thoroughly confused 'From when is asking a couple of questions considered technical?'

He looked at me with an expression that was suggestive of disdain. Alas! I had found success in disappointing him again. But, I wasn't going to abate his vexation by lying through my teeth. I couldn't understand his strange theory and instead of being constrained by the shackles of false pride, I opted to be honest enough to voice my confusion, point blank.

'Anything that requires skill is called technical. Interrogation techniques require a lot of skill and hence it is a technical job, too. What is so difficult to understand about this?' he asked with a touch of impatience.

'I never thought like that before. Well, you must be right. If you say so, it must be so,' I said, still a little dubious over my own admission.

'I know you are still confused. But let me confirm that sometimes a suspect interview is even more technical than a forensic job where you have simple physical objects that easily tell you all they know. In an interrogation, on the other hand, we are dealing with a manipulating person. One has to be very; very skilled when one is dealing with the most sophisticated creation of all.'

'In which you are an expert?'

'Well, my reputation precedes me.'

'And how do you do that?'

He was silent for a while, as if searching for words to express himself better. 'You play chess, don't you?' he said at last.

'Yes, sure I do.' I replied, intrigued. 'So?'

'Tell me, what does it take to become a grandmaster at the game?'

'Why? The ability to read your opponent's moves to the nth degree. The better you can do it, the more difficult you become to beat.'

'Precisely the words I wanted to hear. Suspect interview is the same, too.'

'How?' I asked, this time thoroughly perplexed.

'A person who becomes a grandmaster is almost invincible because he can predict the moves of his partner and thus the game, in such a way, that he almost knows, even before the game has commenced, that he is going to win. You know how he does that, don't you, Sutte?'

'By strategising, of course.'

'Yes, or in other words, he anticipates or reads his partner's moves in advance. I call it a foresight.'

'Yes, that's what the game is all about.'

'You agree with me that this foresight or perception is only found in gifted players?'

'Absolutely. Not everyone can predict long sequence of moves.'

He nodded his head in confirmation. 'And you know, don't you, that every player's strategy is unique and can be broken?'

'Yes. Computer scientists have built chess-playing machines and computer programs that can even break the game of a grandmaster. Take the example of the supercomputer Deep Blue vs. Gary Kasparov match. Deep Blue had defeated an almost invincible Kasparov.'

'I know about the Deep Blue. This computer is the perfect example of the fact that no one's defences are foolproof. You should just know theirs well enough to break through them. If a computer can do it, so can a human. For me, the Deep Blue is the quintessential of a grandmaster,' he said with an impish smile. 'Well, to cut a long story short, I am also like a, please excuse my vanity, a grandmaster. The difference is that while a grandmaster uses his skill or technicality to defeat an opponent by reading his moves, I use mine to crack a suspect by reading his mind and mannerisms. In other words (and this was going to be his most famous catchphrase, cited by every fan of his), *Suspects are like pieces of chess. Read them correctly and be ahead by one move only. You will win the game.* My questionnaire is an important tool to help me with the process. The responses given to my questions help me to understand the nature and mental makeup of the suspect and also to plan my next moves in a way that he starts losing his game that he had carefully planned by making mistakes and there comes a time when caught in his own lies, he confesses or makes a serious blunder. That is checkmate for me.'

'Despite your views to the contrary, I always thought that you had a gift for reading people's thoughts!'

He gave a short, spasmodic laugh and said, 'I don't read thoughts. Why should I? Everyone is entitled to privacy regarding what they are thinking. I just bring from the depths of psych that which people force with all there might to stay hidden.'

'But while dealing with a people.' He added after a thought, 'It's very important to understand one basic fact. Kindness and understanding puts them off their guard, making them comfortable and thus vulnerable to a session. It's a myth that people respond best to coercion. If not anything, it has often led innocents to confess to things they never did just to escape the tortures of an interrogation. As the English jurist William Blackstone had said, 'It is better that ten guilty persons escape than that one innocent suffer.' You know, the principle itself is derived from the Holy Bible. I liked the passage so much that I memorised it. Do you want to hear?'

'Yes, of course,' I said at once.

His eyes shone with the sheer brilliance of compassion which I had always associated with his character. 'Abraham drew near, and said, "Will you consume the righteous with the wicked? What if there are fifty righteous within the city? Will you consume and not spare the place for the fifty righteous who are in it? What if ten are found there?" He (The Lord) said, "I will not destroy it for the ten's sake."' he said, quoting each word with reverence.

'I didn't know you have studied the Bible,' I said, surprised again.

'I came upon the passage in a book that I have, called "The best legal trials of the 21st century". Well, the point that I am trying to make is that useless, medieval methods of interrogation, bodes no good. And. . .' he stopped and I could detect a dull pain in his voice, 'this, as you well know, was the reason I left the police force.'

'Don't think about it now,' I said. 'Let the past be past.'

'You are right,' he said dully and lapsed into his work again.

We were silent for the rest of the journey and I was trying to absorb all that I had heard. It sounded to me fantastic and logical all at once. After all Bhrigu had proven what he had just said. I remembered the articles about him in the paper. It had clearly stated that 'Inspector Bhrigu Mahesh's talents defy the ordinary' and 'As a magician he charmed the shrewd businessman to confess to his crime as if he was conversing with a long lost friend'. Was this the secret behind the moniker, the magic, and the charm?

My thoughts were put on hold when the road ended to reveal a group of low-roofed concrete houses. I knew that one among them belonged to Indumati, our suspect number two. The driver dropped us near a grand Peepul tree as he himself went off to take a shot at a beedi from a nearby shop. A couple of tough-looking Muslims were lounging under the tree, apparently taking an afternoon nap. Judging my apprehension, Bhrigu sallied forth to ask for the directions to Indumati's house. At first, the couple looked quite intent on adopting a zero-tolerance policy towards us but no sooner had Bhrigu as much as breathed the name of Indumati, they shot up straight as if jolted by a high voltage shock.

'Indumati? What do you want from her?' asked the younger of the two. His voice was surprisingly soft but the unseemly creases of irritation that now marked his face didn't provide much scope to appreciate the timbre of his voice.

'We are distant relations,' Bhrigu replied, putting on his poker face as was his custom while questioning people on a case.

'Distant relations?' barked the other. 'Sure you don't look like one.'

'Nonetheless, we are,' Bhrigu said calmly. 'Now, if it isn't too much of a bother, please give us the direction.'

The two of them regarded us with challenging eyes. 'Go straight and you'll come to a fork. Take the left one, walk down it, and the second house with a mighty big wind chime is Indu's,' said the older one in his staccato speech 'Make sure that you don't offend her with your unwanted comments. She has had enough of them already.'

I was on the brink of sounding the man off for his uncalled for belligerence when Bhrigu motioned me to stay quiet.

'Thank you,' he said stiffly and grabbing my elbow, led me away.

'Why did you not say anything?' I asked. 'We did nothing to warrant such a reaction. What is wrong with those people?'

'Charm of a temptress is the most potent weapon known to mankind. And this woman here,' Bhrigu said, looking at me meaningfully, 'knows how to wield hers.'

'She must be very beautiful.'

He didn't reply and we kept on moving at a brisk pace. We knew we had reached our destination when we came to a wooden door, freshly painted and hanging over it was the biggest wind chime I had ever seen in my life.

The door was open and it led to a courtyard. We teetered on the threshold speculating whether to enter or not. As if in an answer to our dilemma, a woman came out of the house with a bucket full of water and started watering a dozen odd potted plants arranged beautifully around the porch. She looked up in a minute and spotted us immediately. As she made her way towards us, I noticed that she was a plain-looking, thin woman, wearing an old, jaded, beige-coloured Salwar Suit. She had sharp, lucid eyes, but nothing else was even remotely beautiful about them. Her cheeks were sallow and her flat nose was an added blot to the unseemly landscape of her face. I thought that she must be the sister of Indumati's husband.

'Yes? Who do you want to see?' She asked cordially

'We are here to meet Indumati,' I said.

'You are looking at her,' she replied with a smile.

'What?!' I shrieked with shock.

'I am Indumati.'

11

I was still gaping at her with an open-eyed wonder. How could this plain Jane possibly be Indumati? The temptress? I looked at Bhrigu hoping for an expression mirroring my incredulity, but I was surprised to find him as poker faced as ever, looking intently at Indumati.

'I am Deb and this is my friend and partner, Shekhar,' he said. 'I am sure Jayanti Devi told you about us and our business?'

'Yes, yes. Of course. Bali informed us on her behalf. I am surprised that Jayanti Bhabhi even considered us for such a wonderful proposal,' she said. 'She never liked me much. Much less still when I remarried. I don't know what caused her change of heart.' She then shrugged and said, 'Avdoot was very happy to hear about the news. We can really do with some extra money.'

'Avdoot? But Jayanti Devi said. . .' I trailed off.

'Amrood. Right?' she laughed sweetly. 'These village folks can never handle an unusual name. Please . . . do come in.'

She took us to a small but tastefully furnished living room. The walls looked newly painted and a giant calendar with a magnificent view of the Caribbean stood facing us. On a cabinet, under it, there was a small, secondhand Flatron TV. A bright yellow curtain was drawn against the window to keep the sun out and the vivid, colourful patterns painted on them accorded the room a very cheerful appearance. It was all bright and sunny in there and I could feel my spirits soar after the hard, bumpy ride that we had to undergo to reach here.

She politely motioned to us to sit on the two cheap, upholstered chairs, and switched on the cooler for our benefit. In no time, the lady had also served us with refreshing orange drinks. We thanked her for her hospitality which she accepted without comment.

'It's a very cosy place that you have got here,' I said, sipping my drink lazily.

'Thank you. It's not much and I can't do much with our frugal means but I try to manage with what I have,' she replied with a smile.

'And you have done a wonderful job at that.'

'Thank you,' she said again.

'Where is your husband?' Bhrigu asked.

'He was having his afternoon nap but is awake now. He is dressing himself and will be here in a moment.'

'Very well, then,' Bhrigu replied.

'If you don't mind, sir, can I ask you a question?' she asked with a slight hesitation.

'Yes, go on,' Bhrigu said.

'I don't really understand your proposal. I mean it will be very fortunate for us to get it, but I can't help thinking that why did you ever think of enlisting the help of people like us, who have little experience in matters like this, when you could surely take the help of professionals.'

I eyed her askance. I had never expected that a rustic, village woman would have the intelligence required to ask such questions.

'Well, our company is a small one. We are but in our infancy and don't have the funds to pay the grand wages they'll require. We have just enough capital to start this business in a handful of villages, including Senduwar, where there is a thriving market for Paan-Masala. The work is not very difficult anyways. Anyone, with proper guidance, can be trained well enough to handle the business. The matter was about getting people we could trust and Jayanti Devi solved this for us when she volunteered the names of her relatives.' Bhrigu explained.

Indumati sat absorbing the piece of information with interest. 'So, basically, it's about handling a Paan-Masala shop, isn't it?'

'In a way. But it would require other duties as well like local advertising through loudspeakers and posters, providing free samples to generate potential buyers and also sending back detailed three monthly reports on the sales of the brand. If all goes well after a year and the brand creates a market, we will start providing regular salary to the handler.'

I could see a question flicker in her eyes even before she had voiced it. 'After a year? So for a whole year, are you going to keep him busy for free?'

'There would be remunerations for sales generated, of course. But we can provide a regular salary only after the product hits off. Let me assure you that we remunerate our handlers very generously.'

'Oh, I understand now. It's the old ad hoc system with benefits. Well, my husband is a very intelligent, though, untrained man. Under your guidance, I'm sure he will be the best man for the job,' she replied, beaming.

'We'll be the judge for it,' Bhrigu replied curtly.

At that moment, a handsome young man in his mid twenties, made an appearance. He was smartly dressed in a white Kurta Pajama which I saw Bhrigu (who himself was wearing a mauve-coloured one that day) eyeing with pleasure. He had a beautiful mane of soft, glossy black hair and his black, lustrous eyes shimmered in the light coming through the window as he surveyed us. His complexion would be quite fair had he not tanned himself so thoroughly in the sun. He was tall with sinewy limbs and the way that he carried himself while he walked bespoke of a certain delicacy that one often attaches with a gentleman or a dandy.

'Oh! You are here at last,' said Indumati cheerfully. 'What took you so long?

'I couldn't find the comb,' he said in a rich, soothing voice that made me reminiscent of a gazal singer I used to hear in my college days.

'I had kept it in the drawer,' she said and then looked at us. 'Sir, this is my husband Avdoot Lekhi.'

The man greeted us politely and said in a gentle pitch, 'I am sorry I was late for the interview. Why did you inconvenience yourself by making this journey? I would have come at your slightest notice.'

'It was no problem at all,' Bhrigu replied and I nodded my head. 'Let's get to the matter at hand. We are already late for a rather important meeting.'

'Of course, as you say,' said Avdoot as he sat on the chair vacated by his wife.

'You can stay for the interview if you like,' Bhrigu said.

'Yes, yes, of course. I was going to get a chair for myself,' she said and appeared in a moment with another of her black plastic chairs.

Bhrigu started the session with his regular questions. 'So, Mr Avdoot, what are your academic qualifications? How far did you study?'

'I have done my intermediate from the government college. I wanted to study engineering but couldn't arrange for the money. And my father died the very year leaving us in a lot of debt so I had to abandon my studies to go and look for jobs.'

'What kind of jobs? Any useful experience?'

'I have worked in the kiln. At first, I was a worker but with time I rose to become a junior overseer. They said I had lots of potential and if I could complete my graduation, I could rise high in the managing field.'

'So you have good management skills?'

'Yes.'

'Can you provide testimonials?'

'You can ask the people working at the kiln. They will give me a good testimonial.'

'You still work at the kiln?'

'No.'

'Why?'

'It was not a very paying job and I had to pay off my debts. The creditors had begun threatening me with my life. So I had to go looking for a more lucrative job.'

'And you did find it, did you?'

'H . . . how do you know?' he said taken aback.

'The condition of your house is a fitting testimonial to it.'

Avdoot's silence greeted the deduction.

'Please, tell me about this lucrative job. What did you do?'

The stolid, magnificent frame of the young man shook slightly and I was aware of an uneasiness enveloping him. It was apparent from his reaction that whatever this 'lucrative job' was, it wasn't a white-collar affair.

His wife came to his rescue at once. 'Please, don't judge him harshly. It was a very difficult period for him. He was absolutely desperate. You don't know these creditors and one of them was nothing less than a loan shark. They threatened him and abused him, never left a moment of peace for my poor man. He couldn't help it.'

'I understand. But you have to be honest with me. What did he do? I promise that I won't judge him harshly. I know of what turn of mind these creditors are. They would harass their own son if it came to that.'

'He . . . he worked with an illegal *daaru-bhatti*. The money was good enough to pay off the creditors.'

'Hmm. Well, past is past. I am sure he could never have done such a thing if his hand wasn't forced. People have killed for less.'

'Thank you for understanding.' Avdoot said with a slight tremor in his voice. I knew that he was mortified about this singular lapse of his morals and would do anything to mend his past.

'That is all about your professional background. Now comes the part about your background. Jayanti Devi and Mutukul Kumar have told me all that there is to it, by the way, I am very sorry about Malthu, I heard of his sudden demise in an accident. It was such a shock to the family. You two, I am sure, were attached to the poor boy, weren't you?'

Bhrigu had dropped the bomb again and that too so subtly and skilfully wrapped in the body of decoy questions that if I hadn't known already, I would have believed it to be a polite, innocent query following a gentle commiseration.

It looked as if the couple had been paralysed for a few seconds but then the infirmity was fleeting. 'Malthu was a dear child,' said Indumati. 'I didn't know you knew about him.'

'Jayanti Devi told us.'

'It was a terrible shock to her. She never speaks to anyone about him. You, sir, must be very close to her. It is well enough. Finally, she found someone to unburden herself. She can heal now.'

I noticed that her husband was conspicuously silent throughout this whole conversation. He was looking ill again and I could detect him shifting uneasily in his seat.

'Avdoot loved him, too, didn't you dear?'

'Y . . . yes. The boy was very good,' he replied as if lost for words. I saw him drying his perspiring palms on his trousers. What was the reason for his discomfort? This tender-looking man couldn't hurt a fly let alone a boy! I knew that much about human character to safely conclude this.

I saw Bhrigu observing the man with keen eyes, but apart from that, I could detect nothing in his expression to betray that he was the least bit puzzled.

'I think we have come to the end of this interview. But there's one last question.'

'Yes, sure,' Indumati said politely.

'The question is for your husband.'

'Yes, go ahead, please.' Avdoot replied. He looked slightly better now and his flushed face was resuming the original pallor.

'What was the profession of your father? Pardon me, but you know we have to cover personal background, too.'

'He was the village Pundit,' he replied.

'Well, that concludes the interview,' Bhrigu said. I could detect a dull satisfaction in his voice but whether it was real or my wild curiosity stoking the fires of imagination, I couldn't say. 'Thank You.'

12

'**D**on't you do that again!'
       'But. . .'
'No.'
'Just a hint. . .'
'What?! What do you think I am? Stop it!'
'You are so adamant!'
'Look who is speaking!'

I gave up. It was the Great tortoise theory all over again. Once his neck was safely tucked under the carapace, no amount of outside pressure could pry it open. He did it with Mutukal Kumar and was following the same rigid doctrine with Indumati and Avdoot, too. The guy just wouldn't crack! I know he had collected quite an assortment of delightful insights into the lives and characters of his suspects but was bent on keeping all the juice to himself alone. I apologise for sounding more like a gossip columnist writing for a sleazy cinema magazine than an acclaimed author of quite a reputation but I refuse to stand on a moral high ground by being a hypocrite and lying that I am averse to what could amount to a colourful conversation. To me, it is called being human, but to my esteemed friend, it is nothing short of hearsay. Undaunted, I tried to approach the matter by another, less provoking angle.

'Okay. I understand your logic of not discussing anything before we arrive at what you call "The Ripe Point" but still you can shed some light on one question that's been troubling me.'

'Indumati and her charm, isn't it?'

'Yes. I knew you had noticed my surprised look as the "tantalising creature" drew near! Please, tell me. How could she exercise such control over men?'

'She didn't and I was in error to suppose so before,' he replied simply. After a thought, he added, 'Although, according to my standards, she was pretty attractive.'

'What do you mean?' I shrieked, ignoring the latter part of his comment. Jayanti Devi's testimonial and the men in the village . . . you heard them, didn't you?'

He smiled enigmatically and observed a silence of two minutes. I knew he was building suspense as usual. I could do nothing but wait for him to get over his occasional thirst for dramatic effect and commence.

'Didn't you notice? It was as clear as a picture. They were his brothers of word!'

'What?! Stop gibbering!'

'Yes. It's the truth.'

'How?'

'Didn't you see how possessive they were for her? Are not all brothers?'

'And are not all jealous lovers?' I barked back. He was definitely on the wrong turn this time and I wasn't going to back off from rubbing his nose in it.

'You missed one crucial point.'

'What?'

'Despite their religion, they were wearing a *Rakhshasutra*.'

I couldn't get his drift. 'What are you trying to say?'

'In Indumati's courtyard, didn't you notice the vestiges of a *Katha?* There were the incense sticks, the camphor, and the empty burnt out vessel where they must have performed the *havan*. I also noticed a stray strand of *Rakshasutra* entwined around one of the incense sticks; just like the one those Muslims were wearing. The inference is that the men attended the Puja in Indumati's house. Noticing that the courtyard was still to be cleared of the holy articles, I would wager that it was under a week ago.'

'So what? It's not above normal for young ladies to call on their lovers under the security that such occasions afford.'

'You didn't let me finish,' he replied, smiling impishly at me, savouring my bewilderment as always. 'Only brothers are called for such a *Puja*. It's meant for their long life.'

'But how the hell do you know that?' I replied with a mixed feeling of impatience and anger.

'Do you know what festival it was a week ago? You city types can never keep up with festivals, can you?'

'Cut it, will you?'

He smiled broadly again. 'It was *Rakshabandhan*, my city slicker.'

My mouth literally fell open on hearing this. In my defence, I was the only child of my parents and my female cousins were scattered about in every city of this country, well, all except the one where I happened to live. Brought up on the gay side of the teachings of the Western civilisation, they never cared for posting the Rakhis for me so naturally I could never understand the importance of this festival, let alone celebrate it. So how was I to remember it? And even if I did, I could never have connected the dots as efficiently as my friend had done, to see the bigger picture.

'You're right,' I said exhaling the air of defeat. But then I was assailed by yet another nagging question. 'But what did those men mean when they said that and I quote, 'She has had enough of unwanted comments'? Why were they so cross?'

'Ha! That troubled me, too, but only for a minute. Remember that this is Indu's second marriage and second marriages are tabooed in this orthodox village. She must have drawn flack from a lot of people and got deeply hurt in the process and hence the men, who truly love her like a sister, have grown protective about her, warning people even before they meet her, to guard their lashing tongues around her.'

'Hmm,' I said. 'That explains it, but not the reputation of Indumati, who is of a whore!'

'It's the prejudiced thinking of her relatives,' he replied, looking thoroughly piqued. Gone was the atmosphere of delight that had surrounded him till now. 'I have a lot of respect for Jayanti Amma, but she is an old school as far as the rules of matrimony go. It's not her fault really as she was raised on such dogmatic beliefs and the same beliefs coloured her views for her sister-in-law. She thinks that marriages are ordained by god and the husband is god incarnation called *pati parmeshwar.* If misfortune strikes and he dies, the widow has to lead her life in exile, living off his memories like a piteous scavenger.' He stopped and looked at me meaningfully and I instinctively knew that he was searching for a confirmation for the expression that he had just used. I was genuinely impressed and after I had nodded my approval, he began a trifle brightly. 'She should abstain from every joy in her life like Amma did herself. Indumati, though, disregards such tenets and supports the modern view that all said and done, a widow is a human being too and so deserves to get her share of happiness. The woman is no chattel. She is intelligent and has a mind of her own. That's why I had to be doubly cautious with her today. I had to go through the pains of giving her a detailed account of everything because one lapse on my part and she would have been quick to smell a rat. Now, when her husband attained martyrdom, she grieved for him no doubt, but then Avdoot came along and alleviated her pain. She was thankful to marry him as it saved her from the loneliness and incapacitating grief. That's all there is to it. Indumati is a good, intelligent woman who knows what she wants and where her happiness lies. Instead of wallowing in misery, she opted to live. If that is a flaw in character, then she is guilty and so is the entire human race.'

'But Mutukal Kumar's wife? She wasn't very favourable of her either.'

He made a wry face and said, 'Women like her are never favourable of *anybody*. It's a handicap they are either born with or cultivate it over the course of their maiden years.'

'Hmm,' I said. 'Are you saying that you are clearing Indumati as your suspect?'

'At your tricks again, eh?' he asked with a lopsided grin. 'For your information, I should tell you that I never clear a suspect before I have caught the culprit.'

It was then that the fateful happened. Nirja Masi entered our room carrying a steel tray with two steaming cups of tea and a plate full of delicious onion pakoras with green, mint chutney. The aroma wafted through the air and reached my delicate nasal passages. It revived the pangs of hunger and I prayed to god for the ring master to just serve the snacks and leave. But was it ever going to be? No. She sat down at the end of the cot on which Bhrigu was relaxing, causing him to jump as if struck by a powerful lightning bolt.

'Eat these pakoras while they are still hot,' she said and I knew that it was not for this one sentence alone that she had affixed herself to a comfortable seat and was now in the act of hoisting her legs on a stool. I knew from recent experiences that the more comfortable her sitting position, the more time she was going to grace us with her presence.

'Bhriguji, I have an important matter to discuss with you.'

With every fibre taut with discomfort, my friend was sitting upright on his cot.

'Yes Amma?' he asked feebly.

'I know you will be leaving soon so the matter is to be arranged without delay.' she said in her characteristic grating voice that so offended the auditory system.

'What . . . what matter?' Choked Bhrigu. I was very disappointed to see that despite my long motivational lectures, he was still strongly under her evil grip, behaving once again like a mechanical robot programmed to obey the commands of his creator. It proved once again that the scars of childhood never completely healed. To add to the burden, Bhrigu's gift of perception had come with a curse. He was highly sensitive himself and I guess that was the main reason why he was still struggling to overcome his fear. My heart surged with pity at my dear friend's wretched condition but I kept my mouth firmly shut. He had to break free from her grasp by his will power alone or else he would never heal.

'I have a few photographs of good girls from our caste. They are from well-to-do homes. Select one and I will begin the negotiations.'

Bhrigu was struck dumb. I could see in the quiver of his lips and the rapid blinking of his eyes that he was struggling to come to terms with this announcement. No word escaped from his mouth.

'Did you listen? Select one photograph. Now let me give you a little introduction of these girls and their background,' she rambled on. 'This first one. Her name is Vidisha. Her father is a clerk in the transfer division of Bihar Health Department. He earns a lot; you know what I mean. He has promised to provide a very fat dowry. He will do anything to get a chief inspector as his son-in-law. The other one . . . her name is Usha. . .'

She rambled on in her high pitched monotonous voice while Bhrigu and I cringed under the unbearable piece of litany.

'So. . .' she said finally. 'Who do you approve? Be quick because I have many matters to settle when you once decide,' she added after a little. 'It would do you good if you take the dowry offered as an important deciding factor. The money will come to your own use.'

I knew without being told that this was purely rhetorical. The one thing the woman ever cared for was her own well-being and the charade was for her profit only.

'I . . . I will think about it,' Bhrigu muttered under his breath.

'Fine then. I'll leave the pictures with you. Tell me once you decide and don't take too much time. Good girls with good dowries are fast to tie the knot. Dilly dallying will serve no one,' she said and left the room, shuffling her feet as was her custom.

We exhaled audibly when she left. Bhrigu looked much shaken up and I put a comforting hand over his right shoulder, 'Get a grip on yourself, man. She is not a devil but a cranky old woman only. There is no need to be so frightened of her. She smells it and then works it to her benefit. You know it, don't you? Who can be a better judge of character than you?'

'I know.' He said in a small voice. Beads of perspiration clearly stood out on his forehead. 'But I can't help it. The reaction is almost involuntary. I have no control over it. I have said the same lines to myself a million times before but to no avail. Just looking at her brings out the worst phobias in me. I . . . I don't know why.'

This statement was so ironical that I almost gasped with surprise. Bhrigu Mahesh, the mental magician, whose one look was enough to read anyone like an open book had failed to read himself.

'What are you going to do about this marriage business?' I asked again.

'I don't want to marry ever. You know my thoughts about it, don't you?'

'Yes. Your reasons are strange, though,' I said as his words from the distant past came floating to the surface of my mind. 'Sutte, I don't believe in the institution of marriage,' he had said. 'I am more of a champion of free love. Marriage stagnates love and makes a mockery of it so much so that one day without even realising you become two people sharing the same roof with no remembrance of why you came together in the first place. Love should never be bound by laws, even marital ones. It was and should always be free.' I had been shocked to hear him attack the sacred institution that had brought bliss to the lives of many. I wonder why he had such radical thoughts about it. Was it something to do with his parents? Who were they? And how did he end up living with a cold, apathetic aunt? I never volunteered such questions because I could understand almost intuitively that he hated to be burdened by personal questions. He always had such a thick, impenetrable blanket of privacy wrapped around him that one could never even begin to think of asking anything that he had not even remotely encouraged. His doubly sensitive nature compounded matters further. So, as he gave me no room for a question anywhere, I had to bite my tongue to quell my curiosity.

'So, what answer will you give to the woman?' I asked.

'I will think of something,' he said, and I was aware of the same nervous energy in him again. 'But let's concentrate on this case first. Tomorrow, we will be meeting our final suspect, Bali. I have my questionnaire to prepare,' he said and slowly walked out of the room, with the bearing of a man saddled with a heavy burden, to sit on the porch and brood.

13

I never knew that even before we could find Bali, a series of unfortunate events would find us. It was a little before seven when a shrill phone call woke me up from my dreamless slumber. Cursing inaudibly under my breath, I looked at the screen with foggy eyes and saw, to my utter chagrin, that this was none other than the person who was soon to get a Nobel Prize for his constant and untiring efforts in irritating people at all ungodly hours.

'What is it, Your Highness?' I mumbled in a heavy voice.

'Why is Mahesh's mobile off?' An agitated voice sounded from the other side of the line.

'I dunno. Not everyone is an owl like you, I guess.'

He snorted haughtily, 'It's almost seven in the morning, smart ass.'

'Where do you want to send us this time?' I said, irritated at being rudely jerked off my slumber. 'To hell and back and to hell again for nothing.'

'If only you had said that not on the other side of the line but to the face, God's my witness, self would have made you regret it bad,' he growled in his thick Mumbaiya accent. 'Self got the dirt on Kala Shahi's next. Pass this to Mahesh first thing after he gets his eight hours. He has been behind self's freaking ass all this month for this bit of info. Self obtained it after great pearl to life. Tell him to deposit the good old currency in the account too. God only knows how self slaves for those green notes!'

'For the umpteenth time, it's "peril" and not "pearl",' I said, mockingly. I still couldn't bring myself to forgive him for his last debacle that had landed us in the soup. 'It won't kill you to use "I" while addressing yourself instead of 'self' either.'

I could hear him cursing in his native Marathi language that I couldn't grasp 'Don't you go all fancy pants on self, you son of a gun. No wimpy English teacher can do the kind of job self does. Now, don't forget to give him the said info,' he said and the line was disconnected.

This call had roused me from my sleep completely and I now made my way to Bhrigu's room. He was a person who woke up with the first cry of the rooster and I wondered why he was still in bed at this hour. Well, before I proceed further, I would like to give a character sketch of this fellow whom I had just addressed to as 'Your Highness'. He was as much a royalty or a blue blood as a guard who claims to be the owner of the property he is guarding. No one knew his real name but just that the man was once the logistics and strategy expert of the crime lord Kala Shahi but had parted ways after a major dispute. He, as is the custom with the Shadyworld (note-not to be confused with the Underworld. Shadyworld or Kala Shahi's world is a sophisticated though ruthless organisation that works on the motto that anything that cannot be proved illegal is legal) with the people who betray them, was now the most wanted man on their list but the man's razor-sharp wits had outsmarted every move that his enemy could make and why wouldn't he? He was the one who had devised those moves in the first place. He sprinted across seven states, fleeing for dear life and finally found himself in a cheap room of an obscure motel in Patna where he went into hiding. Still, there comes a time in the life of a hunted man when he finds himself at a fork in the road and has to decide whether he wants to survive by hiding in the cubbyhole forever and die a slow, pathetic death eventually by starvation or to go out in the free world in search of his daily bread, taking the bullets well in his stride. Either road was wrought with self-destruction with dim chances of survival and hence discouraged, he was on the verge of throwing the towel in when he discovered that he had one last option left that would not only provide him with his much needed loaf of bread but protect him from the bullets, too. The very next day, he gladly took that option and surrendered himself to the law. It was then that he met Inspector Bhrigu Mahesh, doing his stint at the Patliputra police station. Bhrigu, during the interrogation, convinced the man to act as his snitch and help him nab Kapil Shahi, the crime lord who had his syndicates in India and abroad, helped and aided by corrupt bureaucrats and politicians who had their own vested interests to nurture. Kapil Shahi alias 'Kala Nag' was the man behind many high profile intrigues of such sophistication and intricacy that had it not been an act of crime, it could have easily amounted to sorcery. The man was a criminal mastermind or mental sorcerer as he loved to put it, with an evil genius that could shame the brightest and most brilliant that the country had to offer and his business acumen was such that could shame any industrialist under the sun. The upshot of the matter was that while the police and CBI worked day and night to gather evidence enough to nail the man, Kala Nag continued to make his public appearances in his fineries at white-collar parties with the grandeur and bearing of a giant who had nothing to fear from the scurrying mice in uniform, nibbling at the soles of his leather boots. Your Highness had been one of his right hand men who knew more about the Kala Nag than anyone else who they knew and Bhrigu had lost no time in enlisting his services. The man, after a couple of sessions, relented and agreed to do his part, but in return, he asked for three wishes of his to be fulfilled. First, that he should be promptly released from jail, second that he should be properly reimbursed for his efforts that would border on suicide and third that no one would keep tabs on him ever. He would call from payphones or secure lines when he seemed fit and he would henceforth be addressed to only as 'Your Highness'. This would serve the twofold function of keeping his identity safe and would also boost up his confidence whenever he would hear them. Bhrigu had another term for this confidence that needed boosting and he called it *megalomania*. Well, the merger served both parties very well as Bhrigu could now get information on anything that had even the faintest suggestion of the involvement of Kapil Shahi, however well concealed, and in return the Shadyworld encyclopaedia alias Your Highness would get to live a life with a steady income without the need of endangering himself by going out into the world where he was nothing more than a hunted prey.

When Bhrigu left the police force, Your Highness had refused to comply with the other officers. He had said that if he was to remain as a valuable snitch working for the law, it had to be through Bhrigu Mahesh alone. He would deal with no one else. The police superintendent had requested Bhrigu to help them nab Kala Naga through Your Highness's help and that the police force was more than ready to provide the dough required for the latter's services. Bhrigu accepted gladly as the ingenious evil kingpin of the Shadyworld, working on not one but ten brains was his greatest challenge and he had been studying him and his machinations for a couple of years now, trying to find a chink in his armour that he could exploit to his advantage and the one person who could help him was someone like Your Highness who knew the ways of Kala Nag's world at the back, well, almost at the back of his hand.

When I finally got to Bhrigu's room, I noticed that he was not in his bed but was standing near the headboard gazing at a dry leaf with concern and a slight trepidation. After wondering about the origins of the leaf, I went up and looked at it only to be shocked into absolute silence. On the ventral surface of the leaf, the following menacing words where scrawled in dried, congealed blood—'YOU DISTURBED MY SLEEP. NOW YOU DIE.'

14

'Wh . . . what's that?!' I asked hoarsely.

'A warning,' he replied, running a light finger over the words 'Its human blood alright. Judging by the degree of clotting, I should say that it was written not more than two hours ago.'

I gaped at him with disbelief, 'Is that your only concern? Haven't you noticed what it says?'

'Yes, Sutte, I did. How couldn't I? The writing is legible enough,' he replied, now feeling the dorsal surface of the leaf. 'It isn't fall yet and they have found a leaf dry as a bone. Or have they?'

I was thoroughly piqued. 'I would again draw your attention to the hieroglyphics carved on the leaf, and if you haven't grasped the meaning yet, I should tell you that it says we are soon to be in the company of death.'

'Yes. So what do you propose we do? Shriek with fear and run around the house as if our trouser seats were on fire?

No thanks. It would be better advised if I employed my time learning what I can through this singular leaf.'

'And what did you learn?' I asked with the touch of the sarcasm.

'A few vital points. First, someone is carefully plotting to spook us enough to leave this case. Second, the threat, most definitely, is not from the witch and third, that the writer is half literate. He had only a few words to write and still he managed to make about a thousand grammatical mistakes.'

'How did this end up in your room?'

'Through the window. I always sleep with it open, a habit I now think I should revise.'

'It sure is crisp and dry. Very much like the leaves that we used to dry for projects in our botany class by pressing them in our books,' I said, running my finger over the dried veins of the leaf.

'Correct. The same process has been applied to dry this leaf as well.'

'But why would anyone go to such extremes? Why not write a threat on a regular leaf?'

'If you think before asking a question, I am certain you would nail the answer yourself,' he said irritably. 'Green leaves have moisture on their surface. No ink would stick on them, let alone blood.'

I was suddenly aware of being in the sixth grade class with my science teacher glowering and towering over me, ready to explode any second for my silly mistake. I am sure that the man who had written this threat had meant to cause fear and alarm and not to initiate a lecture on the anatomy of the leaf and the study of its salient features.

'I somehow get a feeling that this is a first of what is going to come. Three things to infer from this episode.

First; we have stepped on someone's shoes; second, that someone knows who we are. Third, we are going in the right direction,' he said, carefully placing the leaf over a book and clamping it down with a black paper weight.

'It's a first of what is about to come?' I asked, my mind totally skipping the things he said subsequently, 'You think?!'

'Yes. Clearly someone is trying to get us off the case. They won't stop until we do and we won't so they will continue.'

This time I lost it. 'How can you state this with such sangfroid? And who is threatening us? One of Jayanti Devi's relatives? I am sure it's that Mutukal. He looked the epitome of evil or his wife.' I croaked, 'But aren't you the least bit concerned?'

'I am but I don't go bleating about it,' he conceded. 'We have to be very cautious from now on. Our every step is being watched. If I am honest with you, I should say that I have no definite clue whatsoever as to who wrote that stuff. An idea, but then again nothing definite.'

'But . . . but you have interrogated them! You should know!'

He looked at me with disdain. It was evident that I had found success in galling him yet again. 'I am not a clairvoyant, Sutte,' he said heatedly. 'How do I make you understand? I don't have supernatural powers. I am as human as human goes with a little extra something that you call perception. Yes, it's true that I have observed the suspects and collected valuable information; I cannot give you a final answer until the investigation is over. If I do it before, to quote myself again, I will be leaving room for doubt.'

I sat there smarting with the bruises inflicted by his red hot words and to change the matter to a relatively lighter topic, I said, 'Your Highness called an hour ago. He said your mobile was switched off and he wanted to pass on an important lead on Kala Shahi that he has procured, as always, by putting his life in 'pearl'.'

He bounded from his seat as if an invisible spring had suddenly come loose in it 'Damn! I missed it! I was so engrossed in that freaking leaf that I completely forgot to switch my phone on! Now it will take ages for that useless bounder to call me again. How terrible!'

There were only a very few things in the world that could elicit such a show of passion from a man who was so in control of his emotions at all times, especially when on a case, that only the word 'poker faced' could describe it succinctly. Those few things being Nirja Masi and the evil supreme Kapil Shahi alias *Kala Nag.* I sometimes wondered whether the two shared a bond carried over from the past life. Anything that even remotely hinted at the Nag was enough to bring him to life as if Jesus Christ newly resurrected. What caused this well of passion is something I have thought of often with only one explanation. Kapil Shahi was Bhrigu Mahesh's alter ego. He was gifted with the same powers of perception and acuity as Bhrigu, bordering on the surreal, but whereas Bhrigu used it for the good of mankind, Kapil Shahi had vowed to use it for wreaking destruction where he stood to profit alone. Their powers were matched perfectly and hence they always ended up running parallel, one nullifying the effect of another and never getting the edge that is required to defeat and conquer. Your Highness was the only advantage Bhrigu had over his arch nemesis and so he was rightly disappointed in missing that all important call that could very well have given him that extra edge required to squash the fang of *Kala Nag* once and for all.

'It's probably nothing at all,' I said, trying to soothe him. 'You remember, in his last correspondence, he said that the CBI would kill for the kind of Intel he was about to provide us with? We went to Shigupha, trusting him explicitly, braving the chilly winds for days, living under disguises in motels where rats would also screw their nose, forced to become finicky; ate horrible food, if you could call it food, for what? Nothing. He called you after a week to inform that Shahi's most trusted aide won't be coming to Shigupha after all. We went to bring down *Kala Naga* and brought wild goose instead.'

'It wasn't his fault, man,' said Bhrigu. 'The aide already got tipped off somehow and he didn't show up. You wouldn't believe the strength of the intelligence network than runs through their ranks. Your Highness is never wrong, but he cannot predict an unforeseen event. It can happen to anybody.'

'You are far too tolerant of that beasel. I don't trust him at all. Sometimes I think he's just using us to get to his pot of gold.'

'He's avaricious and suffers from megalomania, yes, but dishonesty is not one of his peccadilloes. If he commits himself to a job, he sticks. I have probed him thoroughly and you know that I am a better judge of character than you.'

'Can I ask you something?' I said. A question had formed itself in my mind and I felt the urge to voice it but was apprehensive as to how Bhrigu would take it. I had never questioned his capabilities point blank before.

'Yes?'

'I have immense respect for your talents but don't you think that people as shrewd and sharp as Your Highness can find ways to bypass even you? I mean he was once Kala Shahi's right-hand man. That ought to figure in.'

I was relieved to find him smiling at my question. Somehow my scepticism had been received in good humour.

'He is Kala Shahi's right-hand man as like the hundreds of others that work under him.'

I was confused and I said as much, 'I've lost you, I'm afraid.'

'Your Highness is sharp and possesses his wits alright but don't forget that Kala Naga is the kingpin of an organisation that is so huge and complex that it can anytime be declared an independent country. He has many such people like Y.H. working under him and I am certain not one of them has met him personally. We are fortunate that we got Y.H. as he is the first 'inside man' that we have gotten our hooks into. He is resourceful, let me assure you but he is as in the dark about Kala Nag as us. It will be a very long and arduous journey indeed before we even begin to get close to the man.'

'But I see Kala Nag almost every day in the papers, partying with officials and dignitaries. They know all about the menace but are still forced to shake a leg with him. That's a mockery of law right there.'

'Ha!' he said, impassioned. I could see the colour rising to his cheeks. 'You're right there. That's the irony of it all. The man has been so successful in creating two contrasting personalities of himself that sometimes it feels as if they are two different people. All thanks to his ingenious brain and the touch of the artist that makes all the difference. He has so skilfully coated the black with the white that no one can as much as lay a finger on him. You know, most of the people that work under him at one time had been white-collar men who were fired and subsequently ostracised by companies for their embezzlement or inside trading. These people were recruited and so effectively brainwashed by the man that now they would do just about anything for him. Y.H. too was one of them, although, he hasn't said anything about the subject. Kala Shahi has laundered his money into school trusts, big corporate businesses, political campaigns, commercial banks etc that it's become almost impossible now to separate the legal from the illegal. Don't you have a proper phrase to describe it?'

'He has painted the black collar, white.'

'Great!' he said, impressed. 'You have nailed it, my scribe!'

As I blushed, he continued, 'Y.H. was just a foot soldier working in the strategy and logistics department. He is helping us to the best of his capabilities. He has no other option other than that and let me assure you that he is trustworthy.'

'As long as he doesn't send us on wild goose chases again,' I said, making a wry face.

Bhrigu let out a sigh and said, 'Y.H. should be the least of our worries right now. This case is getting interesting by the second. We would be well advised to keep all our energies focused on it and all our senses on the red alert. Tomorrow, we visit our final suspect, Bali.'

15

BALI

The next day dawned fresh and clear. There was not a speck of cloud to be seen anywhere in the skies above. I was immensely relieved as the tipsy weather had started to take a toll on me. The wet, slippery dirt roads, the overflowing drain waters inundating the said roads, the long hours of power cuts (Where I could not charge my precious I-phone and laptop), and the long hours of being trapped inside the house with ring master Nirja Masi were proving burdens that my nervous system was having a hard time coping with. Bhrigu, though, looked quite unconcerned and I could see that his mind was lightyears away from these problems. He had grown pensive, detached, almost in his own shell and sat brooding for hours with that gum of his giving him a constant company. I had seen him slipping into this behaviour many times before when he was involved in a particularly baffling mystery. It was as if his consciousness had vacated his body, awakening in the suspects he was studying and to an extent that I sometimes found him almost like a statue cut in stone, with his glazed eyes fixed on any inanimate object, unfocused and unseeing. In such moments you could be shouting in his ears or having a battle, he wouldn't even notice; almost like a true yogi in meditation. This was the time when he needed me the most to take care of his little needs like charging his mobile, getting him his favourite mint flavour gums, and seeing to it that no one disturbed him in anyway.

Well, as I was saying, I was no longer under the weather as it had cleared to reveal a beautiful morning and Bhrigu and I were all set to meet our last suspect, Bali. As we were about to make for the door, I saw someone struggling with the gate, trying to force it open. I couldn't believe my eyes when I saw that it was none other than Mutukal Kumar's daughter Meena Kumari.

I rushed to open the gate for her and called her in to sit on one of the chairs kept on the porch. Bhrigu was looking intently at her but there was not a sign of surprise in his eyes. We took the chairs facing her.

In a bright red sari, Meena Kumari was looking a sight. Her fair complexion stood out in the vibrant colour and the rose in her cheeks became pronounced by the second. She was blushing and her pale skin did nothing to hide it. Her thick black hair had been beautifully done in a plait, tied neatly with a black ribbon and her heavy, lidded eyes where drooping in inhibition. I couldn't help but marvel at her luminous eyelashes that fell like a canopy over her eyes. She had a curvaceous body, slightly on the pudgy side but the elegant, proportioned limbs and the graceful fall of the curves more than compensated for it. She was a very attractive girl and I found myself gaping almost involuntarily at her once again but could only thank heavens that Bhrigu's whole concentration was focused on her and not me.

'Meena Kumari' said Bhrigu. 'That's your name, isn't it?'

She nodded her head in consent.

'What brings you here?'

She was silent for a space, struggling for an answer. Her lips opened and closed for more than what could be considered normal and she rubbed her one foot over the other for an unusual number of times. Even with my average acuity, I could clearly ascertain that she was very nervous and unsure of her position.

'Please,' I said, hastening to make her comfortable 'You can tell us your problem. Is there something weighing on your mind that you would like to discuss with us? Don't be shy. Please, consider us to be your friends.'

This time Bhrigu did throw a meaning look at me, his lips curling in a suggestion of a smile or a snarl I couldn't tell.

'What's the matter?' Bhrigu asked, ignoring my concern for her well-being.

'I . . . I wanted to talk to you about . . . about. . .'

'Yes? About what?' Bhrigu asked again.

'But . . . but you won't tell anyone that I told you this. . .' she stammered, raising her eyes to Bhrigu's and I could just marvel at their beauty. I had yet to see a pair so perfectly round and beautiful like hers. 'Twin stars' is the only expression that jumps to the mind. The apprehension that lurked in their depths was only contributing in enhancing their delicacy.

'No. Rest assured. You can trust our discretion.'

'Yes. Totally.' I piped in even before I could hold myself.

She relaxed a trifle and said, still a little hesitant. 'I know that you are considering Avdoot for the job too.'

'Avdoot? Why, yes. He is a very strong contender.' Said Bhrigu 'But what has that got to do with you? Your father will get a fair chance too. Don't you worry.'

'No, that's not why I'm here.' She said a little impatiently. 'I am not here to plead for my father.'

'Really?'

'Yes. I am here for Avdoot. You would be better advised to cancel him as a candidate for the job. He is a very lecherous man.'

'We didn't think so. He appeared to be quite a genuine and trustworthy person. What are your reasons for such accusations against him?'

She shifted a little in her seat and then said in a voice barely above a whisper 'Avdoot is anything but trustworthy. Had he been trustworthy would he betray my trust like this?'

'Betray your trust?' I asked, surprised, 'How?'

'What would you call a man who promises to marry you and then ends up marrying your own aunt?' she said with a flash of anger in her eyes.

'Avdoot? He was to marry you?' I almost shouted with surprise.

'Yes,' she said and, looking at Bhrigu, continued, 'I am telling you the truth, god's word. Avdoot loved me passionately. Even though I spurned him at first, he persisted in his efforts, surprising me with little tokens of sweet nothings. Being of a tender disposition, I melted and soon found myself falling fast and hard in love with him, too. We started spending time together. God only knows how

I managed it with my mother always at my back but love finds a way and it did for me, too. We saw each other for a whole year and . . . and before this relationship could go anywhere, he . . . he . . . that rascal . . . he married my aunt Indumati! I would never forget that dreadful day,' she said in a heavy voice with eyes tinged with red. 'I was so shocked that I thought I could never breathe.'

'That must have been very hard, indeed,' said Bhrigu softly.

'You have no idea!' she said and this time losing all self control, sobbed bitterly into her palms. My heart went out to her and I couldn't stop myself from patting her lightly on the shoulder.

After a good ten minutes, she raised a tear soaked face and continued. 'Malthu knew all about us. We often used him as a courier for sending and receiving love letters to each other. He died in that accident a day after delivering the last love letter of Avdoot to me. Poor boy!'

This time I noticed that Bhrigu did register a modicum of surprise and needless to say, I was beside myself with disbelief.

'What?!'

She nodded her head again. 'I was very fond of the boy. It came as a double shock to me. That year, I wanted to die myself but you know my brother Vinod. He is much attached to me as I have practically raised him. The only mother he knows is me. He won't survive a day without me.'

'Those letters, said Bhrigu, 'Do you still have them with you?'

'Yes, I had the letters with me but the box in which I used to keep them, vanished altogether. I searched for it but could not find it anywhere.'

'Did it vanish after or before Malthu's death?'

She thought for a while and then said, 'I am not sure but I remember depositing the last love letter to the bundle and till then the box was there. But when I searched for it a week after Malthu had died, in order to burn its contents and vent my anger and grief, I found my letters scattered on the ground with no sign of the box anywhere. I searched for it in the house but couldn't find it anywhere. As I got my letters, I did not care about it much but it struck me as very strange. Who would want a petty cardboard box? Although I had decorated it beautifully with colourful crepe papers and ribbons in the shape of little hearts.'

'Did anyone in your family take it?'

'Only my brother knew about it and he swore on my name that he didn't take it. I knew he was telling the truth because I know instinctively when he is lying.'

'I see.'

'Please, please see to it that Avdoot doesn't get the job. He is a very foul person. He will bring nothing but ruin to your business.'

'We will definitely keep your word of caution in mind,' said Bhrigu and rose to his feet. 'We have to attend to some urgent business, so if you have nothing else to say. . .'

'Oh! Yes, surely,' she said, reluctantly getting up. She left sulking but not before throwing a meaning look at Bhrigu. I knew that she wanted full assurance that Avdoot won't land the job but Bhrigu's evasive answer had done nothing to pacify her.

It was ten minutes since she left but we found us still rooted to the spot. I thought that the first thing Bhrigu wanted was to leave and round up Bali, but apparently he stood there like a man lost in thought.

'What are you thinking now? Meenakumari's confession has surprised you not a little bit, I can see.'

'Hmm.'

'Now what is that supposed to mean?' I asked a little irritated 'What do you think about her? Was she lying to remove competition and help her father get the job or was she telling the truth? That vile Mutukal could have sent her on his behalf.'

This question was more than enough to bring him out of his reverie. 'Sutte, I am fed up of your silly questions. You have got it into your system that I am some kind of a clairvoyant, even after me telling you a thousand times to the contrary. You just don't get my method, do you?' He snapped angrily 'How am I to know whether she is lying or telling the truth?'

I was a little stunned at his reaction. I think I should mention here that whenever we got to the thick of any mystery, he almost always became lost and whimsical, ready to pounce on the slightest notice. Knowing that this was something he had no control over, I ignored his outburst.

'Alright, I am sorry,' I said, 'should we not leave now?'

He was lost for another couple of minutes and then said 'I have to go make some important inquiries. You stay here. Tomorrow we'll go to meet Bali.'

I was about to ask the nature of such inquiries when I checked myself. The onset of his mercurial disposition held my tongue in check, lest I unleashed his wrath again. In a moment he was out of the gate, making rapid strides towards the village.

I stood there watching him till he took a turn and disappeared from my view. The chair looked inviting enough and gladly, I lapsed into it. My mind was still turning over this latest piece of information handed to us by Meenakumari. She and Avdoot. Was it really true? And then why not? Meenakumari looked honest enough. Why should she lie? She appeared to loathe her father as I could see the marks of disgust creasing her face as she mentioned him. She was apparently fed up of her parents, too. To me, she appeared to be a very decent girl, caring and affectionate. That Avdoot must be a total rascal to play with the feelings of such a nice girl like her. The nerve to marry her own aunt! He looked suspicious enough during his interrogation. His palms had become all sweaty and his whole aspect shook with nervousness and an unspoken fear. Till date, I had all along suspected Mutukal to be the man behind the tragedy but the point of suspicion was now strongly in favour of Avdoot. But why would he kill Malthu? Was he fearful that he would talk about the affair to his wife? Meenakumari could use the testimony of Malthu to support her argument against Avdoot in front of Indumati. But Malthu was an imbecile! Who would believe his story? He could be easily trained to lie. Was there something else that caused Avdoot to take this step? Did Malthu pose a greater threat? But how? This mystery was taking the turn for the worse. The degree of complication was increasing by the second and I could do nothing but to let myself get caught up in the tangle.

I tried to sort this mystery by putting together the facts we had collected till now. I thought that if I could write the points systematically, then maybe some clues could present themselves that could help clear up the mystery to a certain extent. Feeling a little more confident, I took out my note pad and wrote:

1. Sequence of Events—

   a) The legend of the witch of Senduwar. The Haunted Garden of Jiyashree. Abandoned site.
   b) The discovery of golden nuggets by Malthu that led to the Gold Rush.
   c) The active participation of Malthu's relatives in the rush. Malthu's demand rises.
   d) Sudden death of Malthu said to be due to an accident that broke his neck.
   e) Jayanti Devi suspects otherwise. She is pretty confident that one of the relatives (Mutukal) is behind the tragedy. Reason for her suspicions, a strong hunch (or distrust?)
   f) The menacing warning scrawled on a leaf- Confirming that Malthu's death wasn't an accident but the consequence of something very sinister. Validating Jayanti Devi's hunch.

2. Reasons behind the crime-

   a) Someone wanted all the treasure to him/herself- The theory was cancelled because we found an exquisite corner of a necklace and other precious odds and ends of precious jewellery at the site. No one had bothered to clear that up and it has probably been collecting on the flood plain for years, undisturbed. The odds and ends of the treasure were totally abandoned by the villagers as inauspicious.
   Conclusion—The murder was committed not for the treasure

b) Other reasons are still in the womb of the mystery.

Suspects-

1. Mutukal Kumar—Very unscrupulous and avaricious. A pure ruffian who is controlled by his wife. Can do anything for money and has always felt wronged because he didn't get a share from Jayanti Devi's husband's pension. But can he kill for it? Strongest suspect. Could he have aggravated matters that led to Malthu's death? Likely.

2. Indumati—A modern woman with progressive thoughts. Doesn't believe in old traditions. Strong and intelligent. I don't think she can kill anyone but Bhrigu has his lips sealed on this topic. So I can't say anything for sure.

3. Avdoot—Handsome, soft-spoken, but apparently has many sides to his personality. Ex lover of Meenakumari. Gets nervous when asked about Malthu and the tragedy. A likely suspect in my opinion.

4. Bali—Jayanti Devi's lone support. By Jayanti Devi's testimonials, he is a warm-hearted person who cares for her deeply. Tomorrow, we'll be meeting him. Not a likely suspect according to me.

I looked at the paper again and again but no clue presented itself that could untangle the knots and help clear the puzzle. The most important mystery for me had been whether Malthu was murdered at all. Even during our interrogations, I had a nagging feeling that this was after all an unfortunate accident and nothing else. But the warning note had at least helped clear that mystery. It was a murder all right and as Bhrigu said, we were headed in the right direction but what direction that was, I couldn't tell. Frustrated, I pocketed the paper and went inside the house to rest awhile and stabilise my buzzing mind. I didn't know when I drifted to sleep but when I woke up I found that Bhrigu was sitting by a stool beside me, chewing his gum peacefully. His eyes were closed and his face looked relaxed. When he saw that I had awoken, he said in a ringing, cheerful voice 'Oh! You are up! Good. Get ready. We have to go meet Bali.'

'But . . . but you said we'll go tomorrow!'

'Why tomorrow, if today's as good a day as any? Now get going. It's almost one o'clock. If we hurry, we can still make it to lunch on time.'

I got up thinking what had occurred to enliven his spirits so significantly. Had he discovered anything of importance? Obviously he had and as usual was keeping it a secret from me. It was no use coaxing him to tell because I knew from experience that he wouldn't speak a word unless he was ready. 'I will come clean once all the threads are in my hand,' he would say. Just to make sure, I asked him, 'Don't you owe me an explanation first?'

And out came the cliché line that had become his catchphrase, 'I will come clean once all the threads are in my hand.'

I chuckled quite unabashedly and left for the washroom, leaving him (and to my delight) with a question stitched between his brows. I revelled in the idea that it was not just him who could be enigmatic. I had my own bag of tricks, too.

Bali's house was situated not very far from Jayanti Devi's house. She had told us that if we move in a straight line from her house for about five minutes, we'd come to a large and bustling ration store, run by an obese baniya who was in the habit of remaining half naked from the torso up, flaunting a belly that could be the source of shock and chagrin to any innocent who chanced to look at it for the first time. We had to take the narrow and congested by lane that ran from this shop and opened to a cluster of two-room houses, all joined end to end. The second one, painted in mauve, would be Bali's. We had no trouble at all in locating him. Bhrigu rang the bell and we stood there patiently waiting for our final suspect to answer the call.

'Who is it?' A thin voice asked from somewhere inside the house.

'I am Deb, with my friend Shekhar. I hope Jayanti Amma told you about us?' Bhrigu replied in a loud and clear voice.

We could hear a deep thump inside as if someone had slipped off the bed and landed clumsily on the ground. 'Please wait. I am coming,' the voice said, but this time, it was earnest and excited.

In a moment or two, the door opened and framed in the doorway stood a tall man, dressed in khaki pants and a white, full-sleeve shirt clumsily tucked in. He had curly, unruly hair and the good part of his face was obscured by the undergrowth of thick beard. The only feature clear to us were his dull, lustreless eyes, watery but almost opaque. Somehow, the excitement in his voice, hadn't reached his eyes. I could detect a hint of pain in them but was it only my imagination working overtime, I couldn't tell.

'Bhabhi told me about your impending visit.' He said in the thin voice he had used to address us before. This time, I could detect a slight quavering in every spoken syllable. It looked as if the man was either ill or on the verge of a serious malaise.

'Please do come in.' We went inside and seated ourselves in the barely furnished room with just a couch with a spring in it that had come loose, a small cot, a low wooden stool, and small-sized TV. There were no windows in the room at all, save for a ventilator. The only attractive feature of the room was a beautiful parrot in a gilded cage, kept on a stool beside the TV. He sat there looking at us with the same dead look that his keeper carried; making me acknowledge the article I had once read that your pets eventually come to share some of your traits. He saw my object of interest and offered 'This is Chameli, my parrot.'

'Why does she look so morose?' I asked, unable to keep out the curiosity. 'Aren't parrots supposed to be lively and talkative, too?'

'Oh! She's hungry, that's all. I will give her the green chilies she loves and she would be alright,' he said, his answer noncommittal 'Now, I take it that you are here for the interview. Would you like a cup of tea first?'

'Please, no need for formalities,' Bhrigu said and I noticed that he had once again donned his poker face. 'We would appreciate it very much if we could start off with the interview right away. There are other pressing matters that we have to attend to.

'As you say,' he said in an almost breathless voice. I don't know much of respiratory diseases, but I was forming the diagnosis that he might be suffering from asthma.

'So, Mr Bali,' said Bhrigu, after taking a seat on the hard couch. 'Tell us about yourself.'

The man gave him a profoundly dumb look and said, 'About myself? What?'

'Everything. You were working at the mill, I am given to know. If so, why were you ready for the interview? Don't you find your present employment satisfactory?'

'Oh!' he ejaculated. 'Jayanti Bhabhi has given you all the details. I see.'

'Yes, but only a sketch that you have to fill in.' Bhrigu said leaning forward in his seat and waiting for Bali's answer.

The man coughed twice and began breathlessly. 'The . . . the mill shut down permanently a week ago. I was rendered useless. When Jayanti Bhabhi told me about you people, I . . . I thought I could get a job decent enough to support my expenses.'

'But why did the mill shut down? Wasn't it one of the main sources of local employment?'

'Yes . . . yes it was. It was a shock for all of us. Many families were dependent on it for their daily bread but . . . but. . .' He exhaled deeply.

'But why?'

'I . . . I can't say for sure but there's a rumour going round that . . . that *Malik* sold the land to a contractor for a hefty sum of money. They are demolishing the mill and building a cold storage instead.'

'Hmm. Who is this '*Malik*'?'

'Our employer. *Zamindaar* Ghanshyam Singh.'

I thought I had heard that name before, but as if reading my thoughts, Bhrigu answered it for me.

'Ghanshyam Singh. Yes, the Gram Pradhan told us about him. He is one of the richest and influential men of this village, isn't it?'

'Not only of this village but fifty villages combined.'

'Right. Now tell me about your past life and employments.' Bhrigu said easing back in his seat.

The man stared at him with his opaque eyes. He looked lost and out of place in his own house. He didn't look anything like the kind and hearty person that Jayanti Devi's accounts had given us to expect. Not even close. We came looking for a warm, affable young man and found instead a lost, deeply troubled youth, possibly in the throes of depression. It's a shame what unemployment can do to a happy, about town youth. If it can make hardened criminals out of them, ready to slay for a couple of bucks and a packet of meal, this man was still better off than most . . . or was he?

'I . . . I did my matriculation from Sardar Vidya Peeth and then dropped out of school. I was friends with a guard of *Malik*'s kothi and he recommended me to one of *Malik's* deputies. He got me a job first as a guard and then shifted me to the mill where I had been working till now.'

'Did you like working there?'

'It . . . it was tough job but the pay was satisfactory.'

'Jayanti *Amma* gave us a glowing account of you. You love her dearly and helped her lot during her time of need, is it not?'

He seared us again with those hard, expressionless eyes and said, 'Yes. I love her and did everything to help her.'

'You must be getting a good pay for all the trouble you took for Jayanti Devi. Bought her new furniture too, is it not?'

'Y . . . yes. I thought it would be a pleasant change for her.'

'You should have brought some for yourself, too' I said even before I could check my ill-timed candour. 'Your house could do with a good, soft couch. This one has rendered the seat of my trousers totally numb.'

Bhrigu and Bali stared at me with a 'What was that' expression and then the unimaginable happened. Bali was riddled with peals of laughter. As his whole body shook with it, I noticed the transformation that was brought about in him. Warmth and light returned to his eyes; as the opaqueness gently melted away, we got a fleeting glimpse of the Bali, Jayanti Devi had told us about. I was relieved to know that his former self had not been completely obliterated but was temporarily absconding under the adverse circumstances. It was a wonder how the simplest of smiles could melt the stoutest of hearts. But this transformation was short-lived and as reality struck the poor fellow, he lapsed back into his painful, robotic routine again.

I saw Bhrigu observing him intently but apart from a slight smile curling his lips (or was it again the product of my overworked imagination, I couldn't say), his impenetrable mask didn't help in revealing much.

'Do you have any testimonials that could prove that you would do your job to our satisfaction?' he asked.

'I . . . I don't know. I was a good worker at the mill but I don't know what kind of . . . of job I am required to do.'

'That's okay. We will give you the details tomorrow. If selected, you will be kept on a temporary basis for six months and if you produce desired results by that time, we will be providing you with a permanent job with proper remunerations.'

'T . . . tomorrow?' He almost gasped. 'Why tomorrow?'

'Why? Do you have a problem with tomorrow?'

'N . . . no, but . . . I . . . I am not well, as you can see. It would be best if you could conclude the interview to . . . today.'

'I am sorry but today we are hard pressed for time. If you wish, we could come back after a couple of days. You don't look well enough to take the interview even tomorrow.'

'N . . . no . . . do come tomorrow. I will be fine.'

'Okay then. That's settled,' said Bhrigu and he took out a pen from his waistcoat pocket, as he looked about the room.

'Are . . . are you looking for something?' Bali asked, following Bhrigu's gaze.

'Yes. I have to note down my appointment with you or else I would be sure to forget. I forgot my notepad. Could you be kind enough to provide me with one?'

'Oh sure . . . sure,' said the man and stood up weakly. There was a cheap-quality wooden cabinet kept close to the TV. The gilded cage of the parrot was sitting atop it. Caught in the unusual beauty of the cage and the unnatural gloom of the parrot, I had totally forgotten to notice the nondescript cabinet on which it stood. He opened the top drawer of the same and after rummaging in it for a while, took out a thin notepad.

'Is this alright?' he said, presenting it to Bhrigu.

'Quiet. Thank you,' said my friend, gazing intently at the cabinet, for reasons I could not fathom, and then busied himself with noting down the appointment.

'We will be taking your leave now. See you tomorrow at 10.00 a.m. sharp.'

We left his place and it was not more than fifteen minutes that we were back at home but not without the shock of our lives greeting us at the door and mind you, it wasn't Nirja Masi this time.

CHAPTER 5

THE TRAP

16

'Oh, heaven!' I ejaculated. It was a dead crow, stiff with rigor mortis, lying just outside the door. I couldn't help but remember the days of yore when such a sight would easily amount to a very bad omen. Julius Caesar had seen one and the rest is history.

Bhrigu went down on his knees and observed the bird intently. I was never particularly fond of crows and considered them to be a pathetic excuse for the avian species, so it was but natural that I liked it little still in its death. A perfect specimen of hideousness, I might add.

'I don't know how long this has been here,' said Bhrigu. 'We went out the back door and hence failed to notice it. It couldn't be dead less than three hours. Stiff as a rod, it is.'

'What are you doing?' I said with ill masked irritation 'You are talking as if it's not a dead crow but a dead person. Just get rid of it'

He looked at me curiously and said, 'Why are you being such a wuss? Superstitious, are you?'

'Nothing of the sort.' I replied with heat. 'It's not a very nice sight to look at, that's all.'

He ignored my remark and extracting a handkerchief from the inside pocket of his Kurta, lifted the bird gently. I grimaced inwardly. 'Yes, it's putrid alright,' he said.

I noticed that there was something scrawled in red on the floor where the dead bird had been lying. Bhrigu noticed it too and lowering his head over it, read it out loud with some difficulty. 'This omen is the harbinger of your death.'

'Good heavens!' I cried 'Not again!'

'Save your energy, Sutte,' Bhrigu said calmly 'As I said before, moaning and groaning will serve no one. Or shall I book you a ticket back home? This case is getting too much for your nerves, I see.'

'Oh no!' I cried again. 'I am perfectly alright.'

'Reading about dangerous adventures of great detectives in books is very different from actually being in one,' he said under his breath.

'I heard it alright,' I said, hurt again. 'Please forgive me for being human.'

'A very jumpy one at that,' he said to himself.

'If you think I can't hear you . . .' I began but was left with my mouth puckered to make a 'you' when Nirja Masi came out the door of her room adjacent to the one through which we were about to enter, looked at the dead thing in Bhrigu's hand and almost collapsed. I had to rush to her side to hold her from crashing to the floor. She was breathing hard and speech seemed to have abandoned her temporarily. We found this condition quite suitable when flippant speech decided to return, after all.

'Wh . . . where did you get that . . . that bird?' she asked in a hoarse whisper.

Bhrigu was silent. I noticed that what not all the dead birds in the world could manage to do, Nirja Masi had done with just a broken sentence. He was practically trembling with fear.

'I . . . I didn't bring it, masi,' he said, like a kid who had been caught in a mischief red handed. 'It . . . it was already here.'

'Oh lord! Oh my sweet lord!' She gasped 'Such a bad omen! Such a bad omen. . . Such a. . .'

I noticed that her record had stuck.

'I . . . will have to perform a *Katha* or else I am doomed. The sweet lord is angry . . . he is angry . . . for some reason . . .' she said, out of breath, and even before I could say anything to pacify her, she shot out of her room not very unlike an arrow from the bow, crying 'I will go find Punditji . . . He is my only hope . . .'

We stood there watching at her retreating form. Her drama had unfolded so suddenly that we were lost for a couple of minutes trying to digest her recent outburst. I beat Bhrigu to it and said, 'Your aunt didn't take it sportingly.'

'How could she? She never lets any opportunity for melodrama, go unexploited,' he replied sullenly.

'You say all sorts of scandalous things behind her back, but when she is standing in front of you, you become strangely dumb. If you can't say it to her face, don't say anything at all.'

He looked at me in a way that I felt sure I would have to call on the services of the fire squad. His eyes were ablaze. 'Why do you do that?' he almost shrieked. 'Why do you keep taunting me about her? Sometimes I feel you are worse than her. It may look awful funny to you, but it's a very sore topic for me.'

I squarely looked back at him. 'I just want you to understand that she is not a demon incarnate but a lousy human being. You will never come out of her terror if you don't fight back. Come on, man! Muster up the courage! You go after the most dangerous criminals with perfect aplomb and you are scared out of your mind of a stupid old lady.'

I could see that he wanted to retaliate with not little bitterness and I was preparing to brace myself for it when his eyes softened and the anger left him, leaving an inexorable fatigue behind that I had always witnessed in him whenever the question of his aunt arose. At such occasions he looked like he was painfully carrying a ton of burden and for some reason couldn't get rid of it. 'Just leave it,' he said in a tired voice.

I knew that I had reached stalemate and hence left the matter alone, as he had advised me, too. He was still holding the bird tenderly and I asked him what he was planning on doing about it.

'I will bury it,' he said. 'The death of this bird has been a total waste. It hasn't served its purpose. But that doesn't mean it won't get a proper burial.'

'What purpose?' I asked, confused.

'Of scaring us, you dimwit,' he replied and then as an afterthought, added, smiling impishly 'But it did succeed in spooking you. So it wasn't a total waste, after all.'

Bhrigu buried the bird in our backyard and we returned once again to his room. Exhaustion had crept into my bones and I readily sought the relief of the arm chair. Bhrigu sat on the edge of his stool, his every fibre taut with suppressed excitement. He had brought out all his questionnaires and was studying them intently.

'What are you doing? It looks as if you are having an exam tomorrow.'

'It's bigger than an exam,' he said, his eyes still trained on the papers. 'Lives are at stake.'

I was silent for a space and then said, 'So, intriguing character, this Bali.'

'Yes.'

'You too think so then?'

'Yes'

I knew that he wasn't listening to me as his mind was feverishly searching for answers. His eyes were glued to his questionnaires and I could see that he was trying to conjure up the personalities of the suspects by the answers they had given. I could see him closing his eyes every now and then, trying to fill the gaps by his vast knowledge and uncanny knack for mind reading. At such moments, he reminded me of Dupin and his theory of ratiocination. I remember I had once asked Bhrigu on the subject and he had said with a simple laugh 'I have heard of Edgar Allan Poe and his ingenious theory but let me tell you my friend, it's a lot easy to predict criminal behaviour in psychopaths or hardened criminals. Their minds work on a monomaniacal method which is easy to predict. What's difficult is to predict criminal behaviour in ordinary people whose mind is a complicated maze of everyday concerns.'

As was his custom when in the grip of this meditation, I could see his eyes blazing with the sheer fire of concentration, rippling with energy, like those of an addict under the power of a strong narcotic. I knew that whatever I said now would never reach him as he was on an island where he saw nothing but what he wanted to seek.

Leaving him to his work, I took out my lap top and began writing my article as I had to mail it in a week. My boss would chew me alive if I passed the deadline. Soon, I was engrossed in my work and it was not after two hours when Bhrigu almost startled me as he said 'Were you asking anything?'

'Wh–what?' I blurted, slightly disoriented 'Oh, yes. About Bali. He was a trifle intriguing, don't you think?'

'Intriguing? His character was very easy to read. He proved to be the most uncomplicated person of the lot.'

'But he was very different from Jayanti Devi's account!'

'That is exactly the reason why he was the most easy to read.' He replied with a thin smile.

I stared at him for a whole minute, ready to argue what he had said just now. His cryptic answers were taking a toll on my patience and I said as much. 'What can you possibly mean by that?'

'You will see but not after we have had the remainder of our interview with him.'

Gods, it seemed, had ordained to the contrary as when we went to meet Bali the next day, we found a big, fat lock belligerently staring at us. At our wit's end, we rounded Jayanti Devi and it was she who broke the grim news. In the wee hours of the morning, a farmer called Billa, Bali's neighbour, who was on his way to his farm, discovered that Bali's front door was wide open. Piqued and overcome by curiosity, he made his way to the door and peeked inside. It was dark. He called out Bali's name a few times but got no answer. With rising trepidation, he entered the room, and as his pupils adjusted to the dark within, he found a figure sprawled on the ground. It was Bali. Nervous, he shook him gently and it was then that he realised that something was terribly wrong. He ran to his home and came back with his younger brother and together they carried him to the only charitable hospital in the village, built by the philanthropist Dr Vijay Kumar Singh. He was admitted at once. When the doctor arrived, he performed a battery of tests and found that due to excessive tension and anxiety, Bali had burst a vessel in his brain and was now in the powerful grip of a coma.

17

The news jolted me and I could see that it had unsettled Bhrigu as well. A slight pall of gloom had descended on his features and he was struggling with the news that there was a greater chance that Bali would never recover from the coma.

'Shall we go to the hospital?' I asked.

'What's there at the hospital now? It would be better if we let Bali struggle with fortitude, alone.'

I was taken aback at his unsympathetic statement, but at the same time, I was almost sure that there must be sufficient reason to account for his apathy.

'So?' I asked, 'What should we do now?'

'We have to search Bali's room.'

'But it's locked!'

He looked at me dismally 'Locks can be picked, you know.'

I was amazed at the workmanship with which my amazing friend managed to pick the lock. He used nothing but a hair pin borrowed from Jayanti Devi. 'Where did you learn this trick?' I asked him, incredulous. 'Don't tell me that inflation has forced you to moonlight as a thief.'

He shrugged his shoulders. 'I once interrogated a murder suspect who had a strange obsessive, compulsive disorder. He just couldn't help picking locks, whenever he came upon one. He always picked the locks of his house, although he had the keys to the same. Quite an interesting fella. He taught me his skill. Although, I didn't ask for it.' His lips curved into a smile 'Thought he was doing me a favour!'

'What a cock and bull story!' I cried 'You are making fun of me!'

'Nothing of the sort,' he said smiling broadly as the scene from the past tickled his senses. 'You know he was innocent of the crime he had been accused of. His only fault was that the poor man couldn't control his urge to pick a lock and walked right in on a murder scene.'

He pushed open the door and drew a flashlight from his pocket. Bali's house had no windows and therefore was dark at all times. In the light, we saw that everything was in the position that we had left the other day. The deadly calm of the room sent shivers down my spine. Bhrigu was carefully and minutely observing the floor. He went about it inch by inch, grid by grid, not leaving a corner go unnoticed. He once chided me when I pushed past him, getting impatient by his fastidiousness. 'Stay behind me,' he shouted.

He was at it for about an hour and I wondered whether he was searching for a needle in the haystack. Exasperated, I took to the couch and waited for his exhaustive search to get over. From my perch, I noticed that the low wooden stool had been knocked down and it was there that Bhrigu sat down and took out, what looked like a spray bottle from his pocket.

He liberally sprayed the area around the stool. I went near him to observe his handiwork more closely. The florescent powder had clearly brought out a beautiful shoe print.

'Wow!' I exclaimed. 'That's amazing!'

'Yes' he replied. 'And of vital importance. You see here, this print is neither ours nor Bali's who, if you remember, wore chappals. Whose print this is then?'

'Someone must have paid him a visit before us or they must belong to that farmer Billa and his brother who found Bali in the morning.'

'No. I tracked the footprints on this floor. The room hasn't been cleaned for months and the floor is covered in a carpet of dust. The marks are faint but discernible enough.' He then trained his flashlight towards the door and illuminated the area that led from it. 'Bali's body was lying not far from the door. The floor is conspicuously clean where he fell. Billa and his brother carried the body from where it lay and never moved a step beyond. I can detect their footprints. They were barefooted and their trail is clear enough. But this other print is unique. I can spot it almost everywhere I go. The man was probably agitated or restless. He was moving about the house and in his restlessness, knocked this wooden stool. The stool was still standing when we left. This clearly shows that this person visited Bali *after* we left him.'

'So?'

'Don't you understand?' he cried impatiently. 'You deliberately shut off your brain. I repeat for your convenience that this person called on Bali *after* we left and the very next morning he was found as he was.'

'But even if this elusive person came to visit him, what's that have to do with Bali? He suffered from an ailment long due, that's all.'

'From my days as a police inspector, I have closely been working with medical examiners.' He said, now fetching a notepad from Bali's cabinet and making a sketch of the shoeprint on it, 'Patients of hypertension are very sensitive towards any kind of stress. Even a modicum of aggravation could easily tip the scale. When we met Bali his condition wasn't good but it wasn't that bad either that within a matter of hours he would burst a vessel or land in coma. Something happened in the night, something so unnerving that Bali suffered terribly. This shoeprint could help. I am reserving any further comments on the matter but it just might.'

His pen was making careful strokes, copying the shoeprint that shone before him with a gentle fluorescence. I waited for him to finish his work and what I saw made me realise that among the many qualities of my friend, drawing wasn't one of them.

He had made a shabby reproduction of the original specimen but as I peered closer, I saw that there were some marks that he had copied to perfection. It was curious, indeed.

'You haven't got the flourish of an artist, my friend.'

'I don't need to,' he said, giving final sketches to his artwork. 'I have copied the impressions that are unique to the shoe. The rest is inconsequential.'

After he was finished he expressed his desire to meet the Gram Pradhan, who had promised to help us in any way possible. 'Now is the time that he has to step up to his plate.' Bhrigu said.

18

'The man we are looking for is tall, almost six feet two inches, and wears battered secondhand sport shoes of the brand *Piccasa*. His right leg has a shortened ligament because he limps slightly; he looks grungy and has little care for presentation. And yes, he is very thin.'

Chaudhary Sahab looked at him incredulously 'And you lifted this information from one shoeprint, hmm?

'Yes, but of course. There is nothing to get amazed. I was just following common investigation practices. It's part of our training. I am but an amateur in this skill with much to learn and polish.'

'If you don't mind, we would like to know how,' I said and I saw Chaudhary Manendra Singh nodding his approval of my request.

'Well, if you must,' he said, shrugging his shoulders. 'There is a direct correlation between the size of a footprint and the height of the individual. This was the easiest of all. The print made by his right foot was deeper than left and it clearly indicates that the man put extra pressure on the right foot while walking. This goes to suggest that he had a handicap, probably a short ligament, which made him limp slightly. The impression made by the shoe's outer sole was not regular but sported many tears and cuts, proving that the shoe was old and worn out and if a man can go on wearing such shabby shoes, he ought to be shabby himself. I compared the sketch of the print I copied to popular shoe's brands on the internet and it turned out to be a very well known one called *Piccassa*. The man must have either nicked these precious shoes or brought them at a secondhand goods shop. Why is he thin? Well, because in this village the only fat person that I have ever come across is that *baniya* and going by that statistic our man ought to be thin too.'

'Sherlock Holmes,' I said involuntarily.

'You flatter me, old man,' he said with his lopsided smile. 'He was the master of the art, genius to a fault, and most often than not, bordering on the fantastic. I am but a humble practitioner and have, at times, tried to follow in his, if you can pardon the pun, in his footprint only to learn that a bucket load of circumstantial evidence can make many false trails of a case that was very simple to begin with had you first studied the suspects and not what they left behind. In this case too, you'll see that of all the information I have painstakingly managed to collect from the shoe print, it will be the culprit himself and not his print that will give him away.'

'And what do you mean by that?' I asked, confused again. I sometimes wondered whether he ought not to have been a cryptologist. His knack for speaking in riddles was as intriguing as it was irritating.

'I mean' He said with his signature grin that was reserved only for my benefit 'that clues fall into place only when you have nailed correctly the nature of people under suspicion. Physical evidence should *support* a case, not dominate it.'

I knew he had noticed the curiosity written all over my face and a million questions that were swirling in my brain but before I could do anything to act on them though, Bhrigu, most deftly, changed the subject. 'Anyway, we should not stray from the investigation. Time is of the essence. Pradhan Sahib, do you know such a man? After all, to quote you, everyone knows everyone in this village.'

Chaudhary sahib smiled indulgently. 'I will call a *panchayat* meeting, summoning the men of the village. I will ask the man to step forward who had paid a visit to Bali at the said hours. That is a much easier method.'

'No sir, I am afraid not.' Bhrigu replied firmly 'That will defeat my purpose, to say the least. You see, the man we are looking for is not guilty for meeting Bali but for wittingly or unwittingly, being a cog in the machinery that led to Malthu's death. This is a delicate matter with a chain connecting all the events. If we somehow damage or destroy one piece of the chain, it will never unravel by itself and the result, even if positive, could be very messy. The man we are looking for already knows this and hence he will never come forward by himself. If we alarm him beforehand, he will abscond and we will never be able to arrive at a clean end to this misfortune. That's why the suspects should never know, under any circumstances, the real context of their calling.'

'Although I didn't quite understand what you just said, my gut feeling is very strong that you are right, hmm,' said the Chaudhary, looking at Bhrigu with admiration and respect. I could see that he had taken a great liking towards my friend. 'Son, as it happens, I know seven people who fit your profile. What I don't know is the one you are searching for, hmm.'

'Never mind that.' Said Bhrigu 'I will know how to identify him.'

'Alright, then. I will get them together and bring to you at the slightest notice. Just tell me when and where.'

'At the Rohtas police station. I know an inspector there. He has promised to help us in this case, which is now taking dangerous turns. No other place is safe to house seven rogues.'

'But' I said, confused yet again 'Why seven? Only one among them is a rogue and it is him that we are searching.'

'Sutte, you have always to have the last question, is it not?' He said, a trifle irritated 'I will treat all seven of them as one until I pick my man. It's very easy to be led by instincts or gut feelings in any case. It's called bias and as humans we are susceptible to it. More often than not we find cops arresting the innocent just because they look or act bad and letting the guilty go free as he or she was too decent to accuse. This is a practice I clearly steer clear of. Hence, as I said before, every suspect is guilty to me unless I round the culprit.

'You and your peculiar rules'. I said indignantly.

Chaudhary sahib was listening to our light banter with a paternal smile. I could see that he was in high spirits because in the course of this investigation, he had bagged the maximum footage. In a dull, idyllic life of a village, where you can never tell one day from another and where all activities follow each other in an inexorable circle, an intrigue could go a long way in providing the much needed respite from the mundane. As Bhrigu and I were responsible for this breezy change from relentless routine, the Gram Pradhan was virtually smothering us with his affection and food. The moment we arrived at his native house, an army of servants marched in and out of the courtyard, carrying delicacies fit for a king. He wouldn't listen to a word of protestation until we were stocked to our necks with an amalgam of *kachodis, samosas, rasmalais, cholas, dahi-vadas, gajar ka halwa*, and what not. Finally, Bhrigu had drawn the line and announced that one morsel more out of the concoction, and we would find ourselves giving company to Bali at the hospital. This had done the trick as Pradhan sahab got fearful that if he lost us, his role in the investigation would be seriously jeopardised.

'Son, I give you my word that those seven men will be at your service, hmm,' he thundered, puffing his chest 'I, Chaudhary Manendra Singh, am the Gram Pradhan of this village and there is no man who would dare disobey my summons.'

19

THE SEVEN ROGUES

Chaudhary Manendra Singh was true to his word as he gave us seven men who limped in varying degrees. I could clearly see that he hadn't been too fastidious in following Bhrigu's instructions and had rounded up any person who happened to have that handicap. One among them was a young man called Bal Kishore. He was inflicted with polio and limped terribly. I couldn't see him fitting the profile but Pradhan Sahib was apparently a person who believed that one should better be thorough than sorry. To add to our chagrin, four of the fellows were not wearing shoes at all, let alone a branded one. Also, three of them, believe it or not, were of the same height and I could almost tell that their shoe size must be the same too. This definitely compounded the process of easy recognition. I now provide a sketch of the seven men, who stood before us at the Rohtas police station on a clear, sunny morning of 20th June, 2010.

1) **Sarveshwar Yadav**—If ever a hybrid of chimpanzee and a man was to be created, he would definitely look like this man. He had a gigantic face, probably the result of a very heavy skull that could have looked fetching on a Neanderthal man but was a gross misfit on the modern man. He had thick jowls that hung over his small, stout neck almost obliterating it from vision. His yellow, beaded eyes were blank and blinked stupidly. He had very thick lips which were barely hiding a protruding set of mottled teeth. It was hard to imagine that such a man was capable of any kind of speech and I couldn't help but feel that if he opened his mouth, it would be to roar rather than to speak.

2) **Mahendra Chaurasia**—This fellow was a slip of a man whose slightness made him look taller than he actually was. Apart from his weight which was a little more than that of air, he had nothing even remotely remarkable about him. His personality was such that he could walk into a shop everyday without the slightest risk of being recognised. Hell, he could drop a bomb and easily escape recognition. Describing such a man wouldn't produce any impression at all and hence it would be better if I abandon this futile attempt.

3) **Jhalka**-Another person with a nondescript personality. He was tall and lean (like Bhrigu had said, all men were rather thin. Sarveshwar Yadav was of a heavy built but lack of nutrition had robbed him of any opportunity of gaining health). He had tattoos of Lord Shiva all over his arms and this was the only thing that could help distinguish him

from a multitude of men. He had folded the sleeves of his faded shirt to display the artwork boldly. I could see his eyes turning to the tattoos now and then, lighting up with a pride that comes when one is proud of one little achievement in the long list of failures. The tattoos constantly reminded him that he had successfully undergone intense pain to have them on his limbs and the experience had left him with a sense of pride of doing something that many would have shied away from. How could he not flaunt the only thing that added an edge to his otherwise pathetic existence?

4) **Priya Kumar**—This man had a pleasant face, with sharp, clear-cut features. He had unusually lucid eyes, high cheekbones, and a prominent chin that spoke of quiet grandeur. Had I not known better, he could easily have passed off as a man of high pedigree. He could very well have been one whose ancestors fell into ruin by their reckless squandering leaving his lot to wallow in poverty. Nawabs of Awadh, present day Lucknow, are a quintessential of them. I know many in the last line of blue bloods who were reduced to pulling rickshaws in and around Hazratganj. This man could be secretly sharing their fate, too. To attach weight to my conclusion, I should add that he stood with a poise that could only be found in a man of breeding.

5) **Ahmidullah**—The only Muslim in the lot and a very traditional one at that. He had a long beard that covered most of his face and half of his body. The only thing that I can say with conviction is that he

had a very flat and unsightly nose that went halfway across his mouth in either directions and gave the illusion that it was pasted on with an adhesive. He had big, blood shot eyes that protruded from their sockets in a threatening, menacing way. He looked quiet forbidding.

6) **Nain Yadav**—The oldest of our suspects had a thin, sagging face and a bald pate that he had covered in a white turban. His eyes were hidden behind dark, double-rimmed spectacles and a fat, grey-moustache adorned his upper lip. I could find a striking resemblance in a very beat up Chacha Chaudhary. He leaned heavily on a stout cane that he gripped in his right hand and I could see that he was well in the advanced stages of arthritis. Pradhan Sahib, no doubt, had left no stone unturned in his endeavours. I could very well imagine this nice, old man sitting peacefully on a cot outside his humble home, messaging his knees with mustard oil when Sarpanch sahib must have suddenly descended upon him, shouting orders to leave with him at once on an important mission. The man would have been scared out his wits on this sudden crisis, wondering if applying oil on the rusted knees was now a crime punishable by law and meekly followed the brass hat of the village with dread in his heart and a sweat breaking out on his forehead.

7) **Bal Kishore**—A youth in his early twenties. Despite his severe handicap, he was of a muscular built and I could see the contours of his sinewy body highlighted by the tight fitting velvet shirt and old, faded jeans that he wore. He had a delicate face with

permanent lines on his forehead which gave him a rather apprehensive look and a maturity way beyond his years. His eyes were of a dark brown colour and looked droopy because of the heavy lids. He steadily kept looking ahead of him into nothingness and I could read nothing in his eyes but weariness mixed with boredom.

They were all standing end to end against the moss covered wall of the police station's backyard. The area reeked of betel leaves and a pungent; nauseating smell of ammonia from an open but out-of-sight lavatory so suffocated me that I reeled on the spot. Bhrigu, as always, looked quite at ease and the horrid smell seemed to be agreeing well with him.

As I was struggling with my current circumstances, an obese man suddenly strode into the backyard from the single room that made up the police station. He had a puffy, florid face and a smile big enough to make it impossible for anyone to take all of it in, at the very first glance. If one tried, there was the risk of damaging one's retina beyond all repairs. He had beady eyes that darted excitedly in all directions. His uniform, lead by the buttons, was crying to be relieved of the strain that it suffered in somehow containing a hundred and ten ton of fat. This was Inspector Gyaan Gere, the in-charge of this police station.

'So, Bhrigu, did you catch the culprit?' he said, slapping my friend so hard on the back that it was a miracle he did not collapse to the ground.

'No, Gyaan ji, but I will, soon,' he replied politely, trying to message his sore back with his left hand.

He flashed a huge smile and said, 'I am there for any assistance, my lad. Just let me know.'

'Definitely, sir.'

'If any of these scoundrels create trouble' He said, now glaring at the men with such animation that it was hard not to laugh. 'I will beat the pulp out of them.'

'Thank you, sir.'

'Have they created trouble for you, then?'

'No sir. They haven't in the slightest.'

'Good. Good.'

The inspector's legs seemed to give way under his weight and he shouted for a hawaldar to fetch him a chair. He lapsed into the chair as soon as it appeared on the scene and exhaled a breath of relief. I could hear the poor piece of furniture groan under his weight.

'Bhrigu, dear son, please don't hold up the proceedings on my behalf,' he said, benevolently 'I will keep a sharp eye on them from here.'

'I have no doubt about that, sir.' Bhrigu said with deference.

I saw Bhrigu stepping into the role of the true mind reader that he was. The changes that I noticed were a proof of the transformation that was brought about in him. Sometimes, I felt as if this was the real Bhrigu that now stood before me ready to dive into the deepest recesses of a human mind, and the person I knew at other times was someone he conveniently slipped back into. I bet he carried both these personalities together, one alive only when the other was resting, causing a sort of balance which was very vital when someone was as gifted as him. It was true that his face became an expressionless and impregnable mask when he was on the task but now the nuances became apparent to me that I had missed before. His eyes that were usually innocent and kind with not a trace of malice in them would change into bottomless pits that only absorbed whatever they saw. His lips would quiver ever so slightly; excited, I think, at the prospect of exploiting his talent to the full and also in the anticipation of the result that awaited him on the other end. Whenever I witnessed him in this avatar, I say without restraint, that I couldn't help but marvel at the man's unusual genius.

He went near each suspect, looking at them carefully, observing them intently from head to foot. I saw that he wasn't attaching special attention to their feet, as I thought he would, given the fact that the only clue that we were relying on was the shoeprint, and kept staring deep into the eyes of the men as if they were their only modes of communication. Three times he revolved around them, sometimes waiting on a particular suspect longer than the other, and I could see that the lot was becoming puzzled and restless by this apparently crazy exercise. Ahmidullah's features were contorted with anger and it was he who broke the silent interrogation.

'What in Allah's name is all this?' he cried. 'Will anyone tell us what the hell is happening?'

Priya Kumar took the conversation to the next level. 'Pradhan Sahib told us. . .' he began, and I noticed that his soft voice did credit to his elegant persona. 'That we had been selected to participate in an important work for which we would get paid. But we were thrust into this rotten backyard of a police station like a pack of criminals! And now this strange man is staring at us like we were a pack of mad men!'

'Or rather he was!' chimed in Jhalka.

I could clearly see an imminent mutiny in the ranks, feeling pretty sure that Bhrigu could see it, too.

'Gentlemen,' said Bhrigu, now putting a stop to his revolutions to face the men squarely. 'I know you are confused so let me put all your questions to rest. You have not been called to do a job that pays. I am sorry for the disappointment, but you are not. We are investigating a matter in which I would want your assistance.'

'What matter?' It was Ahmidullah again. He had probably self-appointed himself as the chief spokesperson for the group.

'You need not worry about it. Just answer a few questions and go.'

'What's in it for us?' Piped in the small voice of Mahendra Chaurasia.

Bhrigu located the source of this query and said, 'I am afraid, nothing much. But I'll tell you what's there for you if you won't cooperate with us.'

'What?'

'A stint in prison, that's what.'

A hush fell over the men and even Ahmidullah looked marvellously subdued. I was happy that the dissent had been nipped in the bud and hoped that things would proceed smoothly from here on.

'I will be in that room,' said my friend. 'And the hawaldar will call you in the order that you stand. Come in, take a seat opposite me and answer a few questions. That's all there is to it. Any questions?'

Silence.

'Good.'

Bhrigu had trained them like any army sergeant would. His days from the police station had taught him how to deal with recalcitrant criminals. I still wondered whether it was from the tone of authority alone that they listened to him. He hadn't raised his voice, he hadn't threatened them, he hadn't used any kind of force, but there was that compelling power in him that was very difficult to ignore. He just had to be obeyed. This was the kind of magnetic influence that he held on people; a hidden charm oozing from an outwardly ordinary personality which, at moments of crisis, never failed to impress.

With slow, measured steps, he disappeared into the police station, and I followed after him. Inspector Gyaan Gere didn't join us because he had dozed off in his chair and was now snoring like a bull with not a care in the world. After five minutes, I heard the hawaldar call the name aloud—'Sarveshwar Yadav!' through the small window that overlooked the backyard. I noticed the ape man pass a troubled look over his companions, who returned him reassuring glances as he walked with trepidation to face what was in store for him.

20

'Where were you on the evening of 14th June?'
'I . . . I don't know.'
'You don't know or you don't remember?'
'I . . . yes . . . I don't remember.'
'Then think hard. Surely, you don't suffer from any form of dementia, do you?'
'What's that, sir?'
'Memory loss.'
'No, sir.'
'Then put stress on your bean and answer the question.'
Sarveshwar Yadav was sitting before us in a posture that spoke of fear and intimidation. He kept looking around him and in his nervousness almost succeeded in knocking down the glass of water that was kept for him on the table. A frightened ape would clearly pull a correct picture of him.
'It was a Saturday, no sir?'
'Yes, it was,' I replied.

Bhrigu looked at me in a meaning way that said that I wasn't to participate in this interview in any way. I was to just sit quietly and observe.

'Then I was at Pratap's Paan Shop with my friends. Every Saturday evening we meet at the shop, eat Paan and talk.'

'A private club, eh?' I said even before I could stop myself. Bhrigu looked at me with disdain and exhaled a breath of defeat. He knew I could never ever slip into the role of a quite, observant scribe but a voluble one at that.

'Can any of your friends vouch for that?'

'I guess so, Sir.'

'You were there for the whole evening?'

'Yes, sir. We meet at around 4.00 to 4.30 p.m. and stay there till it's time for dinner.'

'Okay,' said Bhrigu and busied himself with a file that was kept before him. Without ever looking up, he asked casually, 'Why are you bare feet? You don't have a pair of slippers?'

The man was surprised at such a question and said meekly, 'I had them but they came unstitched when I went to see the local fair.'

'When was this fair?'

'A month ago.'

'Will you go like this forever? Why don't you buy a new pair?'

'I will, sir, but honestly speaking I don't mind this way either.'

'Hmm,' he motioned to the hawaldar who appeared before him in no time. 'Please take him outside.'

'Outside? Am I free to go then, sir?' The man asked in a tone of relief.

'Not yet, fella. There is a cot in the courtyard. Sit there till I call you again. No need to worry. It is just standard procedures.'

The villager looked crestfallen. 'Okay sir,' he said in a small voice. 'As you say.'

It was the turn of Mahendra Chaurasia next. He came in and sat down quietly in the chair.

'Where were you on the evening of 14th June?'

I thought he hadn't heard the question. He sat there like a statue cut in stone, staring at Bhrigu. I thought of repeating the question for his benefit when he said, 'My house.'

His voice was hoarse and heavy and I accorded this to the little use of his vocal cords.

'Can anyone vouch for that?'

After a minute of staring, he replied, 'Wife.'

The whole interview was very strange because it felt as if we were talking to a wax statue that had eaten an automated machine and chimed at regular intervals.

Bhrigu again busied himself with the file and casually dropped the question 'Why are you bare feet?'

'Like that.'

'Always been bare feet?'

'Yes.'

This man really used economy with words.

'Okay.'

This concluded the few syllabic interview and the man was sent to join the ranks with Mahendra Chaurasia.

Next was the young man, Jhalka.

'What were you doing on the evening of 14th June?'

'Who knows? I might be doing a number of things,' he said cheerfully. 'I have many hobbies, you see. I recently had this tattoo done. . .'

'Look here, young man,' Bhrigu said. 'Just answer the question. We are not looking for a colourful chit chat here.'

Jhalka was slightly taken aback but he recovered miraculously, 'Okay, ask away.'

'Do I have to repeat the question?' Bhrigu said with a touch of impatience.

'No. I heard it alright,' he said, now chewing his nails with his teeth. 'On the 13th eh? It's hard to recall. It was a. . .'

'It was a Saturday, yes.'

'Hmm. Well this Saturday I had gone to see my friend.'

'Friend?'

'Yes.' And then he added with a wink: 'My girlfriend.'

'Can she vouch for that?'

'Oh yes, absolutely,' he replied, beaming. 'She is a nice and pretty girl. Her name is Divya. She loves me very much though her father dislikes me and is always filling her ears with bad stories about me that are all lies. Why? One day he was telling her that I was a thief. Do I look like a thief to you? I would have given that old bugger a. . .'

Even before he could finish his soliloquy, the hawaldar took him by his arm and led him away to join the others in the courtyard.

Our next guest was the elegant and imposing, Priya Kumar.

'Can you tell us where you were on the 14th of June?'

'Yes, of course. I was at the dentist, getting my tooth fixed,' he said with a dignified calm.

'Dentist?' I asked a little surprised. 'Save one charitable hospital, you barely have adequate healthcare services and you are telling me you have a dentist?'

He smiled and said, 'You think I am foolish enough to waste my money on your kind of dentist?'

'What do you mean by my kind of dentist?'

'My dentist does not depend on corrupt institutions for his knowledge. He possesses an ancient knowledge of dental science, passed to him over generations. He can barely write but he administers to our tooth problems like the true miracle worker that he is.'

'Do you mean to say that he has no license or a proper degree?' I said, shocked to the core.

'Why should he? Answer me one question. Are all the licensed dentists or doctors with proper qualifications, excellent at what they do?'

I was hesitant to answer such a question. Obviously, in medical field as in any other, there are practitioners who are no asset to their profession and I said as much. 'No. Not all of them are excellent. How can they be? Talent is not distributed equally.'

'Exactly,' he said with a broad smile. 'Talent is not distributed equally, nor is knowledge. These fancy degrees can give you a license to practice a profession but they can't give you the talent to excel at what you do.'

'You mean to say,' I said, a trifle irritated by the way he had caught me in my own admission 'That these witch doctors are talented at what they do?'

'He is not a witch doctor,' he said with heat. 'He is a talented dentist.'

'But that's what we call someone who. . .'

'Sutte' Bhrigu interrupted me. 'We are not here to participate in a lengthy debate which is sure to go nowhere. Can't you keep quiet for a minute?'

I subsided but this smug Priya Kumar had landed me a quick one between the ribs. I was affronted and humiliated at being told off by a village man, however regal his outward appearance might be. How dare he challenge me, an acclaimed writer, with his dogmatic views?

'Who is your dentist?' Bhrigu asked him and I felt an urge to answer the question by a very sarcastic reply but checked myself lest it annoyed my friend again.

'Janak. He lives across the mini mart. Sir, if you have a tooth problem you can see him. He is a magician at what he does.'

'Thank you very much but my teeth are alright.'

'Oh,' he ejaculated as if almost sorry for it.

'Can he account for your time there?'

'Absolutely. Why wouldn't he?' he replied, beaming.

He then motioned to the hawaldar to take him away. As soon as the man was on his way out he asked, noncommittal, 'Your slippers look new. When did you buy them?'

'Oh them?' he said with visible confusion 'Yes. They are new. I brought them three days ago.'

'Okay. Thank you for cooperating. You can go.'

The next man to join us was the intimidating Ahmidullah. He burst in upon us with the energy and speed of a rhinoceros and left a maelstrom of dust in his wake as he settled on the stool before us.

'What's all this nonsense about?' he thundered in his gruff voice. 'Do you people think that I am a loafer with nothing to do? That you can pick me up like a roadside *mawali* whenever you want? You think you are an important person and I am a nobody, is it not? That Chaudhary tricked me into coming here and I respected his wishes for he has been kind to me but not anymore! There are limits to my patience!'

'You are here to help us in an important investigation. An investigation that has far reaching consequences. How then, can you possibly think that you are a nobody? From where I sit, you look like a very important person to me.' Bhrigu said with a pleasant smile.

Ahmidullah was doubtful for a moment but then he said, 'But . . . but . . . there are six people from the village with me. Are they important, too? Because if they are then I know that you are making a fool of me. Jhalka, Sarveshwar Yadav, Mahendra Chaurasia . . . they are the very dregs of humanity and I wouldn't be associated with them in anyway. If they are important enough for this investigation or whatever then it ought to be a petty one.'

Bhrigu was silent for a space and looked at Ahmidullah with the poker face that I knew was just a façade meant to hide deeper emotions behind. 'You are a person of a high self-esteem, right?'

'Damn right I am,' he replied with part heat, part enthusiasm.

'And why is that?'

'Because I have land. My ancestors were wealthy landlords and although much is gone I still have a reputation which I won't sully by associating myself in anything that is beneath me.'

'Right,' said Bhrigu. 'If that is so, I am afraid you won't change your mind after all. Money can never stand over reputation. Never.'

'Wait a minute,' Ahmidullah said with jolt of excitement. 'What do you mean by money?'

'Well, the people who help us in this investigation are to be rewarded with cash. But you don't care, do you?'

'Really?' He said with a twinkle in his blood shot eyes, making it look bloodier.

'Yes. But you can go now.'

'No, no, sir,' he said dropping his vanity as quickly as if it were a piece of cloth. He was so greatly subdued that it was a trouble recognising him from a moment before. His formidable, intimidating aspect was gone to be replaced by that of an obsequious servant, ready to kill for his master. I thought for a fleeting moment that his eyes too had retracted a little, back into their sockets.

'I will be glad to be of any assistance, sir,' he said in a voice dripping with gratitude and sycophancy. 'It's just that this horrid company totally spoilt my mood. I am truly sorry for that, sir.'

'That's all right,' said Bhrigu, smiling ever so slightly 'Now tell me, where were you on the evening of 13th June?'

'Sir, I am a man of routine. Every evening I listen to the radio. It's the only time of the day when you get to hear good songs.'

'So, you were listening to the radio that evening?'

'Yes sir. Most definitely I was.'

'Can anyone verify your claim?'

'Yes, sir. My second wife. She is quite young and loves to listen to the radio with me.'

'Anyone else other than her?'

'No sir. My other wife and the children go to my mother's house every evening. She is very old and loves their company. My wife cooks her dinner as she tells stories to my children.'

'Your second wife does not prefer to go with them?'

'She would have but sir, you see, my mother doesn't like her much. She is rigid and very set in her ways. She feels that Ishrat, my second wife, is not good enough for me.'

'Why?'

'Because she has given me three daughters and no son.'

'Oh, I see.'

Bhrigu was quiet for a few seconds and as the hawaldar came forward to take Ahmidullah away, he asked, 'Your shoes. They look old. Where did you get them?'

'At the fair. They are 4 years old. We villagers buy almost everything from the fair,' he added. 'Why do you ask sir? Do you like them? If you say, I will get them for you. The fair is due in a week.'

'No, no . . . no need for that.' Bhrigu replied 'It was just an inane question, that's all.'

Before he left, he dropped a hint as to how happy he was to have been of assistance and we knew full well that it implied that now he must be compensated in full. Very avaricious fellow, indeed.

Next to step forward was the local Chacha Chaudhary, the old and meek Nain Yadav. My heart went out to him as soon as he entered the room.

'Sahib,' he began in a quavering voice, as soon as he had occupied the seat before us. 'I was just applying oil to my arthritis ridden knees when Chaudhary ji asked me to come with him. I was shocked, to say the least. What would a man of his stature want with me, a mere blacksmith, was all I could think of. Have I done anything? If I have then I apologise because in this age, memory sometimes fails me. I think I might have committed a blunder while I was in the grip of such a memory loss. I hope the problem I caused is not very serious.'

'Sir, you have not to worry about a thing. This is a routine interrogation and nothing else,' said Bhrigu warmly. 'You just have to answer a few questions, that's all.'

'What . . . what questions sahib?'

'Could you recall what were you doing on the evening of 13th June?'

'I . . . I can't say, sahib. I can't recall events from an hour ago. How can I from such a long time ago?'

'If it's any help, it was a Saturday.'

'Saturday? Which Saturday, sahib?'

Bhrigu exhaled a breath and looked at the man with weary eyes. 'This Saturday. The one that passed.'

'Really? Saturday has passed already?'

This time I joined Bhrigu in exhaling a breath. 'Fella,' I said, trying to salvage whatever we had in the way of conversation. 'What do you normally do? I mean, what's your routine? I guess it doesn't change much?'

I saw Bhrigu eyeing me with appreciation and gratitude. My gesture, I was happy to note, had struck the right cord with him.

'I . . . I was a blacksmith. A very talented one at that but . . . but age always catches up when you are least expecting it. My eyes failed, memory failed, and knees joined their lot soon. I couldn't work anymore. I gave the control of my shop to my only daughter, Lata. People laughed behind my back because in this village; daughters are supposed to get married and settled by the time they are 20 whereas Lata had chosen to become a successful blacksmith with no thought to marriage. They say I have been a bad father by spoiling the fortune of my daughter for a good marriage because who would marry a girl who puts her work as a blacksmith above everything else? Who would care for a girl like that? But I didn't care. What mattered to me was my skill and I wanted it to pass on to my progeny. Lata, too, won't have it any other way. She was determined to learn the skill, polish it, and expand the business. My daughter is very hardworking, dedicated, and ambitious. I am proud of her. She is handling my shop so well that now we have two men working as apprentice under her. She is a gem, my daughter.'

We didn't know till then that the old man's ears had failed him, too. He had somehow misheard the word 'routine' as 'biography' and expatiated on the topic at length.

'Dear fella' I implored the man again 'Proud that we are of your daughter Lata, we were asking about your routine, I'm afraid.' I said putting extra emphasis on the word 'routine' this time around so that if he failed to hear me again he could at least lip read but I remembered with a sense of shock that his eyes had failed him, too. Nonetheless, I attempted weakly at some sort of coherence on his part.

'Oh my routine?' he asked with a mild smile. 'What could be the routine of a man as old as me who has every organ working itself to a failure? I eat, sleep, take my medicines, oil my knees, and sit with my daughter at the shop as she expertly tends to the customers. I don't say anything but observe her silently and proudly. Sometimes, I get worried about her marriage but she eases my mind with her grand vision for the future. There is no stopping my girl.'

I had a nagging feeling that this man was again on the verge of expostulating the thousand and one qualities of his daughter and I could see that Bhrigu had sensed this, too, as he was looking at me with pain lurking in his eyes.

He dropped the question altogether and went on with the next 'You are wearing new shoes, I see. Where did you get them?'

'These?' he asked looking dubiously at his shoes. 'They are not new. They are old but my daughter polishes them every day. She is very talented with leather work. I am telling you, sahib, my girl is very talented. She . . .'

'Stop!' We both cried together as terror seized our chests. The old man had overstayed his welcome. 'You can go now,' said Bhrigu as the hawaldar took the cue to lead him away.

'This Nain Yadav looks pathetic but he is a bore of such calibre that if he is let loose on a decent man, he would prefer to shoot himself dead than tolerate his company for a second more,' I said, wiping my brow furiously.

'You are right, Sutte,' said Bhrigu, exhaling broadly. 'He compromises his failed senses by talking nonstop. That way he doesn't feel cut off completely.'

'Yeah. Right,' I said wryly. 'It was better if his tongue had failed him, too.'

'This time I have to agree with you,' Bhrigu said, cocking a half-smile at me.

We had to take a break for fifteen minutes before calling in our final suspect, the lad, Bal Kishore.

He came last for the interview and hence had gained a lot of confidence from the moment they were first ushered in. His previous apprehension had gone and he looked like a strong and silent youth in his early twenties and if not for his terrible limp, he would have stood tall at six feet. He came purposefully into the room and took the seat that was intended for him. As we surveyed him, he kept looking straight at us with his sharp, penetrating, and almost belligerent eyes, sending a message across that he was not the one to be cowed easily.

'Where were you on the evening of 13th of June?' Bhrigu began the interview.

He cleared his throat audibly and said in a strong, determined voice, 'I had taken the cows out to graze at the *deeyar*.'

'So will the cows give your alibi?' I thought to myself and chuckled.

'Was there anyone else with you?' Bhrigu asked again.

'Yes. My two friends were with me,' he replied confidently, 'Ram and Ketav. We take our cows out to graze together.'

'Can they vouch for you?'

'Most definitely they can.'

'Hmm.'

There was silence for a couple of minutes as we stared each other down when Bhrigu cleared the air. 'Why are you bare feet?'

'Why? What's it to you? It's my feet and I will do whatever I want with them.'

'Look here mister. . .' I started, annoyed at the tone he had dared to take against my friend but Bhrigu motioned me to keep quite.

'Yes. It's your feet and I have no right to pass a judgment. I am sorry if I offended you.'

Bal Kishore said nothing but sat there looking the very picture of defiance. He was a hot-blooded fellow and I am sure that his handicap had gone a long way in aggravating matters further. His short temper was a proof to the fact that he was not one of those fellows who take their shortcomings in their stride and try to make something out of their lives despite the odds stacked against them. He wasn't from the school of thought that if god took something away he was benevolent enough to bestow in its place, a gift that could help alleviate the pain of the loss and was useful only when one was sensitive enough to discover it. Bal Kishore was one of those who believe that if they are suffering, the world should suffer with them and if they are miserable, they won't let a moment pass without spreading that misery around. As I was musing along this line of thought, Bhrigu must have signalled to the hawaldar who led the man away to join the others outside.

'So?' I asked when we were alone at last. 'The interview is over. Did you get what you were looking for?'

'I am not totally disappointed. But before reaching a final conclusion, I have to subject them to a test.'

'What test?'

'You'll see.'

21

TRAIL OF BLOOD

In the throes of an important investigation, there comes a point when one has to learn to be patient. I have had several occasions when I was required to sit quietly by myself for hours at end while Bhrigu was meditating over a case or running about the town, in an effort to collate what he had discovered. In this particular instance, he asked me to occupy myself while he left on what he said was an important errand, accompanied by the Village Pradhan. The seven villagers were silently and sullenly sitting on the cot, detained by the formidable hawaldar. Inspector Gere, in all likelihood, had died in his sleep. To cope with such contingencies which I knew could arise anytime when you have drawn Bhrigu Mahesh as your friend and partner, I always keep a good book handy. This time around I was reading a short story by O. Henry called 'The Adventures of Shamrock Jolnes'. It was a parody on Sherlock Holmes and his friend, (or flunkey?) Whatsup. The story accentuated the almost fantastic observational skills of Mr Holmes so skilfully that I could do nothing but hold my seams and laugh. This gifted writer of satire clearly knew how to hit the funny bone where it hurt the most. The part where he correctly deduces what Rheingelder had had for breakfast, left me shaking with peals of laughter. If only I had read Shamrock Jolnes before Sherlock Holmes, I could never have seen the detective in the same light again.

I jolted out of my seat for the umpteenth time when I heard a voice behind me. 'What are you reading, Sutte?'

'Oh it's you!' I said, holding my chest and panting hard. 'Why have you to always scare me like that?'

'I didn't mean to,' he said, smiling. 'In my defence I should say that you are jumpy all the time!'

'No, I'm not!' I replied indignantly.

'Well, have it as you must,' he replied with a sigh and looked about the room. 'Where's Gere? Is he still asleep?'

'Probably,' I replied. 'Did you get what you needed?'

'Yes. Chaudhary sahib has assured me that he will take care of the matter,' he said. 'I came to look for the inspector but I guess it would be a pity to disturb his sleep.'

'What are you both up to?' I asked.

'Come outside and see for yourself.'

I accompanied him to the porch outside where the seven men were seated. The tension on their faces was palpable as they kept staring at a huge wooden crate dumped opposite them. Nain Yadav and Sarveshwar Yadav looked close to fainting. I thought they expected a particularly venomous snake to spring out of the box and subject them to an attack with its deadly fangs. Pradhan sahib talked in hushed tones to the hawaldar who nodded vigorously in return. The scene was shrouded in secrecy and intrigue which the long shadows cast by the setting sun only helped emphasise.

'What's going on?' I asked, piqued.

As if in answer to my question, Bhrigu, with visible effort, unwound the thick tape holding the box together, emptying it of its contents. I went near to have a closer look and saw that it contained seven pairs of brand new shoes of the brand *Picassa*. They were all of the same size.

'Bhrigu, what's the meaning of all this?' I asked

'They are shoes,' he replied still engrossed in his work.

'But what would you do with them?'

'I would like them to wear it.'

I was getting the whiff of a hint as to what he planned to do with the shoes. I knew from the very beginning that anyone would like to compare the print made by the shoes worn by the men to the one lifted from the scene. But what I could not in the world imagine was that why he had he brought seven pair of shoes of the same size as that of the print after considering the fact that only three of the fellows (Mahendra Chaurasia, Ahmidullah, and Sarveshwar Yadav) had the foot size big enough to match the print. Did that not automatically eliminate Bal Kishore, Nain Yadav, Priya Kumar, and Jhalka? If I didn't know Bhrigu, I could say that he had made a mistake but as I did, I knew with a certainty that he knew what he was doing.

He arranged the shoes in a neat row and called for the suspects to come and wear them. They reluctantly got up from their perch, eyeing the shoes with as much suspicion as they could muster, throwing a nervous look at Bhrigu every now and then. They stood up as slowly as their limbs could possibly allow but no one moved an inch forward to do the needful. The enthusiastic and energetic Jhalka, too, seemed to have lost all his energy and stood like a man unsure of his own feet. They had betrayed emotion that was synonymous with their character until it was wiped away in the deluge of suspicion, leaving them mirror images of each other, each reflecting the distrust in the other.

Bhrigu waited patiently for five minutes but when he saw that there was no locomotion forthcoming, he said in a strong voice, 'Come on now. Your modesty is just delaying things. Start with the one at the extreme right and proceed forward. So, Sarveshwar Yadav, come forward and try on the shoes.'

The ape man cursed rapidly under his breath for always being on the wrong side of the line and with heavy, unsure footing, emulating a good somnambulist, moved forward. He touched the shoes surreptitiously, half scared that they would spring to life and bite him on his rear but then reason prevailed and he firmly took hold of them and thrust his dirty feet inside. After he had donned the shoes, his face shone with the radiance of pride like that of a brave soldier who has just emerged victorious after a difficult battle. Smiling proudly, he moved to take his position. The first step is the most difficult to make. That being covered, men filed one after the other, in an effort to do what was required of them. When the task was over, they stood uncertainly, waiting for their next instructions. The new shoes were happily glowing in sharp contrast to the dull colour of their old, dirty clothes. I bet if the shoes had somehow come to life, they would have made a face and nagged the head off the humble men who had dared to lay their dirty feet into their lush interiors, fit only for a king. The men, too, were quite uncomfortable wearing them and self-consciously kept shifting their weight from one foot to the other.

'Okay now,' said Bhrigu. 'This way please.'

They formed an awkward queue, all ready to march into the police station. As the line came close to the door, Bhrigu said, 'Watch out for the red paint. It was meant for painting the back walls, but someone must have stepped over it.'

There was a clear but curving trail of red paint leading from the door to the table where we had conducted the interviews. If I hadn't known better, I could have easily taken it for a trail of blood. Bhrigu stepped aside and saw to it that the others had made it to their destination. I was wondering what he had in mind and what now was he planning to do with the suspects. I fancied that he would now subject them to his rigorous psychological tests, the ones he had so skilfully designed after carefully studying the personalities of criminal offenders while he was still an officer of the law. I knew that I was about to witness something so awe-inspiring that I would find it hard to control myself from applauding. I knew that I was about to witness 'The Scientist', as his ex-colleagues called him, at work, and I was glad that on our very first case together, this opportunity had presented itself. Imagine my surprise when as soon as the seven men stood opposite us, across the table, in the small room, Bhrigu said, 'Except Bal Kishore, everyone can go.'

I was surprised, to say the least. If he had already shortlisted his suspect, why did he go to such pains to buy seven new pair of shoes? What was the meaning of it all? Well, he gave me the answer minutes after an out-of-control Bal Kishore was somehow overpowered by the *hawaldar* and taken to a room meant for further interrogation.

'It was nothing at all,' he replied modestly. 'You have to understand personalities and then look for any anomaly they might exhibit. The larger the anomaly, the greater is the chance that the person is hiding something.' He sat comfortably on the chair and began: 'Out of all the people, only Bal Kishore was the person who failed my three tests for guilt detection.'

'Which were?'

'He had a perfect alibi, he was very restraint and rude during the proceedings, and . . .'

Here I cut him short. 'Generally, it is the most rude and annoying suspect who turns out to be in the clear. I had my suspicions all along on Bal Kishore, so naturally, I thought that of all the people, he wasn't guilty.'

'That is not you but the overconsumption of detective fiction talking,' he said, smiling. 'I bet you suspected Nain Yadav all along because he was the least suspicious.'

'Well . . .' he had read my mind again.

'This is the most common stereotype, my friend!' he said. 'In real life, a criminal does not follow the rules of fiction that are meant to shock you. As the most harmless looking guy is named guilty, you gasp, surprised, and bewildered. In real life, in order to see the truth, the nuances of a character should be read correctly. It may not be as flamboyant or dramatic, but it is thorough with no room for doubt. That is why I always purport the theory that psychology should and must be treated as an exact science. Science never leaves room for doubt as it is based on sound principles. Human character, allowing exceptions, follows strict rules and is not as aberrant as we are given to think.'

I know he was dithering form the topic at hand, but I let him because it was rarely that he was in a mood to talk about his work. 'But as far as I know, for a science to be exact, you have to be able to measure it accurately and also to fit it into a mathematical expression.'

He smiled. 'I am not a mathematician, Sutte, but I assure you that once I am done with my experimentations, there will come along a mathematician to fit the results into a mathematical expression. You see, all of the results follow a specific pattern, and allowing exceptions, they will all fit in an equation. But, that, I fear is not my area of expertise and I will continue to do what I do best, that is to experiment, observe, analyse, conclude, and then record my results; and then apply my findings to my cases. They are the tools that help me crack my cases, however insolvable they might seem. Not, as you so ardently believe, by my supernatural powers to read minds.'

'Okay. I believe you.' I lied because I could never shake off the feeling that he had powers way beyond the realms of the ordinary and did what I was an expert in—Play along.' But please continue with your explanations regarding this case.'

'Bored with my lecture? Are you?' he said, smiling again. 'Well, Bal Kishore was morose and reticent during the interrogations. To you, he ostentatiously behaved as a criminal so you, following your crime fiction instinct, were all set to cancel him as your suspect. But there is one thing that you failed to notice.'

'What?'

'That he was putting up a front.'

'What do you mean by that?'

'Bal Kishore is not, by nature, a morose, miserable man but an affable, sensitive chap; it was a front, a natural, instinctive defence. As any guilty person would, he, unconsciously, tried to hide the truth by hiding his true self or in other words, projecting what he was not. I call it 'The Cover Effect' (he said that he had researched his findings on this behaviour). It never did occur to him that he would look even guiltier that way. His natural instinct was to behave opposite to what he was and it was then that he gave himself away.'

'But . . . but how did you know that he was an affable man?'

'I noticed it when they were in the backyard. He had deliberately placed himself beside the crippled old man Nain Yadav and was whispering words of assurance to him to keep him from losing his nerve. He looked aloof and uncaring but was anything but. I saw it very clearly. He said those words under his breath and with a straight face that betrayed nothing but I could see the effect they were having on Nain Yadav. He perked up considerably. Had it not been for Bal Kishore, the poor old man would have fainted even before the interview started.'

'Oh my god!' was what I could manage to say.

'And my third clue was in the trail of paint. I wanted to see who was afraid of leaving behind their shoe prints because the guilty knew that the shoes were for just that. I, by asking them about their footwear during the interrogation, made sure that he knew in advance that somehow shoes were important to this interrogation, probably to match prints. When I asked them to wear those new ones, he automatically knew what was happening and his defences were up. Of the seven of them, only Priya Kumar and Bal Kishore avoided the red paint. These people are villagers. When they are comfortable bare feet, why would they care for a little paint attaching itself to their new shoes? Priya

Kumar was the only refined man in the lot. So, naturally, he avoided the paint but Bal Kishore had nothing in his personality that vouched for his finicky behaviour. So, as he failed my three tests, I arrived at the conclusion that he must the one with something significant to hide.'

'But there is one loop hole' I said. 'Bal Kishore's feet are shorter than the shoeprint! Did that not bother you? I was inclined to cancel him as a suspect based on this fact alone.'

He laughed. 'You have never lived in a village and hence you don't know about the ways of the villagers. They are quite comfortable wearing footwear twice or thrice their size. As long as it is free or has come cheap, every size is perfect. The shoe size was not much of a criterion anyways. That's why I did not attach much importance to it from the very start. Now you see why I advocate that physical evidence should *support* and not *dominate* a case?'

I was absorbing what he had said just now when through the back door we saw none other than Inspector Gyan Gere, walking towards us yawning and rubbing a pudgy hand over his huge stomach.

'My boys!' he said with a smile that lifted his fat cheeks into two, big hemispherical globes. 'Where are the suspects, I say? Did you lock them up? Good. Very good. They were no good in the open. My wooden stick here will make them sing like birds. Not a thing you or the Chaudhary has to worry about.'

Bhrigu imperceptibly rolled his eyes. I knew that this man must have reminded him of his days as a police officer. 'Sir, we have found the man. Although we appreciate the power of your cane, it is not of much use as of now.'

'Very good. Very good,' he said positively beaming at us. 'After my slumber, I wasn't feeling equal to the task myself.'

'You never do use your stick, isn't it, sir?' Bhrigu asked unexpectedly.

'What?!' The man blurted out in his astonishment. The smile was totally wiped off from his face. 'I . . . yes . . . well . . . no. . .'

Bhrigu smiled kindly. 'No worries, sir. You do a fine job. Anybody in your shoes should be proud of himself.'

Gyan Gere looked a little embarrassed but as his eyes met Bhrigu's, his good humour stealthily crept back. 'Thank you, my son. I am ready for any help you may need in future. I congratulate you on your success.'

'I am very grateful for your support, sir. Had it not been for you and this station, I could never in the world have managed such a feat.'

The obese inspector flushed a deep red. I could see that he was clearly too pleased with these compliments. 'Not at all, my boy,' he said happily. 'Not at all.'

22

Saving Bal Kishore

We had Bal Kishore in our custody now for three whole days but Bhrigu had not cared once to look in on him. For all intents and purposes, he was now the property of the Rohtas police station and Inspector Gyan Gere. He went about his work with not a care in the world, reading his journals, scribbling in his diary, recording observations, and making charts, graphs, and what not and replenishing his stock of mint gums. I once looked over his shoulder and had a glimpse of his work. He was tabulating his data regarding 'People who suffer from a phobia are terrible liars'. My head spun for what I saw. How could he have possibly observed such a connection? I know if I looked more closely into his diary, I would come across several such eccentric researches that would simultaneously entertain the viewer and also arouse his sympathy towards the poor deranged sod.

Except for the occasional brushing with Nirja Masi, his mood was light and sometimes I thought I heard him humming the tune of a local folk song we had heard while having lunch at a popular *Dhaba*. I tried to contain my curiosity but the bizarre situation soon got too much for my humble strength of restraint to control. I caught him on the morning of the third day when he was busy reading an article from the local newspaper.

'What's the meaning of this?' I asked with a touch of irritation.

'What?' he asked innocently.

'Have you forgotten that we have a suspect called Bal Kishore locked up in a cell?'

'I know, yes,' he replied and got busy in the papers again.

My temper was escalating fast. 'Is this the end? When are you going to interrogate him?'

He put aside the paper and looked at me intently for a few seconds. 'I thought you were finally enjoying the simple delights of a village.'

I thought he had gone mad. 'What are you saying?! We have an important case to solve! You cannot leave the lad indefinitely locked up in a cell for practically nothing! You have to ask him about what happened that night when he met Bali, don't you?'

'The process is in motion, Sutte,' he said before burying himself in the newspaper again. 'Have patience. It's justly rewarded.'

'Can you not explain a little clearly?' I cried despite myself. 'I am sick and tired of your cryptic dialogues. Try saying something that I can actually grasp first off your tongue.'

He reluctantly took his head out of the blasted papers. 'Fine. If you want to know. But my theories bore you, don't they?'

'What? No! Of course not! When did I say that?'

'You didn't but sometimes your face did,' he said, apparently offended for something I had done unintentionally. Well, he sometimes got carried away with his lectures and it is but human and scientifically proven, too, that a person's attention span lasts not more than three minutes. After that you phase out and then wander in space for a couple of minutes before coming back to the conversation at hand, ergo losing quite a bit of what the speaker was endeavouring to say. For a researcher like him, this fact should have been common knowledge but I avoided saying anything lest it made him madder still. He was very sensitive about his theories being taken seriously.

He took a deep breath and said, 'Remember, when Bal Kishore was taken into custody, he was scared and full of nervous energy. His brain circuits and thinking processes are sure to sustain temporary damages and if we try to work them while he is in such a state of stress it could get worse. If I interrogated him at a moment when he was raw and vulnerable, he would sneak back into his shell. Mind it, he is a sensitive lad and such people, under pressure either retaliate violently or retreat into their shells and refuse to budge. I have seen it happen way too often. It would be very difficult indeed to handle him in such a state and if we tried with force, he could snap. Policemen are often faced with such a situation and they have their cane ready to do the needful. The thin skinned are the ones who are forced under coercion into giving a false confession or a twisted account of what actually happened. This must be avoided at all costs. I want Bal Kishore to get his bearings and when he is in full control of the situation he finds himself in, we would talk. I don't want him to go Bali's way.' After a pause, he added, 'And don't worry about him starving in the cell. I asked Gyan Gere to look after him properly. He is their guest for a few days.'

'What you say is true. But what if he thinks of a story to account for his meeting with Bali? Surely, he can come up with a scheme in the time being. In your own words, it's a natural defensive technique.'

'Trust me, Sutte,' he said, relapsing to his cryptic mode. 'That's exactly what I am hoping for.'

It was not until after four days that Bhrigu decided it was time ripe enough for conducting further interviews with Bal Kishore. After a somewhat late lunch that constituted of super thick chapattis (Courtesy: Nirja Masi. She was still distracted because of that ominous incident involving the dead bird and kept repeating that it was just first in the long series of misfortunes slated to meet her, as the Pundit, who was supposed to conduct the *Katha* was very busy, it being the peak *Katha* season, and hence could not give her the *dates* soon. Quite a lucrative career, I might add), some fried Ochre, yoghurt, and some mango chutney, and we set off for our destination. We took a tempo and within an hour, it deposited us outside an abandoned, run-down tempo station from where we set off on foot. The sun was high up in the sky and was beating down at us with a sadistic pleasure. My clothes were soaked in sweat and my scalp discharged such a copious amount of water that I could never have thought it capable of. Bhrigu was perspiring, too, but not so much as me. Other than beads of sweat around his forehead and a slight wetting on the part of his collar, he looked unaffected of the scalding touch of the weather. I cursed my city upbringing for making me the kind of wimp that I was. Delicate darling, I might add. A slight provocation of nature, a little shift from the convivial, was enough to tip the scales of my homeostasis. How I envied my friend's resilience at such times! He was truly the man one with all the moods of nature.

The police station was a little way back from the main road which was deserted save a motorcycle or two zooming past us in a hurry declaring nothing short of a medical emergency. I spotted a bullock cart going at a leisurely pace, loaded with baskets of unripe mangoes. However hard the man tried to goad the quadruped to move briskly, like a truant, it simply disobeyed the orders of his master and continued to take a stroll right there on the road, enjoying the view around. Bhrigu called my attention to the task at hand. 'We have to cross the road, Sutte. You'll have plenty of time to observe later.'

We made it to the other side of the road and with a few quick steps, we entered the police station. Gosh! It felt so good to be out of the angry sun! The fan was whirring quite satisfactorily and I stood directly under it, letting the cool air play on my flaming face. Gyan Gere was dozing in his chair, as usual and we didn't think it fair to disturb his beauty sleep. Bhrigu led the way to the small, dingy cell, located at the back of the station that housed Bal Kishore. The suspect was now calm enough for an interview, 'Bhrigu Ishtyle', for want of a better phrase.

We found Bal Kishore sprawled on the floor of the dirty cell, sleeping soundly. His snores were pronounced enough to assail my delicate ear membranes. I must add that he was adapting to his new surroundings all too well. If all criminals were treated like this fellow here, people would be filling forms and competing tooth and nail for a seat here. As soon as the *hawaldar* ushered us in, Bhrigu called out softly—'Bal Kishore!'

The lad was not in as deep a slumber as I had imagined him to be because on the lightest call, he woke up with a start, gasping and breathing heavily and looking around himself nervously. 'Who . . . who's there?' he cried almost in a faint.

'It's alright,' said Bhrigu. 'We have come to release you. Just answer a few questions and you are free to go.'

The youth looked up at us with red, puffy eyes. I could see that he had not been sleeping well. It was not just the lack of sleep though, that I witnessed in those big, miserable eyes. There lurked behind them a great, deep-seated fear that was indescribable. His all senses were on red alert and his mouth twitched convulsively.

Bhrigu was gazing at the pathetic man with concern rising in his eyes. He wasn't half as shocked or surprised as me but his look clearly betrayed that he wasn't hoping for such a reaction in the youth even after a good resting period.

'It's alright,' Bhrigu said to him soothingly. 'No need to fear. We know that you have done nothing wrong. Just tell me the reason for your visit to Bali and then you can go in peace. No one will ever hold you again.'

Bal Kishore was clearly struggling with himself. It occurred to me as if the answers that he had at the tip of his tongue were locked by fear with the key thrown into the part of the mind that knows nothing but pure, instinctual need for survival. The only way to unlock it was to drive that fear away but as we didn't know the source or the cause of it, we were far from our target yet.

'I . . . I . . .' he began in a tremulous voice. 'I don't think that paying anyone a visit is a . . . a crime.'

'Yes. Definitely not,' said Bhrigu reassuringly.

'Then why . . . why have you locked me up?!' he cried pathetically. 'Let me go!'

'Well, I think we made a mistake for which I am terribly sorry.' Bhrigu said. He moved a little closer to the fellow and then squatted beside him, right there on that dirty ground. 'I just want to know if your visit had anything to do with what happened to Bali. He fell into a coma right after you left. Why's that?'

'I . . . what do I know about that?' The lad was now slowly but surely gaining confidence by the meek attitude of his interrogator. He was feeling as if he was in control of his affairs now. I know Bhrigu wanted him to feel just this way. 'He must be ill to begin with. His condition has got nothing to do with me.'

'But why did you pay him a visit in the wee hours of the morning? Surely it must have been an urgent matter that you couldn't wait a little longer?'

I knew that Bhrigu was throwing him bait. We had no means whatsoever to know when he did pay Bali a visit. All we knew for sure was that he was the last one to see him. He was caught in the net.

'I . . . in . . . my . . .' he spluttered. 'I was just hoping to borrow his pen. I had to write urgently to my mother. I couldn't wait any longer. That's all there is to it.'

'Alright . . . alright . . .' said Bhrigu, rising to his feet again. 'I have got all that I needed. I know that you are telling the truth. I am sorry again for your inconvenience. You can go now.'

The fellow brightened up visibly. His face was quickly losing the dark marks of anxiety that he had acquired in the past few days of his lodging here. 'Really? You will let me go?'

'Yes. No reason to hold you here anymore.'

The verbal release order for Bal Kishore had been signed.

23

An Encounter

As soon as Bal Kishore made his way out of his singular confinement, I saw Chaudhary Manendra Singh affecting an entrance through the gate, closely followed by an old but distinguished looking person. They saw Bal Kishore charging out the door like a bull and quickly made way for him lest he bumped into them in his extreme hurry. The lad looked back at them after awkwardly running a little distance, despite his handicap, and I don't know why but it somehow gave him all the fuel that he needed. He ran like the fastest handicapped man on earth. Judging by his limp defying sprint, I was almost certain he had more than qualified for the Winter Olympics.

I was staring at the man's retreating form, bewildered to the core by his sudden burst of energy when my peripheral vision registered two forms looming closer to me. Even before I had the time to readjust by focus, my hand was being lifted into a strong and reassuring handshake.

'Hello, Mr Sutte,' said the familiar voice of our Village Pradhan, Chaudhary Manendra Singh. 'I can see by your flushed face that the summer heat is proving a bit difficult for you.'

'Oh . . . what? Yes . . . yes . . . indeed. . .' I said slightly nonplussed.

'I was just introducing Bhrigu here to my esteemed friend, Ghanshyam Singh,' he said moving to his side to let the other person step in. I now took him in for the first time. He was almost six feet tall, thin but strong with long hands that reached almost to his knees. He had a graceful, angular face with slanting but sharp black eyes that seemed to register everything that they saw. He had a long, beak-like nose and thin lips that were set into a rigid, unmoving line. It was a kind of face that shines bright in your consciousness even long after the person is gone. He was wearing a simple white bush shirt and mauve-coloured trousers. In the pocket of his shirt I could see the upper portion of the golden box that must contain his glasses. 'I noticed that you were in some kind of daze and figured it out to be the result of the harsh heat.'

'Our Sutte is a lot into day dreaming. Summer or no summer,' replied Bhrigu, from somewhere behind me.

'Don't take notice of what he says,' I said hotly, trying to assuage my pride. 'I should tell you about his trances. He almost becomes comatose! I am surprised that he is the one. . .'

'Sutte, I am sorry . . . alright?' said Bhrigu. 'Can we not leave the matter alone? It's too hot to fight.'

I ignored him and addressed myself to the elderly man. 'Ghanshyam Singh? Pardon me, but I have heard your name before. But I can't quite remember.'

'He is the landlord I told you about,' said Manendra Singh 'And also a very good friend of mine.'

'Oh! Yes. I remember now. You also own the mill, too, right?'

'Yes,' said Ghanshyam Singh. He had a throaty voice and he spoke almost as if he was speaking into a mike. I had heard such quality of voice in one of my Dad's friends before who was a commandant in the Indian Army and rose through the ranks to become a colonel general. 'But the mill had to be shut down. It was running on losses for quite some time now.'

'He is employing the workers to do odd jobs for him. Majority of them are being shipped to the district of Rohtas. Ghanshyam Singh has found them jobs in the cotton factory there. He has taken care of the fact that no one suffers because of this situation.'

'As was my duty to do so.' Replied the man with bowed head. 'I tried to salvage the situation, tried to keep the mill running somehow, but the matter got out of my hand soon.'

'You have nothing to feel guilty about. Even a great man has his share of bad days,' said the Chaudhary, placing a reassuring hand on his friend's shrunken shoulders.

'Please, will you come inside?' said Bhrigu. 'It's much too hot here. We can talk there in peace.' After a thought, he added. 'Do you have something important to discuss with me?'

'No . . .' replied the landlord. 'Manendra Singh here, spoke so highly of you when we last met that I wanted to meet you, too, that's all. In this village, it's seldom that an interesting person stops by.'

'So, what is it exactly that you wanted to know?' Bhrigu asked. We had taken our chairs to the dust laden portico that gloomily stared at the unsightly backyard. Although, the panoramic view consisted of a weed whelmed garden and a crumbling encirclement of walls that were forced to fight a losing battle against the formidable and unforgiving enemies in the form of weather, age and rude neglect; to say nothing of the stench, the source of which I still couldn't locate, there was a good shade there and a gentle breeze was blowing in our direction. I would say unreservedly that it was a small consolation over an AC but I was willing to accept the tender care of Mother Nature for once. After all, before the revolution in technology aided and abetted by global warming and evolution of man, we were completely dependent on her for all of our needs and she, like a good mother, loved and cared for her children, ignorant of the fact that one day we would grow up, arm ourselves with the toys of modernity, and look down upon her simple gifts.

'*Pradhan* ji told me that you were working on a case. Although, he didn't reveal any details regarding the same because you had expressly told him not to, I was intrigued.'

'Oh it's nothing, really,' Bhrigu said. 'I have to settle a doubt, that's all. It's a trivial matter for people as important as you.'

'Isn't important a relative term?' said the good landlord and I became aware of a sinking feeling in my stomach that today, on this porch, sat two people who shared an interest in cryptology.

'Yes. You're right,' said Bhrigu, looking at him as if for the first time.

'What's that supposed to mean?' I asked, out of curiosity's sake. They couldn't go having a private conversation in code language when I was also presiding over the meeting.

'It means that what's important to one person can be unimportant to another,' said Bhrigu.

'So . . .' It was Ghanshyam Singh again. 'What's the doubt you're trying to settle?'

'Well . . . I better not say it, sir. You see I have promised the concerned party of total discretion.'

'Oh . . . that settles the matter then,' he said, with a touch of disappointment in his voice.

'I am afraid so.'

At this point there was a lull in the conversation. To enliven the atmosphere, I was about to quote an anecdote from my professional life as a teacher, the one topic I loved to make fun of whenever and wherever possible, when the unexpected happened. One of the legs of the wooden chair that Ghanshyam Singh had occupied gave way and awkwardly he crashed to the ground. Chaudhary sahib beat Bhrigu and me in rushing towards his dear friend and offered a hand to the unfortunate man. Ghanshyam Singh, however, was too busy to disentangle himself from the mess he had landed in and somehow got to his feet by supporting his weight on one of the other legs that was somehow still standing tall. He brushed his suit, smoothed his ruffled hair, and stood still for a few seconds trying to catch his breath.

'That was quite a fall!' *Pradhan* sahib shrieked. 'The chair looked solid enough when you sat on it!'

'No chair is solid enough when they have been used as acting beds by Inspector Gyaan Gere,' I said under my breath.

'Are you all right?' I asked.

'I am fine,' he said, a little shaken. 'This fall is nothing compared to the one in my own life.'

'What are you talking about, sir?' asked Bhrigu as we took our seats again. Chaudhary sahib gave up his seat for his friend as the omnipresent hawaldar fetched another one from the inside of the police station after having discerned what had happened.

'It was a tragedy that changed me from inside out,' said the landlord. I could detect a dull pain in his voice. The strong, resonating voice that carried a metallic timbre was slowly but surely reducing to a wheezing noise with every spoken word of pain; his articulate speech growing close to a hoarse incoherent whisper. 'I . . . don't share my grief with anyone . . . not even myself . . . but . . . I don't know why sitting with you people today, I feel my heart crying to unburden itself.'

I had seen this happen way too many times. My dear friend's presence was exercising its magic on the troubled man. People just couldn't control themselves when he was around. Even before they knew it, the inmost secrets and painful memories they had buried in the depths of their consciousness, gushed to the surface as if summoned by magic.

'I am very sorry to hear that, sir,' Bhrigu said sincerely. I could see that he was deeply touched by the miserable state of the elderly man.

'Well, one gets what is written in one's destiny,' said the broken man. 'I didn't ask for any of it but do you ever go about asking for pain and misfortunes? However hard you try, if your stars are against you, they will align themselves in the form of every kind of misery conceivable to mankind.'

He was now staring hard at a spot on the wall opposite him. I was certain that if I focused closely, I could see the kaleidoscope of half buried memories playing about in those dull, cold eyes. 'I am a man of wealth and power and I have a duty towards my forefathers to protect the heritage passed on to me. I am the custodian of all that has come down to me through generations. Many a strong man would shy away from such a big responsibility but not I, never I. I never wanted all this . . . no . . . I would have been very happy indeed if I was the son of a humble farmer who toils at the fields, day in and out, with the driving force of feeding and sheltering his family. That is where his true happiness lies. I would have carried out in his shoes and worked for a humble morsel of food, leading an ordinary but honest life. But therein lies the problem. I was not born as the son of a farmer. I was born into a fiefdom. A grand fiefdom, for that matter, that came with a burden almost too great to bear. I cannot afford to remain inconspicuous or hide behind the shadows of others by shirking my duties. No. I had to rise to the occasion. I had to accept what I was, regardless of who I wanted to be.' He took a deep breath, moved his glance to meet Bhrigu's, and began. 'If I say I was the last person on earth who wanted power or wealth, would you believe me? Tell me, son, would you believe me or consider it purely rhetorical? I once confided these feelings in my secretary and his look told me that he didn't believe me at all. "Put this man in a hut for a week" I could hear him say "Then he will understand the true state of affairs". He gave me every kind of verbal support imaginable and cheered me even but I just knew he would never understand.'

'Wealth, status, and power are the things most alluring to the one who is in its presence day and night, but still it passes him untouched,' said Bhrigu. 'Is your secretary ambitious?'

'He is a very hardworking man and his motivation is as old as time itself. To rise high in his career.'

'That's why he could never understand your viewpoint. But I most certainly do.'

The landlord was lost for words for a second or two. He gaped at Bhrigu with something close to admiration, amazement, and respect and then began 'You have a unique insight, son. The Chaudhary here was right. You are special.' Hope glimmered in his eyes for the very first time; a ray of light perhaps that could dispel the deepest of darkness. 'So you understand when I say that if I had a choice, I would never have asked for this life with its pressures and challenges but would be quite content to live as an ordinary peasant. But of the many flaws that I might have, I recognise one virtue; one absolute, unforgiving, and unrelenting virtue. Realising and carrying responsibilities. I just have to bear out with the utmost sincerity and enterprise, any kind of responsibility that has been given to me, no matter what. If I was a farmer, I would have worked hard day and night at the fields; if I was a clerk, I would have buried myself, without a thought to fun, under paperwork and hence, as a landlord of a once grand fiefdom, I am doing everything I can to salvage the most of it because that's my duty and my responsibility. Still, I hear people making snide remarks about my austere nature and lust for money and power. How I want to shout at the top of my lungs what I really am! But what's the bloody use?' Ghanshyam Singh's voice reached a crescendo 'They would never understand!'

Bhrigu was looking intently at him, his eyes flashing brightly. I knew not what inferences he was drawing about the character of this intriguing landlord. He wasn't, at any point, your average *zamindar* whose life evolved and devolved around certain hectares of land; where the sun rose from the east of their fields and set somewhere behind a well marking the end of their fertile kingdom. Ghanshyam Singh, from the way he carried himself to the manner in which he articulated his deep thoughts sounded more like a professor of philosophy with a troubled conscience than one who is happy to flourish the cane of power. At any rate, he must have presented quite an interesting study for my friend and companion.

'It's strange that even after so many years you haven't become inured to these resentments. Wealth and influence surely come with a cost but people wielding them grow accustomed to their situation and take them in their stride,' observed Bhrigu.

'I am not like the rest, I guess,' Ghanshyam Singh said, exhaling slowly. 'And the untimely demise of my only daughter might have aggravated matters for me.'

'The death of your only daughter?!' I shrieked.

'Yes. Everyone in the village knows about it. They talk callously about the circumstances leading to her death, totally oblivious to my own feelings.'

'If it's not an intrusion, I would like to ask why? I don't quite understand what you're getting at,' said Bhrigu. I could detect a faint note of surprise in his voice, a note that struck me as well.

'Twelve years ago, my daughter committed suicide and these villagers readily embraced the strange idea that I was the one responsible for it.'

'Why's that?'

'Why's that. . .' trance-like, he slowly repeated the words to himself as if seeking an answer hidden in their obscure crevices. 'Didn't I give you the answer to that question? These villagers hate my wealth and thus me. . . They would do anything and believe anyone to satisfy their ill feelings towards me. And when that anyone turns out be your own daughter who planted the doubt, I really don't stand a chance to clear my name, do I? My own progeny! Would you believe it?!'

'Your daughter was behind it? But why?'

A flood of unfathomable grief momentarily drowned any expression on his face only to be replaced by something close to mockery intermingling with bitterness. 'Because she hated me . . . Because she would go to any extreme to see my down fall . . . This village loved her and she loved them because they had a common enemy. Me. They made an alliance to ensure my downfall. Oh! How well have they succeeded! My mill is shut down, my lands are on heavy mortgage and my heart could give away any minute!'

There was silence for a space as Ghanshyam Singh stared, breathless with sorrow, at the broken remnants of the chair. 'I don't want to speak ill about my daughter especially after her death but truth is truth, however bitter, and one has to face it.' A painful smile stole across his mouth. 'I will tell you a story now; a story that starts at the threshold of unparalleled joy and ends at the precipice of terrible ruin.'

24

TESTIMONY OF VENGEANCE

'You should know that there was a time in my life when I and my wife, Snehlata, were making rounds to the temple of Mahadev, up at the remotest corner of the Khagri hills, to pray for a child. It was a very difficult journey indeed with the last leg comprising of a steep incline of about fifty feet that we had to cover on foot. But we didn't once notice the exhaustion in our limbs crying for rest or the sharp pebbles cutting us deeply in the foot, as if out to take revenge. No. Why? Because for us these discomforts were trivial. What could hurt more than the agony of not having your own flesh and blood even after thirteen years of marriage? No god could be left in peace unless we got what was justly ours and no effort could be spared until our goal was fulfilled.' The landlord shifted a little in his seat and embarked on his tale again. 'When the trips to Mahadev went futile, I thought that this god of mercurial temperament was not his usual, benevolent self and hence we searched frantically for lords who specialised in the department of granting fertility. Lord Krishna was the one who came foremost to the mind and after carefully and painstakingly marking on a map his temples dotting India, we set forth to pay him a visit, to beg for an issue. We went through all his manmade dwelling places, from Kashmir to Kanyakumari, with a fine-toothed comb and left no place untouched, be it an ancient temple, magnanimous and beautiful with the skilful hands of artisans decorating it in exquisite, arcane designs from head to foot, huge sanctums thick with the fragrance of holy incense that left you feeling small and insignificant, to a niche in a tree where a makeshift worshipping place had been created in haste to serve the purpose of a quick, hassle free worship.' Here I would halt his narrative to report that I noticed traces of mockery and disdain in his voice towards his religion. I felt that somehow he had lost a significant chunk of faith and the death of his daughter could have been an important contributing factor.

'Nothing still. We had lost all hope. The physicians had given up long ago and the gods had decided to follow suit. We were on the verge of giving up when a very good friend of mine decided to pay me a visit. His name was Utpendra Nath and we had gone to the same school together. After that, he had gone to a law college in Delhi to study to become a lawyer. On his visit, he told me that he had some business to take care of in the nearby city and hence he had thought of paying his buddy a surprise visit. He hadn't come alone, though. He had brought along his beautiful 3-year-old daughter. As we got to chatting, he told me that he had lost his wife during child birth and hadn't given a thought to remarrying again. He had a thriving practice in Delhi and was doing well for himself and his daughter. Who would have thought that this was the last conversation he would be having with me?'

'Last conversation?' I asked.

'Yes. You see, it's all well to talk about a thriving career but what about the cost? Utpendra Nath talked ceaselessly of his good fortunes but he deftly hid the torture his health had to suffer in order for him to multiply his money. The hectic life, heavy with heated words of arguments and a head swarming with a thousand statuettes of law and bylaws crammed at the last minute; it was but a matter of time that his heart started to lose the pace that his life had set.'

'What do you mean?' The man's love for cryptology was definitely coming through.

'The very next day when he was to leave us, he suffered a massive heart attack and died on the spot, leaving behind his daughter and some currency in the banks. We did his last rites and paid him a final farewell but we couldn't bring ourselves to part with the little girl, who looked at us with her big eyes that were still in the process of processing the wonders of the world around her. It was then that it came to us. The gods had blessed us after all and we finally had a child to call our own and to love and cherish. We named her Meenakshi, after her big, beautiful eyes. My daughter.'

He stopped and took a lungful of air. I could see that saying his daughter's name had opened a flood gate of memories and as his pupils dilated with love and affection for her, I knew that he was visiting in his mind a happy place in time.

'She was a silent girl, peaceful and happy with herself. I remember she asked after her father just once and to my answer that he was now in a better place, she gave me an unhappy smile and said, 'How can it be a better place when I am not there with him?' I was shocked at her simple, yet thoughtful reply. I just knew that she could see through the euphemism, directly at the truth. It was always like that with her. You just couldn't treat her like a child. She was way too mature for her age.'

'Precocious?' Bhrigu asked.

'No. She had a depth unusual for her age but she was childlike in every other way. She loved her dolls and would spend hours dressing them up and looking after them with tender love and affection. She would bring the house down if we did not take her to the nearby playground everyday where she met other children of her age, who accepted her as their little leader! Oh! You should have seen how they used to follow her around as best as their small feet allowed! They adored her.'

A tear of joy made its way down his cheek, which he flicked with his hand. 'She was a unique child, our Meenakshi, and we felt very blessed indeed to have her in our life. As she grew up, she became even more beautiful than before. She gained in height but her child like face with its depth and innocence remained untouched. We sent her to the government school of this village and the reports from her teachers told us that she was a bright kid, not just good at learning but also eager to learn. One of her teachers once said that she was a very curious child and after every lesson, she had a whole list of questions to go with it and the questions were no flimsy ones on part of a child who is more interested in annoying the teacher than in gaining real knowledge but sharp and accurate that helped study the problem in detail. She was that person. She had that insight.

When I come to see it, in that respect, she was a miniature version of you, Bhrigu.'

'Was that the real reason you wanted to see him?' I asked despite myself.

He was silent for a space akin to a person who is caught in his own admission and said, 'Yes. That was one of the reasons.'

'Sutte, if you are done, can we continue?' asked my friend who just loved to tell me off in public.

On the cue, the landlord began. 'We loved her dearly and she was our devoted daughter. I was planning on sending her to the city to continue her studies. I remember how ecstatic she was to hear of the proposal. When we asked her what she wanted to become when she grew up, she gave us the reply 'I don't know yet but whatever I do, I want to be true to myself.' Her answers where deep and hinted at an innate mystery that prevented us from bonding with her in the most intimate way. However much we loved her, she always carried that barely perceptible aura which told us that she had something in her that we did not quite contribute in putting in. We did not mind it because we loved her just the way she was and even felt proud to have such an intelligent daughter to boast about town.'

Chaudhary sahib said here, 'You boasted about her all the time! How your eyes would shine then!'

'Yes . . . but . . . I didn't know then that small isolated incidents would soon contribute to a crisis that would end up destroying everything that I loved.'

'What happened, sir?' Bhrigu asked.

'It all started when Meenakshi started a committee when she was just 16. We had decided that next year, she would go to the city to pursue further studies. She was very excited about the project and said that it could help solve the problems of villagers. The group would become a platform through which the villagers would voice their problems and her fellow committee members would take it to the concerned authorities and do everything in their power to ensure that their problems found proper solutions. 'We for village' it was called. We supported Meenakshi in the full because she was really enthusiastic about it. I remember how she talked ceaselessly of the good she could do for the villagers. Never once did we realise that this community would one day alienate her from us forever.' He paused to assort his thoughts. 'It started with petty arguments over inane issues like me advising her not to associate herself with the dregs of this village to which she curtly replied, 'I know what I'm doing. You don't need always to tell me what to do and what not to. I know what I want to do,' or when I asked her not to compromise her future for this committee and her reply was 'My future is mine. I will do what I like with it.' It was then that I felt the distance I always knew existed between us growing more than ever and the personality she had brought with her eating away the one she had acquired with her days with us. One day, it was swallowed whole and with it my whole life.'

He looked around him as if half afraid that past would pay him a visit. 'As days turned to weeks, she started getting aloof and withdrawn. She would rarely talk to us and when I spoke to her she would reply in a few syllables or would not care to reply at all. Snehlata, too, was beside herself with grief at such a transformation in her beloved daughter. "The thugs of this village are proving a very bad company for my girl," she would cry. "They won't leave her alone. In the name of the committee they follow her around and fill her ears with all sorts of stories. They are stealing our daughter! Please do something!" But what could I possibly do? Meenakshi was a girl who knew her own mind. She wouldn't listen to anyone but herself. I couldn't tie her up forever in the house, could I? Though, I had to resort to that method as a last act of desperation; a last, pathetic attempt to save my daughter.'

He cleared his throat that had become heavy with the painful recollection. 'The day she met that horrid man was the day everything quickly went out of hands. She was already going through a personal battle, a transformation of sorts, but we had every chance of getting our daughter back once it was complete. It was our misfortune that that snake sneaked into her life through the hole punctured by that difficult period to take utmost advantage of her vulnerability.' He paused for a brief moment and then continued. 'His name was Vidwait. You should have seen him. His outward appearance never once betrayed the rotten, malicious heart that beat inside him. His charm was such that dazzles and blinds before one has become accustomed to it, and even then you seldom find yourself gaping at him in awe of those chiselled features that looked like the product of the masterstrokes a gifted sculptor. Yes, he was like a demigod. He had thick black hair with curls that fell all around his forehead. His eyes were a deeper shade of brown and the way he dropped his eyelids while looking at you was enough to beguile even the stoutest of hearts. He had a sharp, straight nose that spoke of a certain hauteur that runs deep only in the blue bloods. His lips were thin and unremarkable but once they parted for a smile, you had to brace yourself or else the light could easily harm your eyes. Those perfect set of teeth sparkled like pearls. His physique and bearing, too, were regal enough to give any king a run for his money. It is often supposed that such an arresting personality would come with a name, a title or at the least, an inheritance; a retinue of servants to do his bidding and run his errands at any time of the day and a mansion where he could just put his feet up, sign a few quick deals under the careful and experienced eyes of a patient, loyal and hardworking advisor; a life of indulgence for a person whom the cosmetic side of life had chosen to indulge upon. But this is where he fell short. He was a complete broke, a pauper, if you must. He had not a dime to call his own but he had tastes so expensive that a fortune would have fallen short in keeping him in style. This was where his conniving brain and malicious heart joined ranks to search for a victim who could be a passport to the lifestyle befitting him and guess who the victim was? My poor daughter.' His eyes held Bhrigu's as he said, 'It was not until that day that I had to acknowledge the bitter truth that strength of character is often helpless against the force of charm. Because if it was not the case, she would never have allowed him so far an access to her heart that once inside, he could only leave after destroying it and us, in the process, beyond repair.'

The landlord asked for a glass of water and then began, 'Like a shadow, he was with her everywhere she went. We met him when he came with her to our house one day. His charm mesmerised me at first and I found myself gaping at him quite involuntarily. But, no sooner had he spoken to me in his silken smooth voice like the gentle hiss of a poisonous snake, I understood that he was not a good company for my daughter. He spoke in words that dripped with respect and humility but only when you started to pay closer attention, did you notice that there was a threatening undertone behind every word, a warning that once he attached himself to a family, he never left before sucking them dry. As soon as I got the chance, I told Meenakshi to leave his side immediately but she reacted so strongly to my advice, that I was left shell shocked. She yelled at me and almost became hysterical in his defence. She accused me that as she was but an adopted child, I wasn't concerned for her well-being or happiness at all. She went further still to say that adopting her didn't give me the right to treat her like a robot that I could control. What could I say to such an insinuation? I had to eat my words and my worries regarding her welfare. From that day onward, I could see her moving inch by inch closer to her doom but I could do or say nothing to save her. I had been reduced to just a mute spectator.'

'But the money was yours.' I ventured 'You could have refused to give it to her when she asked.'

'It's easy said than done,' he replied with evident distress. 'And she had already gone so far away from us that money had become the only cord that still connected her to our family. If I let that go, too, I was afraid we would lose her forever. So, despite knowing that we were emptying our coffers to the villainous man, I had to keep satisfying her. We loved her very much and if our prosperity was the cost we had to pay for her affections, we were more than ready.' He took a breath and then began, 'The problem reached its height when one day, out of the blue, she declared that she was going to marry him. Could you imagine that? My bright, 16-year-old daughter who had a promising life and possibly a great career before her and who was to leave us next year looking for greener pastures was going to destroy her life by marrying that snake! Now, how could we possibly allow for that?! It was then that I decided that the reins of this crisis that I had abandoned out of my love for her had to be handled again to save my daughter from a perfect ruin.'

He asked for water a second time and then proceeded to tell what I knew to be the tragic culmination of the miserable tale. 'After that terrible news, I asked one of my men to tail her everywhere. I wanted to know when they were going to fix the date for their marriage. One day, my patience was rewarded and my man was able to glean from their conversations, the day on which they planned to tie the knot. When the fateful day came, driven by panic and desperation, I locked her inside her room. She was to remain there unless one of my security guards could threaten the snake to leave my daughter alone and also to let him know that if he dared to do otherwise, the consequences would be very harsh. When the guards informed me that the man had acquiesced and left the village, I let out a breath of relief and unlocked the door to my daughter's room to let her out. You can imagine the shock I received when on entering her room, I found that she was gone! I searched the room for a possible way of escape and observed that one of the rods of the ventilator was askew. She had made her escape with the air.'

'On the desk I found a letter and I became confident that her frantic escape had been abetted by the spurious, inflammatory contents of the letter. I knew the human snake had dropped the letter through the very same ventilator. He had written that by the time she would read this letter, my men would have finished him off for good. He further said that his life meant nothing to him if she wasn't in it and if he had to choose between living without her and dying, he would choose the latter without a moment's hesitation. He said that he loved her with all his being and even if they couldn't be together in this life, he hoped that the gods would bless him with her in the next. I knew that after reading the letter, she panicked and made a very difficult escape.'

He sighed heavily at this point and I could see that his eyes had become bloodshot with suppressed tears. 'It was raining heavily that night. I sent my men to look for her. It was not until dawn that they found her lifeless body lying in one of the fields, two miles away, half buried in the soft, wet earth.'

25

A Shot in the Dark

'The shock was such that I was paralysed for a whole month. I couldn't move. Everything went by me in a haze. The world for me was a blurry mass in perpetual motion. The solidity of life had become a shifting nightmare that tormented me day and night without the faintest hope for relief. I had become a captive of my own blinding sorrow. As I look back, I feel that the paralysis was a blessing in disguise because if it hadn't numbed my senses, my head would have imploded with the explosion of remorse and guilt. After one month, when I recovered, what was the first thing that I heard? I heard that a rumour had it that I had driven my daughter to suicide. I had hardly grappled with this obscene accusation when I heard another. My then manager told me that Meenakshi had confided in the villagers which constituted her group that if I had the chance, I would willingly see her dead. Now, when she was dead and that too under such mysterious circumstances, the rumour gathered in speed and strength and soon everyone in the village was certain that somehow I had been responsible for her death. From that day onwards, the villagers covertly despise me. I know that they work for me for their livelihood but their contempt is only half concealed in their eyes. This was my own daughter's testimony of vengeance that brought about my destruction.'

Bhrigu was silent for a space. I thought he was struggling with some unspoken questions of his own but he smothered them and said softly, 'Sir, I am truly sorry for your loss and added misery. No one should suffer as much as you have.'

The landlord gently nodded his head and said, 'That's destiny, as I said before. You carry your sins from your past and with them the forces of retribution. Well, I have developed my own defences against the situation. I don't seem to mind much anything anymore.'

We made small talk after that where Ghanshyam Singh and Manendra Singh asked Bhrigu questions related to his intriguing profession and then after a round of courtesy, they left.

'That was some story!' I cried as soon as the party had broken. 'Who could say on seeing the man that he carried such a burden with him?'

'That's a valid question,' said Bhrigu. I could detect in his simple affirmation a hint of suspicion and wonder that had nothing whatsoever to do with my observation.

'Well, let it be,' he said again after a brief pause. 'Let's follow the trail where we had left it. Bal Kishore's every movement can be crucial for the resolution of this mystery. But it's dark already. Would you care to come?'

I contemplated the matter before me. 'Would it be very dangerous?'

He rolled his eyes at me in a grotesque fashion.

I was quick to undo my lapse. 'Even if it is, so what? I wouldn't abandon this case for the world.'

Bal Kishore was lying prostrate on the cot outside his little, one room mud house when we met him. He had covered himself up to his nose with a thick *Khadi Chaddar*. He wasn't snoring and I had this feeling that he was just pretending to be asleep. Behind that soiled sheet, his brows were clouded and he would scratch his forehead every once in a while by the little finger of his right hand. When Bhrigu tapped him lightly on the shoulder, he woke up with a visible start and sat panting hard on the cot. 'Who . . . who's it?' he said in a panicky voice.

'It's just us,' Bhrigu replied. 'It's a strange hour to go to sleep, I should say.'

'Oh you again?!' Cried our helpless victim. 'What do you want from me now? What have I done now? Why can't you not leave me the hell alone?!'

'Please don't get us wrong. We came here to see how you were doing. You didn't look too well in the jail, that's why.'

'What are you?' the man cried again. This time he was sitting bolt upright on the cot. The *Chaddar* had slipped to the floor. 'First, you imprison me for no rhyme or reason and then you come to me at an ungodly hour asking after my well-being!'

'We had a misunderstanding for which we feel repentant. We imprisoned you wrongly. We were feeling so guilty about it that we couldn't help coming here to apologise to you personally.'

Bal Kishore was silent for a while as if struggling with himself to believe us or not. At last his strained muscles relaxed and he decided to favour us with the benefit of the doubt. 'It's alright. Please be careful next time. It's not a joke to go about town locking people up as if it was a new pass time.'

'Of course,' replied Bhrigu.

'Who gave you my address?'

'We were passing this way when I located you sleeping here. Thus we came. It's a small village after all. Not at all difficult to locate people,' said Bhrigu.

'Please, I accept your apology. Now can I go back to my sleep?' asked Bal Kishore, irritation writ large on his face.

'Yes . . . we have to hurry too. A new Pundit has come for performing a Puja at the *Mahakali Mandir*. We were headed in that direction. It is said that he has magical powers but the most potent power of the lot is said to have been granted by *Mahakali* herself. It is so miraculous! But why am I bothering you with such matters? I bid you goodbye. Have a speedy recovery.'

Curiosity is the strongest of all human weaknesses, if you could pardon the paradox. Dang the carrot of curiosity over a human and he would follow you to the end of the world in a trance; his world governed by the carrot alone. Bal Kishore was distressed, to say the least, but once his curiosity was whetted, he could no longer feel any other emotion except that of gratifying his curiosity.

'Wait!' he hailed us. 'What power did *Mahakali* herself grant Pundit ji?

'Well, if you want to know,' said Bhrigu, feigning disinterest. 'It is said that after a meditation of over twenty years in a remote cave of the *Bhandan* forest, *Mahakali* appeared in his dream and granted him the power that from then on, anyone who lied to the Pundit in future, would become the marked one.'

'What's a marked one?'

'A marked one was a person who was followed by misfortunes anywhere he went till the day he died. His life would become a tragic existence, with all the luck in the world against him. A few people, who dared lie to the Pundit on his face, were dogged by calamities and they died very unhappy men.' Bhrigu said with the flair of a storyteller, speaking in a hushed tone to strike terror at the heart of the one listening. The effect was evident on Bal Kishore's countenance. It was plain that he was indeed scared of the Pundit and his power.

'Do you want to meet him?' asked I

'N . . . no,' said Bal Kishore feebly. 'You go ahead.'

Well, I should reveal at this point that the dialogue that just took place with Bal Kishore was mere fabrication on the part of my friend; a ruse, if you will, to trap the unsuspecting fellow into admitting that which he had struggled with all his might to conceal. This was the easiest way to get to the truth with as little damage as possible and thus avoiding the grotesque repercussions of a fierce interrogation. If we had put physical pressure on him, he could have either harmed himself in the heat of the moment or could have tempered with the truth to avoid the pain, but if we put a gentle pressure on his mind, working and manipulating his fears to our benefit, he would readily sing like a bird. These are not my words, mind you; I am just quoting the views of my dear friend.

The very next day that we had planted the seed of fear into the mind of Bal Kishore, Bhrigu seemed equipped with a sort of enthusiasm that I had never before witnessed in as calm and collected a person as him. He went around the house, knocking things in his wake and grumbling such a good deal to himself that I was half driven out of my mind. I took his less than contagious enthusiasm with as much aplomb as humanly possible but when he borrowed my iPad and started watching a classic Hindi film involving a Pundit, my wits could take it no more.

'What in the lord's name are you doing, man?' I shouted. 'Today you have behaved like a truant. You are always lecturing me on my unbridled energy but today you have surpassed even me on my best days. And why are you wasting my 4G Internet pack, watching an old, Eastman colour movie?'

At first he ignored me but when I repeated my question he said with his eyes still trained on the video. 'I am observing how a Pundit evokes fear in his subjects in the name of god. I have seen many men of cloth in this village but they never really exhibited any character in any of the religious functions at all. They just went through their mechanical routines of taking a seat opposite the *havan kund*, chanting unintelligibly for a said period of time, collecting the offerings and then disappearing. This movie has come in very handy.'

'For the love of god!' I cried again ignoring the pun. 'Why this sudden fetish? Are you feeling alright?'

'Yes'

Silence reigned for a couple of minutes and I was about to probe him to reveal more when it suddenly hit me. *Fear evoked by a Pundit*, he had said. I saw the pieces of puzzle fall seamlessly together, revealing a clear picture.

'You are practicing for the role of a Pundit, aren't you?' I asked, surprised at my own admission.

'Yes.'

'I never thought you to be an actor?'

'I am not, Sutte. That's why I am observing,' he replied with a hint of impatience.

'But if you don't have the talent for acting, you can never act, however much you 'observe', my friend.'

This time he faced me and said, 'I agree that I haven't acted before but I am not looking to develop a knack for it either. I just want to memorise a few expressions and I am ready to go.'

This was the strangest thing I had ever heard a person say. How could one act by *memorising expressions*? As far as I knew, if you had the talent for acting, you prepared for the role of a character by understanding his life and personality and also by associating oneself with the character to get a grip of his nature. That was how it was done. The expressions that the actor nailed in his performance was the result of a meticulous study of the role, sometimes so much so that he forgot his own self. Bhrigu made this art sound so mechanical and prosaic that I almost gasped. Feel the character and you will get the required expressions; is what I thought . . . but memorising expressions?

'How can you memorise expressions? That's the weirdest thing to say,' I exclaimed.

'I don't have to become an actor to play one role. This cinematic Pundit is giving me all the expressions that I require. I just have to remember them by heart and use them appropriately. My work will be done.'

'Use them?' I cried 'You are making an art sound like mathematics. Don't tell me that you are going to add and subtract the expressions as well.'

'At present I don't attempt at such a thing,' he said, absorbed again in the video.

'Oh yes,' I said. 'Now I can see. If you can treat humans as if they were nothing more than programmed robots; their thought processes as the result of experiments and condense their behaviour into an equation. . . I know you must treat the most subtle markers to their state of mind, which is their expressions, equally quantitatively as well. Will you divide them into laws and make graphs for them, too?'

He wasn't oblivious to the slight mockery that had crept into my tone but he chose to ignore it. 'Why? Someday, I will. I assure you.'

After this one-sided heated conversation, I left him to his occupation and taking out my laptop sat down to finish my article for the newspaper that was overdue for over a week. It was a satirical commentary on the indulgent life of one of the most prominent politicians of our time who was happily using the exchequer's money for his own pursuits of pleasure. I had been at it for the past thirty minutes when I looked up and saw that Bhrigu was gone. I called out for him but got no answer in return. Spent, I thought better to resume my work and not waste my energies on trying to understand what power had taken hold of my friend for him to behave so unusually out of his character. Not more than five minutes had passed when he came into my view and looked at me peculiarly. He had a saffron cloth wound around his head in the form of a turban, a holy mark of ash was smeared across his forehead and his face had darkened considerably, probably the application of some kind of metallic powder. For dramatic effect, I would love to write that he looked startling and beyond any kind or form of recognition but I am an honest observer and I write what I see. Despite his touch of makeup, he was looking totally himself and anyone, who had happened to clap their eyes on him but once, wouldn't have the slightest difficulty in recognising him.

'Is this your disguise?' I asked with a touch of mockery in my tone. I was still smarting from the brusque way he had almost dismissed me a moment ago.

'Yes, my dear friend,' he replied in a chirpy voice. 'Tell me, what do you think about it?'

'Do you want my honest view?' I asked, happy at finding a space which I could use to get back at him for his recent snubbing.

'As honest as they come,' he replied beaming.

'Among the many talents that you do not have,' I said placing a modicum of stress on the last three words 'Disguise is one of them. You look like a darker twin of yours who happens to be a priest. In other words, you look yourself.'

'Thank you for the honest appraisal,' he said, beaming still. 'I knew I had not changed much because I still have one final piece of disguise to wear that will make the transformation complete.'

'Really?' I said, faking disinterest. 'And what would that be, pray?'

'The expressions, you fool,' he said and saying thus he turned his back and after a minute, turned towards me again. If I say that I was almost numb with shock and almost dropped out of my chair, it would a gross understatement. My gentle, and pleasant-faced, albeit a trifle irritating, friend had vanished to be replaced by a man whose cunning was unmistakable in his half-closed eyes. He was looking at me with an intensity that scorched me, to say the least. There was such powerful attraction in those fierce eyes that could intimidate any man into submission. The gentle curves of my friend's brow were now pinched upwards like they had been clipped there by pins. Together with the fire in those hard, unyielding eyes, the sharp ascent of the eyebrows hinted at an austerity and imperiousness beyond belief. He had pursed his lips brutally at the corners and set his jaw in such an immovable a line that clearly betrayed the fact that this man was not used to any kind of insubordination or disobedience. His word or prediction, whatever that might be, was final and fatal. Had I not known better, I would have gone as far as to say that my friend had been possessed by the ghost of a ruthless priest. Oh! I was stunned to see so acute a transformation that had been wrought in him.

'H . . . how . . .?' Was what I managed to speak.

'Silence!' He hissed like a cobra that had opened its hood and was about to strike.

Fearful to disobey the curt command of this masterful man, I sat stunned for a few moments when seeing my pitiable plight, he returned to his normal self. His reversal was nothing short of an exorcism to me.

'See? I told you that expressions are the most potent form of disguise. Not all the fancy make up in the world can pack a punch like that.'

'You said you . . . you were not an actor!' I stammered.

'And I maintain my stand, Sutte,' he replied with a touch of exasperation. 'Had I been an actor, I wouldn't have to sit before that video for the better half of the day trying my best to copy and reproduce the complicated but effective expressions. These people are simple-minded villagers who can never understand subtlety. If you have to be convincing in your drama, you will have to take the help of excesses, sometimes bordering on the vulgar.' He paused for a moment and then said, 'I thought I was sloppy in my act but by your own expression, I can tell that I have finally nailed it!' He cried with the triumph of a victor.

'I will now dress up and take your leave. Don't worry at all. I will use the back door. No, Sutte . . . this time I will have to go alone. I will put you up to date as soon as I come. If I'm late don't wait for me and have your dinner with Nirja Masi. Don't wince, please. I know it is far worse an ordeal than anything else in the world but you'll have to put up a brave front for this evening alone. Take heart from the fact that I am her favourite prey. She'll leave you alone after harassing a trifle.'

Well, I put every ounce of resistance that I could find on my person to force him to take me along but I should have realised from experience alone that when Bhrigu was on a solitary mission, it was more like a crusade. He developed a tunnel vision and saw nothing except the dark, nebulous object at its end, silhouetted against the bright sunlight, enticing him to come and reveal its true form. He would then care little if someone had a Kalashnikov with a hair trigger aimed at him; where the slightest of movement would be enough to kill. Compare this deadly scenario to the one I was presenting; entreating and thus distracting him from his mission on the pretext of a nagging, neurotic Aunt? Well, it may sound preposterous at first but if you had only known Nirja Masi like we did, you would take that Kalashnikov shot any day and at any time over her. At least death would be quick and painless. Bhrigu, though, held the opinion that her talent to become a nuisance flourished only when he was the target and thus I was safe from her bullying. I was surprised to find later that he had been quite right in his supposition because an hour after he had gone, the hunter master looked into the room where I was sprawled on the arm chair listening to some old English songs, muttered something venomous under her breath, probably spat on the floor in disgust and then retreated into her own room.

I had begun to worry about Bhrigu when even after we have had our tense and awkward dinner, he had shown no signs of returning. I had checked my cell phone for a significant number of times but he had not tried to call me at all. It was now well past ten and I was thinking of making a trip to Bal Kishore's house myself when I heard a tap at the door. The hunter lady, as was her custom, had gone to a neighbour's house to indulge in some village gossip leaving me free to welcome my friend from, what I felt confident, a successful operation.

He was still wearing the *geruwa* dhoti and Kurta and I could see the rosary hanging from his wrist but the turban was held in his right hand now. His hair was in a state of mess and the ash that he had smeared on his forehead had mixed with the sweat and run down in little rivulets all over his face. In one word, he looked a sight, a bad sight.

'What went wrong with you?' I cried, after he had entered the house and collapsed on the arm chair that I had vacated. 'You went looking like a formidable, awe-inspiring Pundit and are back like a thug who has just been in a brawl!'

In reply, he exhaled a deep breath and closed his eyes in consternation.

'What happened Bhrigu?' I said with rising concern. I took to the stool that was kept in the vicinity of the chair and put a hand on his shoulder. 'You don't look well.'

He half-raised his tired eyes in my direction and said in a voice of fatigue, 'These village folks. You can never be sure with them. I sometimes wonder whether my work is not foolish and superfluous. In the many years that I have been at it, you know, trying to prove to the world that human nature is predictable . . . That it follows a pattern . . . That it is not complex . . . Well, it was not until today that I realised that I may have embarked on a fool's errand . . . If a simpleton can resist me at my best, what right have I to go on? This failure has raised a lot of self doubts, Sutte. I no longer trust myself.'

I could clearly see that he was heartbroken. He sat there looking a picture of defeat, his will slowly seeping away from him. I had never seen him in this mood before and that alarmed me. 'Come on, man. You can't let one failure decide your whole life! You are not that weak!'

He sighed heavily. 'You don't understand this, Sutte. The world that I am weaving is very delicate. One small lapse is enough to shake it from its foundations and to bring it crashing down. If I allow for one incorrect read, I will be allowing for an exception that has not been proved or validated by my own experience. That would mean disturbing the whole equation. . . As one dysfunctional part, however small, can bring the whole machinery to a standstill . . . One unproven exception can put a stop to my research as well. Unless and until Bal Kishore yields, I cannot move forward and from what he resisted today. . . Well, I don't think he would ever submit.'

'But . . . but. . .' I stammered. 'You may have committed a mistake in reading him. Surely, you can rectify that and approach him from a new angle.'

'No, Sutte,' he said almost in a whisper. 'I have done my best. If he is still inscrutable, I have been defeated by a simpleton. I have no right to continue and even if I tried, my work has been damaged beyond all repairs.'

'Did he not give you the slightest of clues? Was he not intimidated in the least?'

'Oh he was shivering from head to toe but he did not reveal a word. Instead . . .' he said now groping in his pocket and taking out a crumpled page. 'He gave me this. Tell me, what am I to do with this? Keep it as a souvenir for my failure?'

I unfolded the creased bit of paper. On it was drawn the most beautiful sketch of a kerosene lamp that I had ever seen in my life.

26

'This is peculiar indeed,' I said, still staring at the neat and delicate sketch. I couldn't help but marvel at the flourish with which the three-dimensional aspect of the glass globe had been executed. It was beauty itself. 'When we saw Bal Kishore in the cell and afterwards, he was struggling with an acute form of anxiety. I think your role playing did more harm than good. It thrust him right into the hands of neurosis. This lamp, I think, is the manifestation of the onset of this mental illness.'

'You are talking like a psychiatrist,' he said sardonically.

'Oh come on! It's common knowledge. I, too, had once fallen into the clutches of anxiety when I found myself at a fork in the road of my life where I couldn't continue doing what I was doing, that is, teach, and was simultaneously failing to find myself a suitable employment elsewhere. Trust me; I would have soon seen myself in quite desperate a situation if the position of an assistant editor hadn't opened in that publishing company. I talk from experience, my friend. May be your method was wrong only just this time.'

'What would you have done?' he asked in a caustic tone.

I knew he wasn't waiting for an answer by his indifferent attitude but I, nevertheless, supplied him with one. 'I? Well, I would have told him that his friend Bali had cracked before becoming comatose. Just a ruse, that is. Also, that he had named Bal Kishore himself, as an accomplice. That way, seething at the betrayal, Bal Kishore would have tried to save his skin by pinning everything on Bali. He would tell us all.'

'Really? This is a standard trick, is it not? I bet you have read and seen scores of detective fiction where such a trick has been employed with success. I have seen my colleagues apply it recklessly in real-life cases, too, but let me tell you one thing, Sutte, most often than not, this yields the wrong result; a very wrong result. Your fiction is just that—fiction. It has nothing to do when dealing with real people.'

I was flabbergasted. 'What do you mean?'

'Haven't you read Bal Kishore? Don't you know how he is? He is a very loyal and honest person; a trifle lazy, but honest. He would never, ever betray a friend.'

'Even when his friend betrays him?'

'He would never believe a word of what we say! He would stick to his loyalty like an oyster to its shell. No amount of trickery could have induced him to give up his friend! People like Bal Kishore are devoted. I have seen and researched on the type. They will die, sustain terrible injuries to their psyche but would never betray the one they are protecting.'

'Then how did you think that *your* ploy would work?'

'Because. . .' he said, pausing heavily over every word 'I was a man of faith. The only fear that loyalists like Bal

Kishore have over their own life is that of a man of faith and a vivid vision of hell where their soul would land if they dared to affront them.'

'But how did you know that he was superstitious?'

'I picked it up from a few imperceptible signs that anyone could easily overlook. Let's just say that he had the aura.' And when he saw a question rise in my eyes, he added quickly, 'I can't always break into words, Sutte, what I see and feel. I am not that articulate. Let's just suffice by saying that he had the look of a superstitious man.'

'Okay,' I said dubiously 'And what did you say to him?'

He paused for a space as if attempting to nurse his injuries and then said, 'I said that I had dreamed about him last night and in that dream I had come upon a terrible secret which he was hiding from all. I further said that if he did not make a clean breast of whatever he was concealing, I, as a man of faith, would curse him to eternity. If he lies, misfortunes would follow him from this world to the next and there would be no redemption for him. I build the scene ever so slowly. First I was kind and sympathetic and then slowly and in degrees I changed into a person whose displeasure could move heaven and earth.'

'But he still didn't crack.'

'And that's the mystery,' he replied sullenly. 'He has acted opposite to what his true nature is. Isn't that unnatural?'

At that moment, someone banged at the door with such urgency that I was afraid one more minute and they would break open their way into the house. If it was Nirja Masi, she owned us an explanation for her wild behaviour. But it turned out to be our humble client, Jayanti Devi. She was sweating and trembling all over. As she saw us, she gave a cry of horror and said in a pathetic, strangled voice, 'Kishore . . . Kishore is d . . . dead! Someone killed him! It . . . it was one shot in the dark . . . and . . . and. . .'

27

I was too stunned to grasp right away the meaning that the old lady was trying to bring home. I just gaped at her with my mouth hanging open on its own accord. Bhrigu, on the other hand, kept looking at her with an intensity that could have melted, within seconds, the iceberg that had been responsible for the drowning of the doomed ship, Titanic.

'What . . . what are you saying?' I shrieked after I lay claim to my voice again. 'How could this be? Bhrigu just met him!'

The lady was clearly beyond any kind or form of conversation. She kept repeating the lines over and over again in a fevered grip of hysteria. 'He was killed . . . I saw him . . . a shot in the dark . . . I. . .' Before I could make the head or tail of what was happening, she made an awkward dash towards my friend with as much speed as her arthritis riddled knees could allow and taking his hand in hers said in a voice that shook with unspoken horrors. '*Beta . . . beta . . .* has this got something to do with the investigation into the death of . . . of my son? Please . . . please . . . assure me that I have not been responsible for the death of Kishore! He . . . he was a very good boy. . . . A friend of Bali, too . . . I . . . would never forgive myself if I somehow led him to his doom!'

Bhrigu kept looking at her with the same feverish intensity as before and let her tug at him like he was some rag doll.

'Tell me please! Oh! How I wish I had never started this in the first place!'

I intervened to ask a few questions of my own that the lady's inquiry had helped create. 'But how did you guess that his death had something to do with our investigation? I am afraid we never spoke a word to that effect!'

She was breathless with her fear and kept staring hard at Bhrigu with a look that struggled between melancholy and guilt. I thought that my question would go unanswered this time around as well but never once taking her eyes off my friend, she said in a voice that competed with the bleating of an injured lamb, 'I . . . I just have this strong feeling. It's the same as I had experienced when my son died. I can feel it as strongly in my gut as if someone had declared it with hard evidence.'

'A woman's intuition is a wonder,' I managed to say.

Bhrigu was still standing with his hands tightly clasped in Jayanti Devi's, looking like an alien from another planet; a creature who had accidentally fallen out of his spaceship and was finding it hard to swallow the eccentric behaviour of the people of this planet. Jayanti Devi had stopped coaxing him but the desperate look in her eyes continued to ask a thousand questions.

I don't know when it happened but one moment Bhrigu was an intriguing ice sculpture with eyes of fire and the next he had thawed quite miraculously and was gently pressing the hands of the old lady with silent reassurance.

'I don't know anything myself, *Amma*,' he said gently. 'But I will answer your every question once the investigation is over. I must suffice to say that this has come as much a shock to me as it has to you.'

'First Bali and now Kishore!' she cried as her fear gave way to his soothing touch and her anger was quick to occupy that empty space. 'What had they got to do with my son's death? I don't understand! I was almost sure it was that Mutukal Kumar! Oh! I thought he would pay for his sins, now that you had taken over the investigation. But . . . but . . . my tragedy has compounded since then. I see people that I love suffering in the wake of my decision. Why is this happening?'

Bhrigu was silent for a few moments and in his eyes I could see the look of defeat, that he had carried from the moment he had returned after his session with Bal Kishore, getting pronounced with every second. His face had sagged in the light of the stress caused by the shock and he looked as if he had aged by many years.

'I have no answers to your questions as of now, *Amma*,' he said again and this time I could hear the faint note of conviction coming through his tired voice. 'But I will get them. The criminals will suffer for what they did. Their day of reckoning is near.'

28

'What were you doing at this time of the hour around Bal Kishore's house?' I asked as we were making rapid strides towards our destination in the moonlit darkness that added to the discomfort of the lump that was forming and dissolving in my throat at the morbid prospect that lay before me.

'I was on my way home from the *baniya's* shop,' Jayanti Devi replied, struggling to keep up with us. 'I take a short cut owning to my condition and the alley runs along Kishore's house. As I drew closer to his house, I heard a muffled shot and thought at first that it must be from one of the Diwali crackers that the children store for later use. But then I could clearly hear someone scream. I was just outside Kishore's backroom window and I swear it was he who screamed. I peeked through the window, straining my eyes, trying to look in the dim light and what did I see?!' she cried getting hysterical again. 'Bal Kishore was lying sprawled on the floor, his head a bloody mass!'

'Your timing was very bad,' I said and subsided as soon as Bhrigu's cold eye locked over mine.

Bal Kishore's house was as we had left it but in that full-moon night, there was an unmistakable element of romance that only horror fiction enthusiasts could identify with. The pale, eerie moonbeam lightly illuminating the façade of his small, box-shaped house was marking the site as a scene of grave tragedy. I could see our shifting shadows playing about the wall; nebulous at first but gaining in form and feature with every measured step that we took towards the house.

The small wooden door was locked from the inside and as it was already loose at its hinges; one firm push from my friend was enough to conquer our weak obstacle. Surreptitiously and saying a prayer to the Almighty, I entered the dingy room at the heels of my friend. Jayanti Amma trailed behind us. The feeble light from a low voltage bulb fixed just above the switchboard was imparting a dull pallor to the room and in the muted glow I could perceive melancholic shadows lurking behind the sparse furniture, further deepening the signs of a tragedy.

I noticed a single bed at the centre, groaning with the weight of the thick, dirty mattress spread over it and also a *surahi* kept on a stool beside it along with a couple of china clay tumblers. There was a plastic chair tossed carelessly aside, carrying a notepad and three use-and-throw pens. A rack affixed to the centre back of the room had been converted into a neat but humble shrine for Lord Ganesha. I could still detect the fragrance of incense sticks hanging in the air around it. The room was divided by a curtain into two and as we parted the dull green curtain to enter into the womb of the house, I saw a plastic table pushed alongside a wall and on the ground next to it rested the lifeless body of Bal Kishore. Not only was his head a bloody mess but the ground on which he lay had turned into a pool of crimson red.

We looked at the body of Bal Kishore with a painful cocktail of feelings swirling in our hearts. There was a pin-drop silence in the room. I could hear a rabid dog whining outside, sending ripples in the still night air with its pitiful cry for help . . . or had its sharp senses picked up the scent of a tragedy at hand? Who could say?

Bhrigu came out of his reverie first and remarked, 'One changes in death. I have seen quite a number of bodies in my days as a police officer but I still struggle in the presence of death.' His voice was low and I had to make out his words by observing the movement of his lips.

'Don't get unduly worked up,' I said, trying to uplift him and wondering at the same time that it was coming from me. 'In our line of work, deaths are inevitable and we have to deal with it.'

He still looked shaken to his roots but my words helped him enough to compose his nerves and begin his investigation. He bent low over the body, observed the forehead critically and said, 'He has been shot straight through the head.'

'I told you!' Jayanti Devi cried. Her face had drained of any colour and she was clutching my arm for support.

'But you said that you heard a scream,' said Bhrigu, looking at her with disappointment.

'I did!'

'But that's impossible. He was shot in the head. It must have been instant death. There was no way he had any time to twitch a finger, let alone scream.'

Jayanti Devi clutched my arm even tighter. '*Beta*, are you saying that I am lying to you?'

'No *Amma*' Bhrigu said curtly. 'But are you sure that you heard a scream? Was it not just psychological? Think hard.'

'I am telling you the truth!' she cried pathetically. 'I heard a scream!'

He looked at her for a moment or two as if weighing her testimony in his mind and then turned his attention back to the lifeless form of Bal Kishore. He looked intently in his eyes; those bloodshot eyes that were wide open with shock. If Bal Kishore had to spring back to life, the expression on his face would force him to stay rooted on the spot, transfixed with what he saw. It was then that the reason for the scream struck me! But even before I could voice it and earn brownie points, my friend beat me to the race.

'He must have seen his assassin,' he said. 'Grief numbed my senses but it was clear as a picture from his look. He knew he was about to get killed.'

'And hence he screamed before he was shot,' I said trying to salvage some of my wit.

Bhrigu carefully observed the grime-laden yellow plastic table that was carelessly thrust against the wall. I could clearly make out the smudged foot prints of Bal Kishore cutting through the dirt; his last footprint on the sands of time, preserved in the layer of dirt on a plastic table. Bhrigu moved closer to the wall and scanned the area with his sharp eyes. His eyes then trailed upwards and as I followed his gaze, I observed for the first time a narrow, rectangular area that had been made by removing four or five bricks. It must serve for a ventilator. Bhrigu now carefully stood on the plastic table and tried to peer through the ventilator. He looked through it for a few minutes and then he was back on his feet again.

'I can see traces of blood on the wall as Bal Kishore fell. The shot came through this ventilator,' he announced his verdict. 'I don't know why Bal Kishore was trying to look out through this ventilator,' he paused and then said again, 'Well, I don't know for sure but I have a theory that might be well founded.'

'And what's that?' I asked, out of breath.

'Bal Kishore was scared . . . scared beyond his wits and had locked himself up in this room. He was furtively looking through this ventilator to see if he wasn't being pursued. He was used to this routine for the past few days but this time his one mode of contact with the outside world brought him into the company of death.'

'But . . . if he had shut himself off from the world . . . how did you gain entry today?'

'I was a *Pundit*, Sutte. Remember? I was someone he just couldn't ignore.'

'Right . . . I forgot,' I mumbled.

'One another thing becomes clear from this tragic episode.' He coughed slightly and then resumed. 'Our assassin is a crack shot. I presume that he can hit even a moving target. One movement on Bal Kishore's part or rather his head and his time was up.'

He looked at me and said, 'Tomorrow morning, we will have to scan the area opposite this house. I want to know the vantage point from where the assassin took his shot. If we ascertain that, we will have him in the palm of our hands.'

'By pinpointing his vantage point? How?' I asked again.

'You will see, Sutte,' he said with a slow but painful smile. 'I will not let Bal Kishore's death go in vain.'

29

THOSE WHO DIG PIT
FOR OTHERS . . .

We informed Inspector Gyaan Gere about the incident and he, for once, was quick to respond to the situation. In the wee hours of morning he arrived on location with a cadaverous police surgeon to take over the body for autopsy.

The police surgeon whose name was Venkat Raju was a south Indian and how he managed to land in this corner of north India was more than I could imagine. His movements were precise and elegant and with one minimal gesture, he had removed the bullet that had been lodged in Bal Kishore's forehead.

'Our Raju Bhaiya is the pride of our police department,' said Inspector Gyaan Gere, puffing his chest. 'What we lack in funds, training, infrastructure, and intelligence, we make up with this great man here. He and I are the only jewels on the broken crown of the Rohtas police force.'

'Does he speak Hindi? I have heard that South Indians speak very little Hindi,' I asked, curious.

'He dabbles in Hindi but it is enough for us to understand; although he prepares his reports in perfect English.'

'From which part of South India is he? And how did he end up serving in this remote corner of Bihar?'

'He hails from a village in Kerela. I don't remember the complicated name.' He replied, beaming so brightly that he had almost displaced the heavy, tragedy stricken air of the room. 'As for how did he end up here? Well, that's something of a story in itself. He . . .' He was interrupted by my friend.

'Sir' he said addressing the burly man. 'We are progressing in our investigation. We have come to that point when we need to combine our forces yet again.'

'Sure, my boy, sure,' said the inspector, patting the shoulder of Bhrigu with his paw like hand. 'As I said before, I will be all too happy to cooperate.'

I was confused for a moment at this exchange. It seemed as if Bhrigu was the police here and Gyan Gere, the visiting detective. The Indigenous Santa Claus had nominated Bhrigu in his place and was more than happy to take the backseat. He was a man desperately in need of capable leadership; a leader who could show him the ropes and Bhrigu more than qualified for that position.

Bhrigu addressed the police surgeon next: 'Dr Venkat, I have a request to make of you. As I am investigating the case and have carte blanche on the matter from Gere sir here, I think I can count on your cooperation as well.'

The stringy man nodded his head that made me reminiscent of a robot I had seen in a Hollywood movie that moved his head in precisely the same fashion when it was asked a question.

'Sir . . . I don't want you to cover the body completely as is the custom. I want you to attach a drip bag and to all outward appearances it should look as if we are carrying an injured man to the hospital. You can discreetly take it to the autopsy house by following a detour, but no one beside yourself and the inspector should know about it.'

There came for a second a quizzical look in the doctor's eyes but it was gone as quickly as it had come and he soon became busy with his work. A true professional the man was.

With the help of two *hawaldars*, Dr Venkat Raju hoisted the body on a stretcher (following the instructions of Bhrigu), and loading it in a white minivan, was off to the autopsy house.

Bhrigu next took Gyaan Gere by his arm and they went out of the house together talking like old buddies. Clearly, there was a plan that my friend was trying to set into motion. I knew from his determined look that he had this mystery in the palm of his hand and knew exactly how to get to the bottom of it. The sudden gushes of enthusiasm that erupted from his melancholic mood also said a lot about his urgency to catch the killer. I knew intuitively that the mystery of Malthu's death was coming to its dramatic conclusion.

Sun was shining brightly over our heads when we began our search in the neighbourhood just opposite Bal Kishore's house to know the exact location from where the fatal gunshot had claimed a life. Bhrigu selected a line from where he thought a clear aim could be taken at Bal Kishore peering through the ventilator. There were seven mud houses roughly arranged on the line. When we called on the owners of those humble abodes, the simple villagers where so intimidated and over awed by our polished presence at their doorstep that they were very happy to wait on us and also offered us the best of their hospitality. We just asked them politely to let us use their roofs to which they promptly agreed. We observed that two of the roofs offered a perfect aim for the sniper. The first belonged to a family of eight: mother, father, and their six children. The other belonged to an old man of 70 who lived alone. When we inquired to the father about whether he had let a visitor in their home around ten at night, he shook his head in the negative. It had been a while since they had entertained any guests. The old man, though, was not quite so sure. He said that he is sound asleep at 10.00 p.m. and the door to his house is broken. Anyone could have entered his house with a drum beat and made himself at home and he wouldn't know. He wasn't much concerned about his security because he was a pauper and even thieves shy away from paupers. We now knew how easily the sniper had made use of the old man's infirmity and of his roof to get rid of his threat.

Bhrigu said later that he was now on his way to Chaudhary Manendra Singh's house. He told me to take my day off and that he would call once he had made further arrangements. I did not fight with him on our parting ways because the exhaustion of the night was creeping into my bones and I was feeling disoriented by the second.

The next two days went in a daze. I was feeling a little under the weather and hence Bhrigu went on his business alone. I tried to pressurise him into taking me along but he put his foot down. On the evening of the third day, he brightly marched into the room where I was reposing and said, 'I don't want you to miss this moment. I have laid the trap and now I want you by my side when the big fish gets caught in the net.'

He led me to the house of the elderly whose roof had been made an accessory to murder. I noticed we used a different route to reach his house and entered through the back door. It was twelve o'clock noon. I couldn't help but notice the stealth mode in which he had led me to my destination. I asked him to that effect, 'Why the secrecy?'

'You'll know soon,' he replied.

As we entered the mud house, I saw that the elderly man whose name I was to know was Bhawani Malto, had company. On the bamboo cot with him sat three men and as I looked at them closely, I realised that I already knew two of them. First was Inspector Gyan Gere dressed up in casual clothes. Not until this moment did I understand that I had underestimated the way he looked in his uniform. At that time, I had thought that he had set the standard on what to avoid when you had the weight equivalent to the combined weights of an elephant and a hippopotamus. The number one on that list was any job that required you to wear a uniform. Now, I think I might have to revise that. I will tell you now what you should avoid if you had the weight of the aforementioned. A red shirt that is so tight for your size that it refuses to come down beyond your chest, leaving others to feast their eyes on your gigantic stomach that heaves and rolls at the slightest movement on your part; a pair of cream-coloured jeans that are so loose that it can pass off as a skirt with no one the wiser. I stood there for a couple of minutes waiting for my pupils to adjust to the vision that they were seeing. After the initial shock wore off, my eyes took in the other companions. One was a tall, stringy man with eyes of a hawk and hair like the mane of a lion. I had never seen him before. The last one was the *hawaldar* who had helped us to conduct the interview with our seven rogues.

'So, what exactly are we going to do?' I asked after I had taken a seat on a low stool that was the only furniture in the house beside the cot.

'In a couple of hours, the clock will strike ten. Our vigil begins from that moment on.'

I was confused at his answer but refrained to ask any more questions. Clearly, the atmosphere in the room was all charged up. I couldn't have possibly imagined that this humble hut could transform in a heartbeat. It was still communicating its wretched state in the language of poverty but the pitiful tone now shook with occasional vibrations of thrill. The modest begging bowl that never saw more than an odd assortment of change was now surreptitiously hiding an exotic jewel.

The old man was nowhere to be seen. Bhrigu told me that he had been removed to another location for security reasons. We sat there in the dark, poorly lit room in silence. Our lean shadows played on the mud walls and I could see Gyan Gere flinch once at the movement of his own shadow. He was the one most stressed and I could see his brows darken with anticipation and fear. He was continuously mopping his brow with his handkerchief. The stringy man, whom I came to understand was the police inspector in whose jurisdiction the case fell, was sitting in a ramrod posture. He sat so still that it looked as if he was doing an impression of a statue. My friend Bhrigu restlessly paced about the room and kept checking his watch every now and then.

As soon as the clock struck ten, Bhrigu motioned us to move to the back of the house from where started a short flight of broken, uneven stairs that led to the roof. He looked about himself cautiously and then began climbing the stairs by pressing his foot to avoid making any sound. The three of us followed his lead silently. We had left Gyan Gere hidden but alert in the dark room to warn us with a cat call in which he was surprisingly good at, if he noticed any movement on the stairs. Once on the roof, I noticed that there was a huge cardboard box carelessly lying on the floor. On closer inspection, I saw that it once contained a big LCD TV. Bhrigu told me that the old man had brought it from one of his sojourns to Rohtas where his relative lived. He was an on and off salesman for the said brand and once he had allowed the old man to earn some money by carrying a TV to the customer. How its box got here was something to which the elderly made no remark. We bent on our knees and hid behind the box. The stringy man whose name was Pratap produced his automatic pistol as we sat behind our loose cover with bated breath for what was to come.

The moon was high in the sky, bathing us in its gentle luminescence. From our vantage point behind the flimsy cover, we commanded a clear view of the roof. My legs were developing cramps for sitting on my knees and I thought how lucky Gyan Gere was to escape this torture. We waited for what seemed like an eternity but in reality only an hour had passed. I was almost reaching the limits of my patience when I heard a cat yowling at a distance and every fibre in my muscles became taut with excitement. It was the signal for the homicidal intruder.

We could faintly hear muffled footsteps on the stairs; the sound getting louder with their ascent. In a few minutes, the silhouette of a tall man outlined sharply against the moonlight. At first I had trouble making him out and as I saw the look on the faces of my companions, I knew from the way they stared that they were struggling with visibility, too. As our eyes adjusted to the light, he had already gained access to the head of the roof and we could catch nothing but his broad, retreating back. He struck a perfect pose for a sniper and removed a long stick like thing from the inside of his long jacket. As I peered closely I saw to my horror that this was no ordinary stick but, as Bhrigu had foretold, a magnificent hunting rifle that glistened in the moonbeam. He aimed for the ventilator of Bal Kishore's house which shone brightly on the other side, but even before he could curl his fingers on the trigger, Pratap had charged towards him and had him in his power, his pistol pressing threateningly against the back of the sniper's head, he shouted, 'Hands behind your head!'

Bhrigu and I blew our covers soon afterwards and joined the inspector. As we moved round to face the man, the light reflected on his face to reveal a man I had seen once before but the diabolical expression he now wore perverted it past any recognition. It was none other than the *zamindar* Ghanshyam Singh.

CHAPTER 6

MEN BEHIND THEIR MASKS

30

CHANDANI

We stood there staring at the man who now cowered before us, defiant and defensive all at once. He was clearly struggling to come to terms with his condition. His eyes kept searching our faces, as if seeking some confirmation that we were neither the products of a phantom phenomenon nor of a trick played upon him by his tired mind. He struggled to speak but the shock had paralysed his tongue and no sound escaped as his lips parted time and again. We had hounded him into a corner and all that was now needed to be done was to give the man time to accept his predicament. When a full ten minutes had elapsed, the *zamindar*'s shoulders dropped slightly and the look of defeat clearly relaxed his painful expression, slowly working them into a state of blankness. Bhrigu knew that the man had now accepted his fate and it was now only a matter of time and the application of the right amount of pressure to get the truth out.

We were back at the Rohtas police station with Inspector Gyan Gere and our partners in the mission, Pratap and the *hawaldar*. Bhrigu had some work to attend to and hence he joined us an hour late. We hadn't just yet informed Chuadhary Manendra Singh about this terrible affair as the culprit was his dear friend. Ghanshyam Singh was locked in the same cell that had housed Bal Kishore a fortnight before. We took our seats around the table and as the *hawaldar* brought us a much needed cup of strong coffee, I asked my friend 'Now, can you tell me everything? How did you ensure that Ghanshyam Singh came to the roof a second time?'

Bhrigu took a sip from his cup and said, 'Can I not relax a little first? As you can see, the operation has tired me.'

I made no remark to this and he must have noticed the exasperation on my face that led him to change his mind. 'Okay, you win,' he said. 'Although I am surprised that you did not nag me to death!' He cleared his throat and began his narrative. 'As I saw how Bal Kishore had been killed, I came to the obvious conclusion that we were looking for a sniper of outstanding skill. I then decided to use this great talent of the man against him. Remember that when we reached Bal Kishore's house, we saw that the door was locked from the inside. It clearly meant that after pulling the trigger, the man, overconfident in his aim, took for granted that he had killed his target with one clean shot. Hence he did not care to check whether his victim was actually dead. His hubris rejected any chance of failure and in so thinking he made a fatal mistake that I exploited to my advantage. I arranged with Inspector Gere to look as if Bal Kishore was just injured and not dead. Next, we located the roof from where the aim had been taken. I then called for the *Sarpanch* to ensure that he circulates the news in the village that Bal Kishore had been slightly injured by a stray bullet from an unknown madman who had fled the scene and most likely, the village, too. Kishore had been taken to the hospital and as he did not sustain any serious injury, he had returned to his house after a day of recuperation. We started keeping vigil at the house of the old man thinking that once the sniper got the whiff of this news, he would try again to kill Bal Kishore in the same way as before. He took Bal Kishore's and the police's simplicity for granted a second time and thus sealed his own doom. I was confident that he would operate only in the visibility of the moonlight as he had done before and hence we had to wait for a full-moon night. That evening when I called for you, it was a *Purnima*, and therefore, I knew that the killer would set to work on that very night. I had told the inspector to keep the lights on in Bal Kishore's house and as the sniper took his position, waiting for a glimpse of his target, we nabbed him.'

'So Ghanshyam Singh could handle a hunting rifle at his age?'

'It's in his blood and comes to him as a reflex. Ghanshyam Singh is an expert hunter, a skill he had learned from his father in the days when hunting was a religion in powerful feudal circles.'

There was silence for a couple of minutes and I could hear the clock ticking distinctly ahead us on the wall. A lizard played hide and seek with it and I am thankful that my fortitude allowed me to bear the disgusting sight with aplomb. Normally, I wouldn't, even in my wildest dreams have allowed to coexist with this revolting reptile. The low, groaning sound of the ceiling fan, as usual, did nothing to provide respite from the blazing hot weather.

Gyan Gere had collapsed into his reclining chair and was on the threshold of falling into a deep, dreamless slumber. He kept looking fixedly at Bhrigu as if insuring he had nothing further to say. At that point, I saw my friend fumbling inside the pocket of his Kurta. After a struggle for a couple of seconds, he drew forth a book. I wondered whether this was the time for him to indulge in his reading habits.

'Ghanshyam Singh would be called for questioning shortly,' he said, placing the dirty, crumpled book on the table. 'He would try to justify his actions and make us sympathetic towards his conduct. Trust me; he is a very persuasive man. He may very well trick us into believing that he was the real victim. Hence, just after we arrested him on the roof, I made my way to his house to search for something I was very sure he had concealed in his house. Something so incriminating that he could do nothing but accept his guilt. I could enter and search his house without interference as they already knew that their master had been arrested and I was there to investigate on behalf of the police. I thought I would have to search the house with a fine-toothed comb to get to that evidence, but was pleasantly surprised when his wife gifted it to me as soon as she knew who I was. The woman looked as tortured as a lamb before it is slaughtered. She said and I quote—'Take this diary and deliver him from evil. I could not help my daughter when she was alive as I was scared before but not anymore.' This diary holds the key to all our questions.'

We looked closely at the forlorn, gloomy little diary sitting awkwardly at the centre of the table. The black velvety covering had changed colour to a dirty grey; the pages were soiled and looked like old parchment. It was this innocent diary that had somehow been responsible for three deaths and a coma. Bhrigu gently turned the cover and on the first page were written in beautiful, cursive writing the words 'Chandani, my friend.' Apparently, Chandani was the name that Meenakshi used for her diary. I know that when people write personal diaries they often do so by fondly naming it so that they could easily share their inmost thoughts with it, like one does with a dear and precious friend. On the first five pages was written simple but heartfelt poetry on school, mother, and life. The poems were composed by a child but the depth of feeling that was conveyed by those straight, unadorned lines melted my heart and I could feel my face getting flushed with the warmth they carried. On the next eight pages were drawn beautiful pictures of goats, buffaloes, a rough sketch of a younger and happier-looking Ghanshyam Singh, his wife, the fields and her house, her coterie of friends, her school, and a beautiful rainbow rising over a well. The confessions to the diary started after the picture of the hypnotic rainbow. It ran like his—

> 'My dear Chandani,
>
> Today, I am a student of class ninth. Wow! Father says that I am really growing fast. He says that soon it will be time for them to marry me off to a prince charming. I am so angry with him when he says such things. I told him squarely that I want to study and become something good, someone good. . . I don't want to marry ever! He asked me about what I wanted to become . . . and I said I was confused . . .

I have not decided just yet . . . My teacher tells me about these wonderful profesions. . . (It was then struck off by one clear line) professions, I cannot decide which one to pick . . .

Got to go Chandani . . . Mother's calling for breakfast . . . Bye!'

The next entry was after three months and it said—

'Dear Chandani,

I think I have finally decided what I want to become when I grow up. I want to be a social worker just like Suman *didi* who comes to our village every month to provide the poor students with books and stationary. She is a very sweet person and her passion to do good, really inspires me. My teacher applauded me when I told him that I had found my purpose in life. I thought father would be happy to hear it as he is my role model and I want him to be proud of me. I ran to him with the news and waited with delight to see the expression on his face. But Chandani, he wasn't as ecstatic as I hoped he would be. He said that of all the paying careers, why would I chose a profesion, (again it was struck of by a straight line) profession which hardly qualified to be called one? He said that social worker is just another word for unemployed. When he saw that I was confused by his outlook, he tried to cheer me up by saying that he just wanted what was best for his daughter. He said that he could send me to any prestigious school in the country and that I shouldn't think like the poorer students in my class. Their fate was sealed by their birth but I wasn't like them. I had the money and the power to mend my fate to what I wanted it to be. I vaguely understand what he was trying to say and I think that he wasn't wrong either but . . . but . . . why do I feel this horrible pit in my stomach? Why do I find myself rebelling against the very idea? I hope this bad feeling would soon pass.'

The next addition was after eight months.

'Dear friend,

I have decided that I am my own person and that however much I love my father, I cannot let him dictate my life. I respect him a lot but on this matter I am afraid I will have to put my foot down. I know that he loves me a lot and the only way I can show him that I am really passionate about what I am talking about is by proving to him that I have the qualities to bring a change. I have decided that I will form a committee with a handful of my friends that will look after the interests of the illiterate villagers who are exploited every day because of their lack of education and cunning. My team will look after them and will be made responsible for them. I have decided to call the committee 'The Guardians'. Once father witnesses how we are capable of doing what we say, he would relent and give me his blessings. Of that I am very confident.'

The next five pages had been compromised to paste photographs of village men and women who had been helped in some way or the other by 'The Guardians'. Their colourful picture was posted on the left side of the page and the corresponding story on the right. I also saw a group photo of Meenakshi with her community of helpers. She was the girl sitting confidently in the centre. Her kind, bright black eyes, shining countenance and a delicate, sensitive mouth were proofs to her strong, determined but gentle nature. She exuded the calm assurance, silent strength and unassailable dignity of a born leader.

The next addition to the diary came after six months and it read—

'My dear Chandani,
    Our work is gathering speed. We have been successful in helping many poor villagers regarding their diverse problems. Kachani Devi, age 39, was finding it difficult to protect her farm cabbages from the locusts. The insecticide was way too costly for her. Her income was dwindling

as cabbage selling is her only occupation. She brought her problem to us and my team took immediate steps. I told her that the government had subsidised the sale of insecticides for marginal farmers and she could now get it very cheap from a store nearby. We went with her to the store to see to it that she gets the correct price and is not cheated by the unscrupulous, greedy merchants. I am very happy that our efforts are paying off. Educating farmers and local producers about their rights and simultaneously making them aware of the several government schemes run for them has helped these poor people from much distress.

P.S.—I hope Father would now see that my work is as important as the paying ones.'

The next few pages were again plastered with the camera conscious pictures of villagers who had been helped in some way or the other by the committee. The diary was serving the dual function of recording the memoirs of a young adult and documenting the progress of her work.

The next piece was added after three months.

'Chandani,
      Today I met a man called Mahesh Yadav who I think is suffering from some sort of delusion. He came to me looking for

help and when I asked about his problem, he related to me a bizarre cock and bull story involving my own father! According to this madman, my father has somehow been responsible for the disappearance of his younger brother. One day, he went to the fields to collect the harvest and never returned! At first I scolded him soundly for spreading such vile stories about a very respectable man of this village and then I suggested that the only help that I think he needed was to see a good psychatrist (it was then struck of with one clear line) psychiatrist. He took offence at my levity in the most ungentlemanly manner and said that many people of this village had lost their young sons to my father's illegal operation, whatever that was and due to the fear of their lives they have not dared come out into the open. Everyone in this village who has a bonny son reaching adulthood, lives in the fear that one fateful day he will disappear from the face of this earth leaving no breadcrumbs on the trail behind. I lightly asked the clearly deranged person about how he could be so sure of my father's hand in the involvement and he laughed. He laughed hoarsely. Another sign of mental deterioration. He said that he 'put two and two together'. To my next question as to what the illegal operation was, he gave me a long look and quietly retreated. This episode made me realise that in my line of work, running against such loafers who have nothing better to do with their time than to indulge in poor gossip was certainly a problem.

He gave me a good laugh though.'

After two months—

Chandani,

After that Mahesh Yadav incident, a few villagers came to me corroborating his outrageous story. They said that Yadav had lost his marbles due to the disappearance of his brother but the crux of his story was legit. My father, they said, is involved in a scandalous operation involving the illegal transportation of coal from Senduwar to Palamau. They said that he was hand in glove in other smuggling operations, too. He recruited youngsters as bonded labourers and worked their hide off at merely a pittance in such smuggling activities. I was shocked to my core and reeled at the spot. My mind could not process what it was hearing. My dear father . . . a smuggler? How could that possibly be? I know he wasn't supportive of my work but I have always known him to be a kind man and even though I was but an adopted daughter he has done everything for me that any loving father would. It is impossible to believe them. If a person such as my father can be a criminal, then any good person walking on this earth can very well be a criminal, too.

The villagers said that they had kept their mouths shut all this time to protect themselves as my father and the mafia he works for are ruthless and could easily make them disappear, too. But now as they see me, his own daughter working night and day for the betterment of people like them, they could not help but approach me for the biggest problem plaguing their lives in the form of my own father. They felt that as I was his beloved daughter I could coax him to release their loved ones from labouring forcefully in the smuggling operation. I write about this ghastly episode with trembling fingers, a throbbing heart and a mind that has become numb with the blunt force trauma caused by this terrible news. I hope against hope that this be nothing more than a misunderstanding and the fog of confusion clears before the sun rises again tomorrow.'

After a month and a half—

'Chandani,

I have struggled for the past one month to come to terms with the fact that my father is indeed a criminal who has been responsible for ruining many lives. My heart rebels against this, even in the face of concrete proof but my brain has to acquiesce to the stark, naked truth. It's hard to believe that only a month and a half ago, I was so close to my father . . . he was my pillar, my strength, my idol . . . despite our small altercation regarding this work, I always looked up to him . . . but . . . now I look at him and he feels like a total stranger . . . I miss my mother, too, who I still love dearly but . . . but . . . how can I go to her for comfort when I see how proudly she flaunts her beautiful *Mangalsutra* and adorn herself with jewels in the name of my father? How can I make her my confidante when I see her glowing with the sheen of my father's affection? How can I? The truth will take all happiness away from her but . . . but . . . what am I to do then? I am sick at heart Chandani and sometimes life seems such a burden . . . It is as if an earthquake has shifted the very ground on which I was confidently standing. How I long to escape the misery, the pain, the injustice of life . . . How I wish I was never born . . .'

Three months later—

'Chandani,

I have met a man called Vidwait. He has come to visit a distant relative who lives in the village. He is a very kind man. I met him at the school when he came to see a student off who happened to be his cousin. I don't know why but from the moment I saw him it felt as if I had known him for ages. He looked so familiar. He, too, was staring at me from a distance. When I passed the school gate, he introduced himself like a gentleman. Chandani! He is wonderful! He is not only handsome but very soft-spoken too! My life has been in a turmoil these past months as I still struggle to accept the truth about my father and with every passing day, the distance between us keeps growing . . . For the first time after that incident, the dark days of confusion and chaos have cleared to admit a beam of sunlight. I am glad for this respite . . .'

With every addition that I read, I became more and more uncomfortable under my own skin; the same discomfiture that possesses you when you unwittingly walk into the most private moments of a person . . . The struggle within the mind of this young girl, standing on the cusp of a breakdown, was almost too much to bear and I gently moved my head to a side, unable to continue with the perusal. Bhrigu was quick to notice my plight. He looked at me with eyes that shone with sincere emotion, almost mirroring mine. Well, whatever the differences in our natures might be, we both fundamentally shared the characteristics of an empathetic human being. Our group had become unsettled, too. The passionate words flowed from the book and saturated the very air that we breathed, threatening to suffocate us. I knew that if I had the choice, I wouldn't have liked to continue with my unpleasant task.

The next addition was after fifteen days—

Chandani,

I have a feeling that my father suspects that I know everything about his nefarious activities. For the past one week, his attitude has completely changed towards me. He no longer asks me how my day went and he no longer inquires about my health. Almost always he used to come to my room at night to wish me goodnight but he has stopped doing so in the past one week. When I tried to talk to him over breakfast, he gave me curt replies and I felt as if he was deliberately trying to tell me to leave him alone. Mother also notices his coolness towards me and tries to make it up for him by showering me with her love and care. As I see closely, I can clearly make out the creases on her gentle, beautiful face that weren't there a few months before. I know she knows nothing but her female intuition is strong and she can very well sense that something's amiss. As she cannot quite put a finger on it, she is all the more perplexed and troubled. How I blame myself for her pitiful condition! How I wish I could undo everything! Father is not making matters any easier for me. I have sometimes even caught him looking at me with such hate in his eyes that I fear he is waiting to make his move. Chandani, I feel as if slowly and steadily my father and I have begun to fall into the roles of adversaries and I very much fear that the day of our clash sits snugly in the future. . .

P.S.—I am thankful to god that in these troubled times, where I fear my own shadow, a great guy like Vidwait is my ally and friend. I now meet him frequently and we share so much! I am thankful that apart from you, I now have a person in my life with whom I feel so loved and secure . . .

After two months—

Chandani,

My worst fears have come true. My father confronted me yesterday and threatened me not to associate myself with the villagers. He also said that if I did not put a stop to my 'nonsense work', there would be dire consequences. Chandani, it was so frightening to see the change that has been wrought in him. I could scarcely recognise the man towering over me with red, angry eyes as the loving one that I always knew my father to be. His face was contorted with rage and hatred so supreme that I thought he would explode any second. How can anyone change so? I kept pleading my case and he kept repeating one line over and over again. 'Leave the nonsense behind,' he said, 'and everything will be as before.' But will it, Chandani? Will it? How can I go on living with the burden of the truth that I now know? How can I? I am not that person and father knows it too and that's why he's so angry at me. . .

He has also come to know of my meetings with Vidwait and forces me not to see 'that pauper's son' ever again. I was quite in the face of his explosion that was long overdue but I will fight back. I know my time will come. As I said before, he will not decide the course of my life or my actions. No, he won't.

After one month—

Chandani,

The past month has seen a cold war developing between me and my father which is threatening to freeze any warmth of feeling that we ever had for each other. I know my father is expecting me to break this ice by apologising to him for refusing to obey his orders, but he knows as well as I do that I am made of sterner stuff. It's ironical when I think that it was *I* who was expecting a full explanation from him regarding how the villagers have gotten confused and mixed matters up . . . but his cold and morose behaviour has only helped to prove beyond all doubt that the poor people were telling the truth. I sometimes feel that if I wasn't his adopted daughter, he would have wasted no time in sealing my fate with them. But I don't know how much longer I'll be able to enjoy this privilege as his contempt for me gets stronger with every passing day, replacing his love little by little with pure hate . . . I can see it in the way he turns his back towards me if I happen to be in his vicinity and hurriedly sums up a light moment with my mother if I happen to call in on her. He is displacing me from his life and it's only a matter of time when this irreversible process gets completed . . . leaving me all alone again . . .

P. S. Thank God I have Vidwait to share my troubles with . . . He and I have really grown very fond of each other and . . . and I may very well have already fallen deeply in love with him. . .

The last poignant entry was eighteen days later. It ran like this—

Chandani,

I . . . I can't believe he could do something as terrible as this! I knew I had started to repulse him but to take that out on Vidwait! How brutal is that! I have no doubts now that my father is a monster in disguise. He could see that he could not harm me owning to the love my mother bore for me . . . and the one person we both are deeply attached, too. I, too, tried to turn a blind eye to everything . . . I suppressed my character . . . I shared in his sins by keeping quiet in the face of his atrocities out of concern for my mother but . . . but . . . he did not leave the matter alone. He just could not tolerate that I was helping his poor victims by doing everything that I could to find the whereabouts of their loved ones. I did not seek to destroy him! I was just trying to help! But his inflated sense of self-importance could not digest that . . . His iron fist had to destroy everyone who did not throw the gauntlet in the face of his tyranny. . . . He could not touch me and so he turned towards the one person that meant the world to me . . . Vidwait. You know Chandani; his henchmen beat the poor man to the inch of his life! We rushed him to the district hospital where his life hangs in the balance. . . . Oh! If something happens to him. . . . The thought makes me shudder with an unimaginable fear. . .

My father will now have to answer to his every sin. I was quiet for far too long but the unrelenting din of injustice has chased every peaceful thought away from my mind. Only vengeance can now still my restless soul. . . . I will see to it that he gets his just desserts.

P.S.—A room in our house is always under a lock and key. Only my father has access to this room. He enters it surreptitiously and leaves it stealthily . . . I now know that that room must serve as his office for illegal work. I have decided to break into that room as I know for a certainty that I would find proof of his chicanery hidden somewhere in its mysterious folds. I know a villager called Rama who can pick locks. It's now a matter of time that this vile snake's cover is blown and the world sees him for what he truly is. . .

On the next page was clumsily posted a page out of a file and as we looked closer we found that it was a balance sheet outlining transactions that involved crores of rupees. The money was paid to the concerned parties for the 'Supplication of coal', 'Supplication of cheap labour', and 'Supplication of tendu leaves'. It was a black page out of a black book where the date of operation and distribution of profits to the said parties was meticulously maintained and the balance sheets rapidly approved by the signature of the accountant who was none other than Ghanshyam Singh. The evidence of his complicity in illegal work and thus his subsequent fate was duly stamped and sealed.

The valiant Meenakshi had been successful in her mission of implicating her father and the cost that she paid, a terrible cost that was never mentioned in any ledger . . . was her own life. . .

31

A Full Circle

Ghanshyam Singh sat facing us on the chair, as straight as an arrow. He very much resembled an old violin whose strings had been tightened to the breaking point. The fibres in the muscles of his face where also painfully strained under the burden that threatened to crush his mind. He looked almost at the point of a mental breakdown but I suppose his hubris prevented him from openly exhibiting his pathetic state. He kept staring into space with blank, slit like eyes as if he was just bodily present with us but his mind was far removed from his physical existence, wandering by itself, looking for a sign of hope to cling to. I had a suspicion that he might be visiting the time when his world came crashing down about his ears as he retaliated with a fury, a blind fury that destroys everything in its path . . . his home . . . his life . . . his own daughter . . . The most important question that was now left to settle was that how much his actions were prompted by passion and how much of it was cold calculation. The more the scales tipped towards the latter, the less became the chances of his salvation.

'I know you are not in the mood to talk,' Bhrigu said, trying to pull him out of his trance-like state into the present. 'So, let's cut a deal. Let me do the talking and you, for once, listen.'

Ghanshyam Singh's eyebrows went up a barely perceptible degree but apart from that there was no visible change whatsoever.

'You said before that you were a man who understood 'responsibility' and did everything in your power to protect what was yours. What was yours? Tell me? The fiefdom whose borders where slowly receding or the title of a landlord that was leaving you with your land? You thought it was your responsibility to do everything in your power to hold on to your status and hence you joined hands with the local mafia. Didn't you? You kept justifying your actions and propitiating your conscience by telling yourself that you were doing it to safeguard your inheritance . . . you were so lost in your own perverted ideals that the lives of innocent men became just a thing that you traded for your selfishness. The road to crime is very slippery. Once you put your first foot, it does the rest for you; it carries you smoothly to your doom. You took a small step by illegally transporting coal and ended up doing everything that was as black as your soul that now hides behind your polished exterior.' Bhrigu's face had become flushed with this impassioned speech. He took a deep breath and then began. 'You became so lost and disillusioned that the life of your daughter whom you loved and cherished became insignificant when she threatened to destroy your house of black cards. You forced her to take her own life and then took a sigh of relief. But when the past threatened to resurrect itself, you went on doing what you did best and that was removing everyone who stood in the path of you and your grandeur. Well, from what I see, I don't find anything grand about you; I just see a bent, pathetic old man who lost his way and his head. Not very grand is it?'

The heat of the words thawed the ice as Ghanshyam Singh came out of his trance and looked at Bhrigu with eyes spitting fire and I was afraid he would strike him hard, but to my relief, he just glared at him for a couple of seconds and fell back into his comatose state again.

'Just to bring you up to speed,' said Bhrigu, now addressing us. 'I would now tell you why and how this tragedy of epic proportions unfolded. It was this man's greed that ignited the fuse which led to the conflagration.' He threw one look of contempt towards the statue of a man and then resumed. 'Meenakshi wrote in her last addition of how she succeeded in procuring a solid piece of evidence that could help prove beyond all doubts that her father worked for the mafia. The story ends at that despairingly jubilant note and I will now reveal what happened next. Meenakshi, at that time, was under the powerful, almost hypnotic grip of fury and she had decided that while going to school the other day, she would take the evidence to the local police station. But her plans never materialised as Ghanshyam Singh entered his office that very night and quickly discovered that an important page from his ledger book was missing. Meenakshi was unlucky here as she happened to take a page on which her father was currently working out the transactions. Had she taken an old one, of last year's perhaps, no one would have been the better. Well, on discovering his loss, a mad Ghanshyam Singh assumed at once that his daughter must have had something to do with its disappearance. He violently shook his daughter out of her fitful sleep in the middle of the night and demanded that she immediately return the page back to him. To this, Meenakshi feigned total ignorance. Ghanshyam Singh was already simmering with anger for what he thought to be her daughter's betrayal and now in the face of such defiance, he lost all restraint and slapped her hard across her face. To add to the poor girl's misery, he locked her up in her room and said that she could only earn her freedom by returning what was rightfully his. The strained cord that still existed between the father and daughter snapped with this last terrible pull. Meenakshi, when her anger had subsided, was considering in the dead of the night whether she should turn on her father and as she remembered the years of his love and affection, her resolution surely and steadily dissolved. This bitter spat with him renewed the hurt and resentment she was feeling for the past couple of months and as was natural she thought of her only source of comfort—Vidwait. With the thought of Vidwait, she was once again reminded of his pitiful condition and her benumbed bruises spiked with an intolerable pain. In that weak moment, it appeared to her that the root cause of everyone's misery was her own father and as her anger crossed the Rubicon, her hatred devoured her whole. With her skin burning with the fever of contempt, she looked desperately around for a means of escape and finally her eyes rested on the ventilator that occasionally shone into prominence in the dark room by reflecting the lightening outside. It was a space narrow for a girl of her size but somehow she wriggled herself free from her captivity and landed awkwardly on terra ferma.'

'That night, rain was pouring hard and strong and the ground that she touched was slippery with the stagnation of rain water. Despite the challenges of an unwholesome weather, she kept on running with a manic energy until she found a clearing. I must inform you that she had brought her diary along. I guess in her state of mind she just wanted to hide the diary someplace where a villager could easily find it and thus reveal the truth about her father to the world. As the fields of the village where regularly ploughed and sowed she thought it to be a matter of time that the diary was finally discovered. At last, she found a place to her satisfaction and buried the diary in a shallow grave that she had dug with her bare hands. As her work was completed, the torture that she had endured came rushing back to her as an avalanche and crushed every reason for her to continue living. Before leaving the room, she had pocketed the sleeping pills of her mother that were always stocked in Meenakshi's room. These she took in full and within an hour her soul was finally light and free from the agony again.'

We were listening with rapt attention as Bhrigu called for a glass of water, sipped noisily and then began his narrative again. 'The very next day, they discovered the body but even though Ghanshyam Singh combed the house in search of the elusive page, it did not reveal itself. How could it? As he and his men were searching the house inside out, the little diary was lying in its shallow grave, dark and distant from prying eyes.'

'Meenakshi's intention was clear but what she did not know was that the land she was submitting her diary to was no ordinary land but that of Jiyashree, the mythical witch. In the night, she must have walked right past the board. It was an alleged haunted site and hence no one came to venture there. Thus her diary remained in its resting place until the gold hunt began and greed overcame phantom fear.'

'Malthu was the one who, after being egged on by his friends, arrived first at the haunted site and discovered the nuggets of gold but nobody knew that he had found something else, too. It was the diary of Meenakshi that was sleeping undisturbed for a long time. Had he been any ordinary boy, he would have thrown the revolting looking thing and gathered the shining trinkets instead but as he was a special kid and was gifted with a childlike curiosity; unique and endearing, he was overjoyed at the sight of this old diary with its beautiful pictures within. For him, it was much more precious than the worthless golden scraps. He shared the nuggets with the world but hid his precious diary from everyone but his mother.'

'He was very possessive about his lucky find and spent hours poring over it, trying to understand the beautifully crafted words written with a feminine flourish. Needless to say, he could not understand much but going over the lines gave him a certain pleasure shared by the keeper of secrets when they have the luxury of knowing something that is hidden to the world. Intrigued and inspired, he even tried to jot down his own ill assortment of words which you would have found had you cared to look at the last pages. No Sutte, don't interrupt me by looking at it now. It is most distracting. Now, as days changed into months and the rush that had come with his little adventure began to subside, he felt the yearning to share the delights of his find with someone whom he trusted and loved. After his mother, Malthu was close only to one person, Bali. So, he ran to his uncle and with his face beaming with the exultation of a victor, showed him his coveted prize. Bali was more than happy to feign interest to please his nephew whom he genuinely liked but as he began turning the pages, colour drained from his face as he realised the insidious potential of what his hands held. You see, Bali already knew everything about Meenakshi and how she had secreted away the black page to oblivion. He at once understood that where Ghanshyam Singh had failed he had succeeded.'

'But how did he come to know about everything?' asked Pratap and I secretly congratulated him on voicing my question.

'Isn't it obvious?' replied Bhrigu. 'He worked for Ghanshyam Singh; not as a mill worker as he told us in the interview but as his guard and henchman.'

'Oh!' I ejaculated.

'Yes. He was very happy at the prospect of getting rewards from the landlord once he presented this gift to him and he tried hard to borrow it from Malthu for a day or two. Had the boy done the needful, he would still be alive but with the obduracy of a child who cannot bear to be parted with its most precious toy, he refused to oblige his uncle. He snatched the diary from his hands and ran in the direction of his house. On the wings of desperation, Bali gave him a good chase and soon overtook his nephew. He tried to wrestle the diary from Malthu's hands but he protected it against his bosom and nothing that Bali did, help him pry the diary from his interlocked arms. Exasperated and exhausted by his futile effort, he lost his temper and pushed the boy violently to the ground. I assume it was an accident but Malthu fell at an awkward angle that caused a severe injury to his cervical vertebrae and within a couple of minutes he was dead.'

A hush had fallen over the group and in the overpowering silence we could distinctly hear our rapid breathing, trying to keep up with the breathless pace of this tragic story. We kept looking at Ghanshyam Singh almost as if he were a celebrity out of a motion picture. The man was still a living statue with all of his life concentrated in the smouldering of his eyes.

'Bali checked his pulse and after finding none he so panicked that he forgot all about the diary and ran towards the security of his home, away from the scene of the accident. In a few hours, a passing villager discovered the body and somewhere, a loafer gossiped about the witch punishing Malthu for riling her resting place. As is the destiny of rumours, it soon became common knowledge that Malthu had succumbed to the dead witch's black magic.'

'When the danger had passed, Bali's fear of being caught was overcome and he soon became thirsty for the rewards and recognition he would receive once he favoured Ghanshyam Singh with what he had sought for so long. He figured that if he had ever a shot at finding at again, it would be at Jayanti Devi's house but the question was how to search her hut? She would become suspicious if he boldly attempted such a thing. He racked his brains and soon came up with a plan. He disguised his intentions with fake affection and started showing up at Jayanti Devi's house inquiring after her and looking after her health. Within a month, he had earned her full trust. Now he borrowed some money by selling a few of his possessions and advised Jayanti Devi to shift to a better house that he had arranged for her. He also asked her to leave all her furniture and belongings behind as they would always evoke the memory of her beloved son. The idea behind this devious plan was to search the house thoroughly once the old lady had vacated it.'

'So did he find what he was looking for?' I asked despite myself.

'I was coming to it, Sutte,' he said with a hint of exasperation he always kept handy for me. 'Yes, he did find the diary. It was concealed in a colourful box in some obscure part of the hut. Once he had discovered what he thought was his employer's unholy grail, he ran to hand it over and earn his reward. Ghanshyam Singh was glad indeed and in return he gave Bali two things. First, his well-earned reward, and second, a warning that he would lose his life if he dared let his tongue, slip the contents of the black page to anyone else.'

'The matter, again, had the scope of ending then and there with no one the better, but it is said that the dead have a way of rising from the grave and demanding justice. Jayanti Devi, Malthu's mother, started having a strong suspicion; an intuition, if you will, that her son had not died in an accident but at the hands of someone she knew and hated. She suspected that the greedy and unscrupulous Mutukal Kumar was somehow responsible for her loss. She had no one to share her fears with, when I knocked at her door. You already know the rest, Sutte. You can brief our friends about that interview later on.'

'Do you remember that Jayanti Devi had a strong suspicion of someone watching her? The reason why she did not divulge anything concerning her relatives? Well, she was right but it was not her bete noir Mutukal Kumar who was trying to eavesdrop on our conversation but Bali. From the moment he had accidentally caused Malthu's death, he had become paranoid with guilt. He irrationally thought that Jayanti Devi might suspect something any day and hence had fallen into the habit of stealthily following her around. His fears escalated to mania when he heard that the old woman was enlisting the help of a detective in solving the case of the mysterious death of her son. He panicked, ran to his house, and shut himself in. You see, Bali was a mentally weak person. He worked as one of Ghanshyam Singh's henchmen, owning to the recommendation of a friend but he never really appreciated the dangers lurking behind the profession. He preferred to hide behind his other colleagues and let them do the dirty work on his behalf. This arrangement worked and he got to have a decent living, too, but he was always in awe of the *lathi* bearing, fearless strongmen who protected the *zamindar* and always thought what a powerful man he must be to command such a force of brutes. The day he went to collect his reward was the day he actually got to meet the man and his menacing manner had chilled his spine in a moment. He swore never to bother him again.'

Bhrigu again had a sip of water and continued, 'The fact that the case was being reopened exposed his raw nerve and the fear of getting caught took him in its powerful grip. He wanted to warn Ghanshyam Singh about the matter as in a way, they had become confederates in the same crime but the mortal fear of the man kept him in check. After many troubled, sleepless nights he finally decided on what looked like the only course of action left for him to pursue. He was going to take the matters in his own hands and somehow try to nip the matter in its bud.'

'Sutte, you remember the threatening note on the leaf and the dead bird? Well, that was the handiwork of Bali. It seems that his only ally in his difficult time was the dead witch, with whose help he tried to scare us away, but sadly our rationale defeated the man-witch team.'

I remembered the ghastly incident that had scared the wits out of me. Clearly, the combination of a morbid specimen of a dead crow and a leaf, expressing the less-than-friendly intent of a popular witch was a trifle more than my weak nerves could handle. It was a relief now to know that the alleged preternatural occurrences were just the machinations of a troubled man who himself was half scared to death.

Bhrigu was still explaining. 'I then focused my attention on my last suspect Bali. By what Jayanti Devi had told me about the circumstances following her son's death, I already half suspected him but after the interview was over, I was fairly certain that Bali had somehow propagated the sad affair. (I asked the reason and he said he would give the particulars later.) That night when we left, Bali was very troubled. His nerves were frayed and he could barely breathe out of fright. He was scared less of us and more of what would happen to him, lest the truth got out and our dear friend in trance here, *zamindar* Ghanshyam Singh, took him to task. His fear reached its lofty height when the very next morning, his best friend Bal Kishore, paid him a visit. He came to ask after the health of his sick friend and also to deliver the news that the landlord wanted to see him presently. Bal Kishore worked odd jobs for the *zamindar* and he sometimes used the lad as his messenger. Bali almost panicked after hearing this news as he thought it must have had something to do with the investigation. Out of sheer nervousness, he told everything that he knew to Bal Kishore and appealed to him to talk to the *zamindar* and try to convince him of the fact that he did not divulge any of his secrets regarding the black page. Bal Kishore was a good-natured lad and he readily accepted Bali's entreaties. You see, Bali wrongly suspected that Ghanshyam Singh knew all about the affair. He had some other work that he wanted Bali to handle. It was through Bal Kishore that he came to know of everything. Meanwhile, Bali's mental strength finally gave way and he fell into a peaceful coma after many a frightful night.'

I glanced sideways at Ghanshyam Singh. He was still as stiff as a rod. I felt that if I lightly touched him, he would trip over like a statue. I was sometimes having trouble coming to terms with the fact that the depraved villain in the story was the old, broken man sitting right before us.

'We then came upon the scene,' Bhrigu was saying, 'and I subsequently figured out the involvement of Bal Kishore. Ghanshaym Singh knew that the poor lad had been caught and detained for questioning and hence he was on his case. He was now a threat far too great for the landlord to be allowed to live. You remember, Sutte, when Bal Kishore saw Ghanshyam Singh as we met outside the police station, he ran like fifty ferocious dogs were behind him? Well, he was scared as he knew the dangerous predicament he had unwittingly landed himself into. He was now in mortal fear of his life. He ran home and tried to barricade himself from that terror. He only checked on the outside world through the ventilator which eventually got the better of him. If I wasn't a Pundit, he wouldn't have let me in too.'

As he paused for a breath, I knew that he had concluded the story and as the four of us sat there making a half circle, shrouded in the shadows of intrigue, Ghanshyam Singh's tremulous voice rose from the forgotten chair on which he sat and said—'Meenakshi was my daughter. I loved her but . . . she . . . she . . . she destroyed me. . .'

32

THE PIECES FALL TOGETHER

'She did not destroy you,' said Bhrigu looking at him with eyes spitting fire. 'You destroyed yourself; you and no one else. You cannot assuage your guilt anymore by repeating your lies to yourself. You tortured a poor girl beyond all human endurance, traumatised others who unwittingly shared in your dirty secret, and still all you can think of is yourself. I don't have to go into my researches to understand people that stand in your lot. It's very clear. You are a cold-blooded narcissist who is capable only of thinking about himself. I know you will never feel any remorse for what you did and that's why I will not tolerate another word that falls from your lips. Sir. . .' He said addressing the portly man, 'Please show him his new headquarters.'

We were sitting on the porch outside Bhrigu's house. It was a bright, sunny day and my friend sat on his favourite stool, scribbling intently in his diary. I looked at him for a minute or two and ventured to ask.

'There are many points in this mystery that you have still not revealed.'

'Such as?' he asked, never once looking back at me.

'You solved the mystery but you did not reveal the key that helped you find the solution.'

He smiled and said, 'The key is human behaviour and a keen eye.' With this cryptic response, he disappeared into his notebook again. 'Please don't do that again. You know how much I hate it!' I said with visible irritation. Tell me in detail. My first question is that how did you first suspect Bali?'

He exhaled a mock breath of defeat and began, 'I first suspected him when Jayanti Devi told me with how much zest he had helped her in moving from her house. Bali is a poor man. He had trouble making ends meet and so it stands to reason why, out of the blue, he became so sympathetic for the grieving widow, helping her in a way that was well beyond his means. It was fairly obvious to me that he wanted the house to himself and as it was not for tenancy, it could only mean that he was desperately searching for something hidden in the house. He was the only one in the list of suspects whom I found contradictory from the very first. I would now enumerate the three points that led to it—

1) Why would a struggling man spend unnecessary amount of money on buying a new house and furniture?

2) Why the sudden concern for Jayanti Devi?

3) Why was he so adamant that Jayanti Devi leave all her stuff behind?

The points which led me on to him during the interview were—

1) Why was he so afraid to continue the interview the following day? Obviously he wasn't comfortable with the idea.
2) Why did he appear on the point of collapse?
3) Where was the kind, happy-go-lucky man Jayanti Devi had described to us?
4) Why was the parrot looking so morose? Had it witnessed something that led it to feel afraid of its owner? For ex—Brutally killing a crow that was used to threaten us?
5) I also observed a thick book lying in his shabby cabinet. He could have easily used it to dry the leaf that we found the other day. (Here I remembered him asking for a notebook and then intently observing the cabinet as it parted to reveal its contents. Now I knew why.)

'These points were enough to put me on his case,' he concluded.

I weighed what he had said in my mind and sifted the evidence. It looked clear enough now that he had said it.

'But I observed suspicious behaviour on the part of Mutukal and Avdoot, too. And remember Meenakumari's tale? From what she told me, Avdoot had a pretty solid reason to kill Malthu. How did you get around that?'

He coughed gently and said, 'You observed how both Mutukal and Avdoot became nervous when we questioned them about Malthu, didn't you?'

I nodded my head and waited for the perfect analysis of these colourful characters that he had refused to provide at the start of the investigation.

'Mutukal is a ruffian who is very much under the power of his wife. This we deciphered before. He is a slacker as well but the big question is how his character would allow him to behave if he had done anything wrong. Mutukal Kumar is a brute but that is an exterior only that hides and protects a weak heart inside. His every action is prompted by external influence which is his wife. If he had anything to do with the murder, on questioning, he would have panicked and relapsed into his ruffian mode, in order to hide that raw fear. But when asked about his nephew, he started—a) simpering, b) flushing, and c) stammering, which meant that he wasn't making any effort to hide his weak nature and hence it can be concluded safely that he was hiding nothing. The nervousness that he exhibited was only because he thought he wasn't doing well in the interview and his wife would therefore be mad at him.'

'And you have a name for your theory here?' I asked almost involuntarily.

'Yes, I do,' he replied looking sceptically at me. 'But I have a feeling that your question is more jocular than serious? You never have any special regard for the names I give to my theories.'

I smiled slowly and said, 'You underestimate me, my friend. I appreciate those titles and if you want, I can offer my literary expertise to name a few.'

'Please . . . leave that domain to me alone,' he replied hotly. 'If you care for it, the name I have given to this behaviour is "the turtle effect".'

It was more than enough that I could do to suppress a loud guffaw. I have oft times wondered that if his R&A is so perfect, why the hell has he to let it all go down the drain with such preposterous names?

'The turtle effect uh?' I replied, applying the power of Hercules to control my laughter. 'And why is that?'

He was looking at me with eyes that were turning a deeper shade of red. 'Because, Sutte, Mutukal Kumar hides his weak nature behind his tough exterior the same way as the turtle hides his soft body behind a hard carapace. Now you get it?'

'Rather,' I replied, trying hard to control my insides from exploding with laughter.

His mood had become surly. 'I don't think I should say anything else. You guess it for yourself.'

It took quite a lot of coaxing, cajoling and to be candid, begging, for him to change his mind.

'All right. All right,' he said crossly. 'No need to embarrass yourself. I will now move on to Avdoot.'

He cleared his throat and said, 'Avdoot is a weak man with a nervous disposition. He is insecure and requires someone to be his strength and keep on assuring him that all is well. This support he has found in his wife, Indumati.'

'Now, how would Avdoot behave if he had something to hide? Avdoot is a sort of person who, when threatened, hides behind his source of strength and lets that person take charge. He is completely unable to function by himself. His major concern was Indumati getting to know about his love affair with Meena Kumari. Hence, in order to get rid of the dread he was feeling of his wife discovering his secret from an outside person, he, himself, told her everything. Indumati, being a broad-minded, modern woman, accepted his past graciously and Avdoot heaved a sigh of relief. This I call "the creeper effect" as Avdoot is a creeper who can only stand erect by entwining to a rigid support.'

This title I had no trouble digesting and everything was well in my world.

My friend was saying 'Avdoot's weakness was the reason he had to leave Meena Kumari. At first he got attracted to her charm and started dating her but later he came to know that the pretty girl was just as insecure as him. She was fed up by her unsympathetic parents and wanted just about anyone to marry her and release her from the torture of living with them. Hence, as their dating commenced, she became increasingly clingy and desperate. That was what drove Avdoot straight into the arms of a strong woman, Indumati.'

'But if he had nothing to hide, why did he break a sweat when we questioned him about Malthu?'

'Superstition, Sutte, blind fear,' my friend replied easily. 'You observed every detail about Avdoot but you failed to notice the rosary, half concealed in his Kurta's sleeve? That's the reason I asked him about the profession of his father. He was a village priest, as I had half suspected. Avdoot was brought up in a house steeped in the traditions of orthodoxy and fallacies. That's the reason behind his weak, timid nature and also for his unreasonable fear of anything even remotely connected to the preternatural.'

I found myself remembering the events of the past as Bhrigu adroitly placed the people in their respective 'categories', classifying them according to their personalities.

'Meenakumari told us about a colourful box where she used to keep her love letters and of how it magically disappeared. You don't have an answer to that do you?'

'As a matter of fact, I do,' he said. 'Malthu used to visit Meenakumari often as he was her love letter boy. Remember that Malthu was childlike and children often have a weakness for colourful, attractive things. He must have noticed the beautifully decorated box and temptation drove him to purloin it. The reason was that simple. I am positively certain that he used it instead to keep his diary.'

'You understood that part as soon as you heard it, didn't you?'

'Yes. It was pretty obvious.'

'For you, I'm sure.'

I sat there brooding for a minute before another question assailed me.

'After Meenakumari recounted her tale, you took off for a few hours. Where did you go and what did you do?'

'Do you have a page where you have written all these questions or are you voicing them from memory?' he asked with a touch of brusqueness.

'It's your own undoing,' I replied with a touch of triumph. 'If you wouldn't be so stuck up in your philosophy that—'I will reveal all once I have all the threads in my hand' we would have fewer questions to go through.'

He looked at me with a hint of irritation but it soon dissolved into a gracious smile. I would even go as far as to say that he laughed a little. 'You are a marvel, Sutte.'

'Thank you for the appreciation,' I shot back.

'Well, for your answer,' he resumed after curiously looking at me for a few seconds. 'I frankly confess that I was taken aback not a little by the story of Meenakumari.

It had shifted the basis of my investigation. I wanted to nip this deviation in the bud and hence I ran for help to the village's most popular *Dhaba*. It is a place where people usually exchange gossip and make it their business to know anything that should be known about anyone. Naturally, Meenakumari and Avdoot's affair was common knowledge there. The veterans of the *Dhaba* told me about how it started on a romantic foot and ended on the left when Meenakumari literally started giving the man a chase almost everywhere he went. As Avdoot was in the habit of relaxing with two of his friends at the *Dhaba*, she often used to come running to the place, desperately looking for him.'

'I see,' I said, again going through the weighing-what-he-had-said-and-sifting-the-evidence routine.

Silence reigned for a couple of minutes, where I found him scribbling in his diary once again. He then eyed me and said suddenly, 'I didn't give you Indumati's analysis, did I?'

'Nope,' I replied. 'And I didn't find it in my heart to remind you lest it offended you again.'

'You are a piece of work, Sutte,' he said, gracing me with his lopsided smile 'Indumati is a strong willed, intelligent woman who can keep a level head over her shoulders even when others all around her are busy losing theirs.' He paused for a breath and continued, 'She is a smart, strong woman with a modern outlook on life even though her rustic background totally rebels against it. This anomalous behaviour clearly reveals that she is scarcely influenced by the opinions of others and has a mind of her own. If she had to execute a plan, she would do it to perfection and leave not a clue behind.

Now, if such a woman had a hand in murder, she would have so cleverly steered the suspicion away from her and scattered it all over her relatives that by the end of the interview, we would have gone back convinced that anyone could be the murderer but her. And that she would have done coolly, without once losing her nerve. When we questioned her, did she behave in that manner? Was she unusually calm and collected? Was she interested in exposing the skeletons hidden in the closet of her relatives? No. The woman was forthcoming with her answers and also exhibited a normal level of anxiety regarding the interview as she desperately wanted her husband to get it. I could see how sharply she followed our questions and was ready with some of her own. By the end of the interview, it was evident to me that Indumati was clear of the crime.'

Even before I could voice my question, he asked coolly 'If you were to give a name to such behaviour, what would it be?'

I was certainly taken aback at such a direct order. How come he, who is so touchy-feely about this matter, suddenly gives me the carte blanche to say what I pleased? 'Are you sure?' I asked feebly.

'One hundred percent.'

'Well . . . then . . . ummm. . .'

'What?'

'Let me think a while.'

'Carry on then.'

'I got it!' I screamed 'The Margaret Thatcher effect?'

He guffawed so loudly that I almost fell off my seat. He held his sides and laughed till tears flowed freely from the corners of his eyes. 'S . . . Sutte!' He cried between his hysteria, 'You are too much!'

'Thanks a lot,' I replied, confused whether to take this remark as a polite compliment or a vile invective.

'What have you named it?' I asked after his cackle had subsided.

'Your coinage was perfect. Why should I spoil it by offering mine?'

'Hmm.'

Nirja Masi made an entry just then and removing the Puja cloth that she had left to dry in the sun, retreated, muttering god knows what under her breath. She paused at the threshold, looked at her nephew, and said in her usual stern voice, 'I give you till tomorrow to decide on a girl. Sitting here idling and laughing with your no good friend won't help move your life forward.' After issuing this polite warning, she stomped off.

Bhrigu's face drooped like a Mimosa Plant touched in full bloom.

'Cheer up, man,' I said with a ringing in my voice 'Tell me, when you first suspected Ghanshyam Singh? I have this feeling that you weren't easy in your mind about him. His story seemed to touch a few cords in you, I could see.'

I was thankful that my question brought him back from his nightmare world where he was busy running away from a fiend shaped relative. 'Oh that?' He ejaculated 'Yes. After listening to what Ghanshyam Singh had to say about his alleged tragedy, I was certain that he was suffering from the "the Self effect".'

'The Self effect?'

'Yes.'

'What's that?'

'A person exhibiting "the Self effect" can think of no one but themselves alone. They can be very imaginative and enterprising when it comes to saving themselves and putting false blame on people who are completely innocent of the matter.' He glanced at the door to make sure that Nirja Masi wasn't eavesdropping and resumed: 'His story, as you remember, revolved less around how her daughter suffered and more around how he had to endure everything. Meenakshi, even though dead, was projected as the culprit and Ghanshyam Singh himself, the victim. Tell me, where can you find a genuinely loving father, aggrieved over his daughter's death, lamenting over his loss and simultaneously pinning everything on her? He was more concerned that we see him as a victim than he was for us to know how his own daughter suffered despite being loved and protected.'

'Also,' he resumed after a brief pause, 'I saw something that corroborated my analysis. You remember when Ghanshyam Singh's chair gave way and he fell to the ground most awkwardly?'

'Yes. What about that?'

'Well, did you not observe how he behaved in the wake of that little accident? His friend, Chaudhary Manendra Singh, rushed to his rescue. Any other person would have been glad for the help but not this man. He was too full of false pride to let anyone lend him a helping hand. He ignored the help his friend promptly and kindly offered, getting to his feet completely on his own. This was a classic case of someone chock full of the realisation of their own self-importance, so much so that they look down upon anything that remotely suggests to their mind the idea of submitting. This incident put a stamp on my diagnosis that the landlord was most definitely suffering from "the Self syndrome".'

'Hmm,' I said, thinking aloud. 'Now that you have said it, I found myself wondering the same when I saw his reaction to his friend coming to his aid. I found that pretty odd, too. I thought it touched a nerve in him.'

'Exactly.'

We were silent for a space when I asked. 'There are still a few questions that keep fighting for attention in my brain.'

'Call for a ceasefire then,' he replied with a smile. 'Now that the case is closed, I won't take a toll on your patience with my silence.'

I took this opportunity and fired away. 'We all heard what the diary of Meenakshi had to say. What surprises me is that you knew everything that followed right after her last entry. There was no way of knowing that unless you were right there with her. What sorcery was that, huh?'

'Sorcery?' he said. 'You aren't calling me a witch now, are you?'

'Please, answer me.'

'To answer this question of yours, I'll have to ask another question.'

'Yes?'

'Have you ever plotted a line graph?'

'What sort of a question is that? Of course I have!'

'So, you remember how we used to do it, right? We calculate the x and the y; plot the coordinates on the graph and try to find the relation it follows by the line it traces. May it be straight, hyperbolic, parabolic, etc. . . . Once we ascertain the relation, we can know what happened next simply by extrapolating the graph. I did the same with Meenakshi, too. The diary provided enough data to understand the character of Meenakshi and the relation she had with her father. I closely followed the line of action that the events of the diary traced. When it ended, all I had to do was to extrapolate the events further to complete it. I could have made a minimal of error as per the details, but the overall story was quite easy to foretell.'

'You can plot the graphs of human beings, their activities, and relationships, too?'

'It is in the line of my work, yes,' he replied. 'Have you not seen the various graphs I keep working on in my diary?'

I was too nonplussed to answer to this bizarre approach. 'One day you will reduce our lives to a few simple quadratic equations, I am sure.'

'I am trying,' he said with a half-smile, trying his level best to annoy my sensibilities.

'Your strange researches will one day be the death of me,' I cried.

'Do you want me to calculate that day?' he asked, now smiling broadly.

I gave up. 'Now stop gloating and stick to the case at hand. Please tell me everything that the diary revealed to you about Meenakshi.' After a forethought, 'And please . . . stick to Queen's English.'

'Meenakshi had many qualities,' said my friend. 'As you, yourself could have ascertained; she was bright, determined, energetic, a born leader, receptive, fearless, adventurous, and affectionate. She was one of the rare few who put others before themselves; a quality which calls itself altruism. It was indeed a pity that a girl like her could have been under the tutelage of a man like Ghanshyam Singh. She was everything that he feared and he was everything that she despised. They both had forceful personalities which drew power from alternating sources. The nearer they drew towards each other, the greater was the chance that they would repel with a force that would destroy everything that surrounded them. And this is exactly what happened. Meenakshi struggled to accept the real face of her adopted father, but once she did, she knew herself well enough to understand that her father had to be brought to justice. The love for her mother kept her silent for a while but the storm that was slowly brewing and stirring her conscience would never leave her in peace. Ghanshyam Singh was aware of her daughter's nature and hence he became increasingly paranoid about her actions. The love that he had for her slowly dissipated and raw fear took its place. He knew almost instinctively that if he had to safeguard his reputation, he had to crush Meenakshi in a way that she would never recover. He could not touch her physically so he resorted to torment her mentally. He beat Vidwait to an inch of his life in the hope that this would surely kill his daughter's spirit and hence liberate him from the ensuing danger. This was a big mistake on his part because this incident acted as a fuel to the fire of hatred that was already smouldering in her heart for him. It was then that she decided that her father would pay for all his sins.'

'The fire burned her too. What do you have to say to that?'

He exhaled lugubriously and said, 'Yes. That was inevitable. She couldn't have lived a day longer with what burned inside her.'

'And you knew what followed?'

'Yes. As I said before, I extrapolated the events based on her character and the way her relationship was progressing with his father. Trust me; there was only one *definite* way that it could have progressed.'

'And how did you know what happened between Bali and Malthu? Surely, the latter did not leave his diary behind?'

'Bali is a man of drama. He is not a man of action. His timidity would not allow for it. I inquired about him at the mill; one of the days that I asked you to stay behind. They told me about his reluctance in acting as one of Ghanshyam

Singh's henchmen. He was eager to draw his wages but reluctant to work for it. They would often watch him trailing behind the sinewy men, afraid lest he be discovered among them. If he had killed Malthu, he would have no qualms whatsoever to kill us, too. Instead, he chooses to scare us with presents from the witch. That tells you what? Believe me, a person like Bali can only kill a man by accident and not by calculation.'

'And one last question,' I said as I suddenly remembered the bizarre incident. 'You did not by any chance discover the meaning of the lamp that Bal Kishore drew on the paper? It was just insanity on his part, wasn't it?'

My friend looked at me with a jolt and said, 'Oh that? I didn't tell you about it, did I?'

I shook my head in the negative.

'You remember me being upset over Bal Kishore's behaviour?'

'Yes,' I said. 'How can forget that? You seldom look so distraught.'

'Well, it was later that I realised that Bal Kishore had cracked after all and the lamp that he drew for me was not the manifestation of madness but a hint aimed at truth.'

'I do not understand.'

He signed deeply and said, 'Bal Kishore was torn by my questioning. The deep-rooted fear that he had for the landlord was proving it difficult for him to say anything against him. I goaded him to the point where the fear of god finally triumphed over the intimidating mortal. But he still couldn't bring himself to become candid. Hence he drew me this symbol in a hope that I would know who the culprit was.'

'But what has a lamp got to do with Ghanshyam Singh?'

Nisha Singh

'As I have said before, Sutte, if you keep your eyes and ears open, you will know.' He said, 'Did you look at the label of the shirt that the landlord was wearing? Stitched at the corner of his shirt pocket sat the beautiful logo of the prestigious Premium Khadi Empire and you now know what it is, don't you?'

'A beautiful lamp,' I said involuntarily.

'Exactly,' he replied with a sickly sweet smile.

EPILOGUE

I was still having trouble believing what I had just heard from the mouth of a local villager called Hanumat. He had cordially invited us to the brick laying ceremony of The Temple of Goddess Durga, soon to be constructed in the honour of Meenakshi, the brave girl who had sacrificed her life for the good of the villagers. It was because of her efforts that the police were now actively involved in the investigation of the missing villagers as their family members, finally emerging from the shadows of fear that had held them captive for many years, were now telling their pathetic stories. It was not so much the invitation that confounded me but the location where the temple was set to be constructed. The place was none other than 'Jiyashree's Garden', the alleged haunted strip of floodplain that until a week ago was as abandoned as The Great Angkor Vat of Cambodia, one fine morning. Believe me, it's true. One day, the great net of temples were the prime centre of activity and on the very next day, all that was left behind were the great buildings, ready to face ruin for centuries to come. What I am striving to arrive at is that the isolated area was no longer isolated now. It took a tragedy and a number of deaths to restore life there.

We were making rapid strides towards the ground. Chaudhary Manendra Singh, one other VIP, and Bhrigu were the luminaries asked to set the first stone. We could not afford to get late. It was a comfortable journey as the sky was overcast with clouds obliterating any effort on the part of the sun to catch a hole in their defence. It was a pleasant, sun-free day and I am proud to proclaim that I was keeping up fairly well with the jaunty gait of my friend.

Soon, the place loomed closer and I waited for the sign post that read 'Jiyashree's Garden' to appear any minute but instead I found a new one thrust into the ground a little farther from where the original one stood that read 'Site for Construction: Maa Durga Mandir,' I was fairly confused at the contrast that the two sign posts offered. One was an open declaration that you were now standing on haunted premises and the other proudly proclaimed that your feet had just touched sacred ground. The surge of feelings that had accompanied the two signs was also vastly different now. When my friend and I had first stood here, we had been aware of a sinking feeling that gnaws at your insides and leaves you perspiring with fear in its wake. It is a wonder that the ground on which we now stood was the very same but the feeling that I now experienced had undergone a remarkable shift. I no longer felt frightened or depressed but a feeling of joy and tranquillity assailed my senses. I was at peace here and the thought perplexed me no less. Our own thoughts had given life to the witch and created an atmosphere of horror but now the weight of truth had forced them to accept the presence of a divine being, creating an aura of devotion and peace. In a nutshell, it was not the ground that had changed but our mindset and how.

A throng of villagers was present to witness the auspicious moment when the first stone for the foundation was to be laid. The atmosphere was surcharged with the thick fragrance of lilies from the incense sticks as two voices, a mellifluous one and a hoarse one from an old and a middle-aged Pundit respectively took turns singing hymns in the praise of the Goddess Durga. After the *Puja* was over, Bhrigu, Manendra Singh, and one other dignitary from the neighbouring village laid the first stone amid much cheering and clapping from the crowd and one other Pundit cracked open a coconut over it, marking the event as propitious.

All throughout the ceremony, Bhrigu kept looking at Jayanti Devi, who had also come to pay her respects to Meenakshi. Her face hinted at a sorrow but the desperation; the anguish that we had witnessed in her was now gone. It was easy to notice that she wasn't struggling to breathe anymore. My friend was happy to see that he had found the troubled, old lady a peaceful place where she could begin the process of nursing her bruises.

We returned home after partaking of the *Prasad*.

I had noticed a certain change descent over my friend as we made our way home. As soon as we reached the house, he did the unthinkable. Marching straight towards Nirja Masi's room, he knocked at it boldly and tapping his foot impatiently waited for a response. Nirja Masi opened the door after the fifth knock and stood staring at him groggily. It was evident that she had been roused from a deep sleep.

'What is it, Bhriguji?' she said in a heavy voice. 'I was sleeping. What was so urgent that could not wait?'

'I have come to tell you that . . . that I won't marry ever,' Bhrigu replied with grit. 'Burn the photos of those girls, for all I care, but I won't have anything to do with them.'

She stared at him with shock and confusion, struggling to understand what force had taken possession of her nephew.

'What did you just say? I think I did not understand.'

'When did you ever understand me that you will now? I just wanted to say that I am not afraid of you anymore. That's all.'

He turned on his heel and left, leaving a lightening stuck Nirja Masi behind. He later revealed to me the change that had wrought in him. 'Today's incident made me realise that we make our own demons. The haunted ground transformed easily into a holy place as soon as the villagers were ready to let go of their fear. I knew then that only I had the power to let go of the fear that had been crippling me. I confess, Sutte that I have a knack for understanding human behaviour, but it was only today that I got to understand and accept mine.'

My dear friend looked a lot younger that day. No longer could I see the marks of tension creasing his eyes and burdening his existence. He was well on his way of conquering his demons. I knew from his abrupt, bizarre expostulations in the course of our long talks that he had suffered during his childhood and his sensitive nature had prevented him from getting past the hurt and torment. I was thankful to God that he was on the path to recovery as the biggest torment that had plagued him, his aunt, was no more a painful memory now but a valuable lesson. . . . A first among many that my friend was yet to learn and . . . record.